F

X132198201 BLW

PRAISE FOR

"Kerri Schlottman has delivered us the richest of reading experiences. I read *Tell Me One Thing* voraciously with equal parts intrigue and admiration, thinking how did she pull this off? Slinking expertly between time and location and point of view—the contrasts here are bright and nuanced, honest and vulnerable, jagged yet tender. This is a novel of great heart, examining the lines we draw as we become who we are. A devastating and rich exploration of trauma, art-making, love and the unmistakable hauntedness of what we cannot control, yet long to. I want everyone to read this book."

– Chelsea Bieker, author of *Godshot* and *Heartbroke*

"With a clear, empathic gaze, and with a sharp, startling intelligence, Kerri Schlottman's *Tell Me One Thing* traces two paths—that of artist, and that of subject—through the cruel disparities of the Reagan eighties and beyond. The result is a book that asks enduring questions about what art is for and what we, all of us, owe one another. *Tell Me One Thing* is phenomenal."

– Matthew Specktor, author of *Always Crashing in the Same Car*

"In *Tell Me One Thing*, two women's stories begin in an instant—with a shutter click. Divergent yet inextricable, the paths and aspirations of a photographer and her young subject leap and shatter through the passage of four decades and at the mercy of American dearth, all of which Schlottman relays with understated grit and unflinching humanity. As we follow the photographer through seedy 1980s New York to today's commercially sterilized iteration, Schlottman proceeds to vivify a Polaroid snapped in a Pennsylvania trailer park, infusing viscerality and tragedy into a portrait that would have otherwise hung static on a collector's wall. By reframing an object to be admired as a child to be protected, *Tell Me One Thing* will both compel and confront readers with questions that only the finest of novels can posit."

— Jakob Guanzon, author of *Abundance*, longlisted for the National Book Award

"At once the expansive story of two women navigating two disparate, intersecting lives, and a thoughtful meditation on the transtemporal power of photography, Kerri Schlottman's *Tell Me One Thing* is that rare book: an art world novel with heart."

— Rachel Lyon, author of *Self-Portrait with Boy*

"I loved the way *Tell Me One Thing* follows two women trying to find their ways in the world—Quinn, the starving artist whose work rescues her from grinding poverty, and Lulu, a subject of Quinn's photography, whose own ways of working only mire her further into destitution and desperation. Kerri Schlottman's vivid writing skillfully recreates 1980s' New York City and rural Pennsylvania; we're invited to witness both the heady art-world scene of the era and the foundations being set for the opioid epidemic. It's such a smart and well-crafted novel, bursting with life. I couldn't put it down."

— Amy Shearn, award-winning author of *Unseen City* and other novels

"An intimate look at the way art transforms the lives of both artist and subject, and not always for the better. In crisp, descriptive prose, Kerri Schlottman draws a portrait of both rural Pennsylvania and a transforming New York City, as she—and her characters—probe the murky line between inspiration and exploitation."

— Wil Medearis, author of *Restoration Heights*

"This stunning and vivid debut novel is like walking into a late night dive bar, and the blues band inside is excellent. Two women cross paths almost by accident, and the story follows each of their efforts to overcome the hard lives they're living. These characters are so realistic, we start rooting for them moments after meeting them. And the writing? One of the women's homes is so well rendered, I swear I could smell it. Best of all, for all of their hard times, this book is full of unexpected moments of fulfillment, surprising flashes of grace."

– Stephen P. Kiernan, author of *Universe of Two* and *The Baker's Secret*

"Fans of *The Vanishing Half* will love this novel written in alternating points-of-view: each one a perspective rooted in a starkly contrasting experience and yet one that echoes the longings of the other. Reading this was a much-needed exercise in empathy, one tempered by clear, endearing prose. In the parallel universes of two unforgettable characters, Schlottman renders on the page a simple and beautiful expression of our shared humanity. In *Tell Me One Thing*, we see the private struggles of a famed photographer making it in the wild days of New York City and how her seminal work exposes and yet neglects the harsh truth of one of her subjects. My heart broke and rooted for both characters, and long after I've turned the last page, I am still thinking of them."

– Cinelle Barnes, author of *Monsoon Mansion: A Memoir and Malaya: Essays on Freedom*

TELL ME ONE THING

Kerri Schlottman

Regal House Publishing

Published by
Regal House Publishing, LLC
Raleigh, NC 27605
All rights reserved

ISBN -13 (paperback): 9781646033010
ISBN -13 (epub): 9781646033027
Library of Congress Control Number: 2022935685

All efforts were made to determine the copyright holders and obtain their
permissions in any circumstance where copyrighted material was used.
The publisher apologizes if any errors were made during this process, or
if any omissions occurred. If noted, please contact the publisher and all
efforts will be made to incorporate permissions in future editions.

Cover design © by C. B. Royal
Author photo by Kambui Olujimi

Regal House Publishing, LLC
https://regalhousepublishing.com

The following is a work of fiction created by the author. All names,
individuals, characters, places, items, brands, events, etc. were either the
product of the author or were used fictitiously. Any name, place, event,
person, brand, or item, current or past, is entirely coincidental.

Printed in the United States of America

This one is for you, Jason A. Brodak

PROLOGUE

2019

Quinn looks around at the installation, pleased with the result of weeks of work and over a year of preparation. Standing in the center of the Whitney Museum of Art's sixth-floor gallery, it seems as if she has an audience in these subjects. Many are her friends and loved ones. They watch her from their respective photographs, sometimes directly, sometimes as passive observers, but always there, aware. And she can time travel here, among these faces and scenes. They lure her into an elaborate hopscotch over decades or yank her through dense hours and minutes. She closes her eyes for a moment, trying to find some form in the darkness there.

A touch to her elbow brings her back, and William says, "Mom, Gary Radcliff from the *New York Times* is here. Are you ready?" She nods and follows William to where the young man waits near the massive vinyl lettering at the entrance to the show. He stands, hands clasped in front of him under the *Q* and *U* in *Quinn Bradford: A Retrospective*.

He smiles when he sees her, says, "Quinn, it's such a pleasure to meet you." They shake hands. "I really appreciate your time. I know you're not a fan of interviews, so I'm grateful all the more." He's right. She's not a fan of interviews, though she doesn't like how it sounds coming from him, as if she's deliberately challenging. She considers explaining why that is. She could tell him about how she was hounded by journalists after what happened to Billy, but she doesn't because doing so would invite that conversation here. Instead, they exchange the usual pleasantries as Quinn leads Gary to a bench in the gallery.

Workers in white coveralls are busy making last-minute touch-ups to the walls where things have been rearranged, shifted, and rehung. Gary taps the record button on his phone, and something about that formality changes his tone, deepens it to sound more serious when he says, "I'm excited to dig into the exhibition, but first, I want to ask you about *Lulu and the Trucker* after what happened this week." And Quinn thinks maybe this is the real reason she doesn't like interviews, how they can somehow, still, after all this time, make her feel like an impostor. Even so, she assumed he'd start like this. "Well," she says, "it was a surprise, for sure."

"Maybe not," Gary says, misunderstanding her. "That photo has long been considered the piece that launched your career."

"That's true," she says. "Although, it's hard for me to think of it that way. I've done so much work since then."

"Understandably, but considering that it just broke records at auction, I'd say it's an important one." His eyebrows raise, and she realizes he's asking a question with that statement.

"Oh yeah," she says. "I don't mean to diminish it in any way. It's an important photo, and it pushed my career in a direction that I'll forever be grateful for. It's why Eric Hoffman ultimately chose to work with me. I meant that the auction was a surprise. It's challenging not knowing who owns that piece now." What she would never say is there were so many times she thought of destroying the photo, so many times she held its edges and studied the interaction, hoping to find innocence there, but always returning to the dread that set inside her when the Polaroid first processed in the car, in front of her eyes. And the things the photo doesn't show, the monster that she still sees plain as day as if it's a third subject in the composition. How it looms around Lulu, hovering like an aura. She doesn't need to possess the photo to see it all.

"And we may never know who owns it now thanks to the anonymous sale." Gary brings her back to now, and Quinn swallows hard, her dry throat clamping to itself. She wishes she had a glass of water. "It has an almost mythical status seeing as it hasn't been seen in quite some time. Would you tell me about that?"

She shifts a bit, unsure of how much she wants to say, then leans in toward him. "When I first exhibited it, it was all anyone could talk about. I didn't want it to be the thing that I became known for, but I could see that was rapidly happening."

"And so, you gave it to Billy Cunningham." Gary watches her as if he knows he's just treaded into a landmine territory.

"I did." Quinn takes a deep breath. "For safekeeping. I always refused to allow it to be for sale, even though it would have helped me financially. And there were some hard times back then, really hard times. I was worried about what I might do. If I might get desperate enough to sell it. I told him not to let me do that, and I knew he wouldn't. But then..." She trails here because she won't talk more about this, and she doesn't need to because it's well known what happened next. She tries to put the lawsuit with Myles out of her mind, the endless arguments about ownership and rights and estates, the things she never wanted to have to fight about, especially not when she had just lost the love of her life.

Gary nods, and his eyes squint in contemplation. "Do you still think about Lulu?"

Quinn tries to hide her disappointment in this question but then realizes that even though Lulu's part of her DNA after all these years, she's an invisible part, like an extra organ tucked deep inside of her that no one else could possibly know about. Her words come out husky when she says, "Yeah, of course I do." She clears her throat to gain more control. "It's been almost forty years since I took that photo, but I've never stopped thinking about her. Now, she'd be, like, fifty. I wonder what her life is like, if she's still alive, married, kids, you know?"

"In your later series, you followed your subjects for long periods of time. Did you ever think about going back to shoot more of Lulu?"

"I did think about it." Quinn doesn't offer more, doesn't say that she tried, and, surprisingly, he doesn't ask. She wonders if he can see inside her now, can feel the edges of that aching appendage as it pulses throughout her. She's relieved when he shuffles his small notebook in a gesture to move on. "Your work is often discussed in the context of the downtown arts scene. You certainly chronicle a special moment in New York City's history. Many of your friends who appear in your early work became equally well-known artists, writers, performers, and the like. Liv Brown, Micky Hart, Alex Campeau, Myles Wainwright, and of course, Billy Cunningham. You followed them for years, and it's a delight that we get to see them grow up in these images. And then you stopped, which felt abrupt to many of those who were following your career. What happened?"

"Well, I started doing more time-based, thematic series, as you noted. But I never stopped taking photos of my friends. I just stopped showing them." Quinn doesn't elaborate on why. Anyone who was even kind of paying attention could figure that out on their own.

"Do you miss the New York of those days?"

She's been asked this before, and she wonders how old he is, if he's lived long enough to watch something disappear only to reappear as a stranger. She's never sure how to answer cleanly, simply, because there was nothing clean and simple about that time.

"I don't know," she finally says. "That New York is long gone. I mean, it was a free-for-all, like. People doing anything they wanted. Which can be amazing, right, but also dangerous. New York was coming out of near bankruptcy when I started my career. There was so much need, so much desperation. We were all working in these various areas around consumerism, that huge *thing*. And any time you're creating in a transitional space like that, you don't really know something big is happening. So, yeah, there are some things that I miss about that New York City. That urgency. Feeling hungry for everything."

Gary leans intently toward her. "What changed?"

More like, *what happened?* She could blame AIDS, heroin, and crack, which killed so many beautiful minds and devastated the city. Racism, sexism, homophobia. Or the rise of the art market, gentrification, the machine that forced artists who couldn't afford exorbitant rents to move away. She could blame commercial galleries, Wall Street art collectors, real estate tax credits, political lobbyists, and so many other things and maybe even herself. She could tell Gary all that, but she doesn't. Lost now, stuck there, stuck in all of it, she doesn't say anything at all. She knows she hasn't answered his question, but she can't really remember what it was anyway.

LULU & THE TRUCKER

1980

Polaroid 600 Instant, 4.2 x 3.5 inches

"What's this package we're picking up?" Quinn asks. Something in the softness of the dim car lighting makes her imagine a younger version of Billy, the one who was her first kiss, her first everything. When she offered to take a ride in this rusty borrowed car with him, she thought they'd be gone for a few hours. Now, they've crossed into Pennsylvania, dropping up and down the mountains, and the summer sun set some time ago. Quinn welcomes the dusk, though, how immediately it tempers the heat of the day, hushes the sunspots in the reflections of windshields and polished chrome, mutes the landscape. She scratches at a scab on her knee, and it protests by picking up a tender pink coastline of skin with it. Joan Jett's concrete voice on the cassette player sings, "I Love Rock 'n' Roll." Billy puffs a cigarette, making ghostly circles of smoke that pull apart in the breeze from the open windows.

"Just some pills," he says as he tosses the cigarette out the window where the red sparks trip across the lane.

"What kind of pills?"

"The kind that shoot you to the fucking moon." He winks at her.

"I thought this was a little side hustle," she says. "Some weed here and there. Should I be concerned?" But she's already concerned, has been concerned about his rebelliousness and the way it has slinked into deeper recesses that seem harder and harder to return from.

"Nothing to be concerned about." He squeezes her knee, and she watches his expression for the slightest indication of anything outside of confidence, but it stays steady. She exhales and it might have sounded like a sigh except the air gushing from the open windows clears it straight away.

Despite the drop in temperature, the summer night air is thick in the hills and Quinn runs her palm against the push and pull of the wind. Inside, the car shudders and the music breaks apart in the boxing beat of the air. She slips off her combat boots and rests her feet on the dashboard, tries to will the tightness in her back to release. Billy glances her way, his eyes dip down her bare legs, and Quinn whips the Polaroid up from her lap to shoot a photo of him. She knows it'll come out dark but hopes it'll capture some of the light that plays around him.

"Hey," he says, but he smiles anyway, a wide one that pulls his thin cheeks up to his eyes and out to his ears. A smile that makes her smile. In her tiny studio apartment in SoHo, Quinn has collected years' worth of photos of Billy. They chronicle his transition from boy to man, the lanky white arms slowly becoming covered in tattoos, the dark hair growing from a floppy bowl cut to the shaggy twists that can sometimes look greasy but are soft to the touch.

Quinn holds the edges of the photo and watches a ghostly image of him emerge. The light she had hoped to capture illuminates his more dramatic features, frosts his cheekbones, lingers on his lips, puts a bit of glitter in the side of his eye.

"I'm kinda hungry," she says, but she doesn't tell him that she's barely eaten the entire day. She knows he'll worry. She worries.

"We're almost there, I think. We can grab something after." He shifts in his seat and rubs his eyes. Outside, the scenery seems to speed up, the flashy reds and yellows of car lights smudge the awkward darkness of the surrounding trees. Quinn closes her eyes. They were out late last night, well into the morning really. It wouldn't take much for her to fall asleep. The seatback cradles the heaviness of her head. The restless engine's shallow vibrations soothe her. She's on the brink of dozing off when Billy slows down. She opens her eyes as the car labors up the steep incline of an off-ramp, threatens to stall. He guns it through a deserted intersection. Small blinks of light indicate some life around them, but it's desolate. They drive a short distance toward a half-lit gas station and adjoining truck stop. "Jesus," Quinn whispers. She drops her feet from the dash and rolls down the window entirely, leans on the frame. "Where are we?"

"Riverdale," Billy says. He slows the car to a crawl as they pass a motel with a partially lit vacancy sign, a small church with a boarded-up entrance, a dingy diner, a squat bar with no windows, and finally a trailer park with spotty holiday lights strung throughout in a sometimes-broken circuit. Billy turns right, out of the small downtown, and the car heaves over cratered road, jostling them both. Quinn sits up straighter, slips her feet back into her boots and fights an urge to roll up the window. It's too warm to do so. The car air is pregnant with a new humidity.

Billy turns into a driveway with a deeply dented mailbox whose numbers are peeling and caked in dirt. A house squats at the end of the drive, illuminated by a bald yellow porch light that flashes on a sagging roof, bricks stacked in lieu of steps, bulky trash bags that litter the sides of the front door. Bugs sweep the light, bump around in its casted fuzzy glow. Billy eases the car to a stop, turns to her. "Stay here, okay?" Quinn nods, grateful that she's not expected to come along. She watches nervously as he gets out and shouts, "Digger!" And it's only then that Quinn sees the people sitting in various chairs in the dark front yard. She quickly pulls out her 35mm and snaps several photos through the windshield, though she knows they'll turn out grainy.

In the headlights, she sizes up the guy named Digger the best she can, his meaty neck and the bulge of belly that pushes on his flannel shirt, the arms of which have been ripped off. Behind him, she can just make out the features of the others hanging out in the circle of light from the porch. A girl rests lazily on the lap of one of the guys as she swigs from a paper-bagged bottle. Her legs sway back and forth, not reaching the ground.

Quinn looks at Billy, hoping he's almost finished, but it's clear that something has gone wrong. He's shaking his head. Her own leg twitches as she watches him shift from foot to foot, run his hand through his hair, and she looks around the floorboard for something she can defend him with if a fight is about to break out. But then he's suddenly back at the car, and he slams the door, slumps down in the driver's seat. He looks at her. "I'm sorry about this," he says, "but we have to stay the night here. The guy bringing up the stuff had car troubles and can't get here until morning. Digger said we can get a room at that motel we passed."

"Oh fuck, for real?" Quinn rubs the goosebumps from her arms and sighs. This place feels dangerous, more dangerous than the rotting New York City alleys she treks through for shoots. The air is ominously dark, rich with the boozy hubris of the rough-looking guys on the lawn, the sulky slumped shoulders of the girls among them. "That motel did not look good."

"I know, but there's nothing else around here for miles. I'm sorry, I really am. I'm not stoked about this either. I'll come back first thing on my own."

"Can't we just go?" That hope brings her a split second of ease.

But Billy shakes his head. "I have to get this stuff, Q. There's only a few people who supply it." Her concern flares, but she doesn't say anything about that because right now she's more concerned about spending the night in Riverdale. Billy twists to watch the driveway as he reverses out, his arm wrapped around the back of her seat. The cratered road, a turn, and she watches the town repeat, now in reverse.

They check into the motel and toss their things inside, not yet ready to see the state of the room. Quinn leaves the 35 but takes the Polaroid, and as they walk to the diner, she shoots a couple of photos. They're gloomy things when they process. The N in the diner sign flickers and threatens to give out entirely.

They take a seat at the counter next to a trucker whose eyes trail them as they sit. A web of frothy beer clings to the man's beard. He licks at it but misses. Quinn pegs him to be in his mid-forties based on the lines around his eyes. She stares at his dulled yellow wedding band and tries to picture his wife but can't. He notices her noticing him.

"What's that you got there?" he asks, nodding at the Polaroid around her neck. His voice is gravely, older sounding than she anticipated.

"A Polaroid camera," she says. "I'm a photographer."

"For the newspapers or something?"

His attention makes Quinn uncomfortable. "No, for art. I take pictures of people." The heat creeps into her cheeks. She glances around for the waitress, hoping for a diversion to end the growing interest he seems to have in her.

"You want to take my photo, honey?" He smiles, revealing rotted teeth in the back, a layer of brown film in the front.

Quinn hesitates, not wanting to further engage, but there's a tug in her too because she's always looking for a good shot. So, "Yeah," she says, and Billy presses near her, tenting the countertop with his arm. She holds up the camera. The waitress has finally joined them, and she watches from behind the counter, a hand on her hip. "Just be natural," Quinn tells him in the same way she's told many of her other subjects. "Do what you were doing."

He shrugs and starts eating again, and she takes a photo just as he's swallowing a drink, the bottle coming away from his mouth. She sets the film on the countertop to process. The waitress takes their orders for BLTs and beers, and Quinn captures a photo of her as well.

"Can I see?" the trucker asks, pointing to the nearly finished Polaroid. Quinn hands it over. His thumb makes a grease mark on the front corner.

"Fuck, I'm fat," the guy says, and Billy laughs. Quinn reaches out, and he hands it back.

"I like it," she says, ignoring the thumbprint that will never come off now. "You look tired, but relieved. Like, you're almost there, but this beer and food are everything to you right now." She blushes again at the way he stares at her as she says this.

"Whatever you say, honey." He flips some cash on the counter and leaves.

Billy leans his shoulder against hers. "That made me laugh though," he says, "when the guy called himself a fat fucker."

"He said, 'Fuck, I'm fat,' but I like *fat fucker* better." Quinn stares at the two Polaroids. While the trucker ruined the one of him with his thumbprint, the other of the waitress is quite good. The photo captures a twist in the woman's face, a smirk as she wipes the countertop, her yellow and brown uniform blending with the Formica in the fragile outline of her torso's reflection.

After they eat, Billy convinces Quinn to have another drink at the bar. The place is dim and worn, and when they walk in, all faces turn their way. A game of pool stops in the back. A skinny man with a handgun tucked into the back of his jeans chalks the top of his stick as he watches them. Quinn wants to leave, but Billy is already walking toward two empty bar stools. They order from a tired bartender with a messy tattoo of a heart on her chest. She introduces herself as Linda.

Billy clinks his beer bottle to Quinn's and looks around, says in her ear, "This place is freaking me out."

The locals have gone back to their drinks and pool game, and Quinn nods her head. "I should have brought the Canon though."

Billy says, "That guy has a gun. Just hanging out, playing pool, with a gun."

They're quiet for a moment, just drinking. "These small towns are trouble," she finally says. "Not that ours was this small, but still. Look at the shit we used to get into in good old Milford, Connecticut."

Now that they seem to be there for a bit, Linda asks where they're from and seems impressed when Billy says New York City. She tells them about a trip she took with her cousin to see

Times Square, how a man took a shit on the sidewalk right in front of them. Quinn asks if she can take her photo, and she waves by way of a yes, and it's as if she understands what Quinn is hoping to do because she doesn't pose or even acknowledge the camera in any way. Quinn sets the photo on the bar and shows Linda the others.

Linda shakes her head at the one of the trucker, says, "That's Curtis. Look out for him."

When the photo develops, Linda seems to approve as she hands it back with a nod. She pours two tall shots and says it's on her, and then she moves back down the bar to wait on others. Billy looks at the Polaroids. "These are wicked." He holds up the one of Linda, and Quinn takes it from him, studies the angle of the shot, the tilt in Linda's head as she concentrates on pouring a drink. The way the strap of her bra has slipped down her arm. "This camera is all about luck," she says.

"Yeah, whatever." He grabs her shoulder and gently tugs her. "Let's get out of here?" She nods, and he throws cash on the bar, and Quinn is grateful that he always does this as she considers the few remaining dollars in her back pocket. Again, the entire bar seems to stop and watch them as they leave.

Now, there is no avoiding the motel room, the stains on the carpet, the peeling wallpaper, the cheaply framed poster of a sunset. The bedcover is thin and pilled and has an ambiguous pattern that may have at one time been floral. Quinn doesn't bother to pull it back as she has no intention of getting under it. Billy flops down, almost sending her off the edge as the faulty springs recoil. He leans down next to her, looking at her as he's perched on his elbow. "You're fucking cute, Q."

She scoffs and pushes at him. "Stop flirting. This room sucks." She knows he's only trying to make it less awful and for a minute she forgets why they're even here. The ripple of worry eases as she pretends there are better reasons for this.

"I'm sorry," he says. "But I'm glad you're here. This would be horrible without you."

She rolls her eyes at him, but she's only playing at it. His hair flips down to his chin, and she wraps a thick strand of it around her finger, lets it curl away. She wants him to flirt. She wants to not feel lonely. She wants to not feel the hole that she always feels like a dark spot roving somewhere inside of her. He grabs the Polaroid and angles it her way, takes a sideways photo of her blocking her face. Quinn sits up, tilts her head, and reaches for the camera, but he holds it back.

"For real, man, that film is expensive. Don't waste it on me." She motions for him to hand over the camera. She doesn't tell him about the mounting pile of rolls from the 35 that she can't afford to process. It's too depressing to think about here in this already depressing motel room.

"I'll buy you film." He gives her a look that's both exasperation and confusion.

"Yeah, I know." She has never liked taking money from others. Not when her mom died and her dad was barely scraping by and the neighbors would come around with hand-me-down clothes and casseroles, cards with cash tucked inside. Not when she was the only one at school who couldn't afford art supplies. And not now, as a twenty-three-year-old woman who should be able to support herself but seems to be just making it from one day to the next and sometimes not at all.

Billy sets the camera down. He grasps her ankle instead. His hands are warm. She gently kicks at him, and he lets her go. He lays down at her side, and if there was a moment where something might have happened, it passes. He fishes a joint out of his cigarette pack, lights it, and passes it to Quinn. She inhales, settling back on the bed and blowing the smoke straight up into the ceiling where it clouds, briefly obscuring the dirty popcorn plaster there. The moon shines into the room through the threadbare curtains. Quinn hasn't seen the moon look so bright in a long time. It simply doesn't have the opportunity to do so in New York City where it competes with 42nd Street, the lumbering towers downtown, and millions of people who never rest.

"I feel like nothing," she says. Billy leans over her. His skin is blue in the room's light. She hasn't meant to sound serious, but she means what she says. She feels tiny in comparison to the enormity of the space between them and the moon. Between them and everything else. He draws a line with his fingertip from her forehead, down the slope of her nose, over the ridge of her lips. "I wish you wouldn't worry so much."

Quinn shakes her head. "It's this weed," she says. "It makes me think too much."

"It's not the weed," he replies. "You've been like this since we were kids."

He links her hand in his, and in the darkness, Quinn pretends they're young again and in that world, she hasn't yet gone to art school and Billy hasn't started dealing drugs, and everything is much simpler.

Lulu paces outside the motel, bored out of her mind. She watches a wasp flirt with the cone-shaped construction that hangs above room six. It circles and stalls, tucks the front bit of its glossy body inside then pulls back out, buzzes the nest like it's confused, before flying straight into the small hole, perfectly centered, no wings snagging on the edges. She studies the nest, thinks it looks like the papier-mâché they made in school before summer break, hers an ashtray that her ma Maureen flipped over in her hands before tossing in the garbage because Lulu accidentally made the bottom round.

Lulu drags her flip-flops across the cracked cement and shields her eyes from the hazy day with her hand. She's tired of the hot weather, the wet air that makes it hard for her to breathe. And even though she hates school, she's excited that it starts again soon because they get to take care of a class guinea pig, and if you're real good, you get to bring it home on the weekend. She's already made a space for the cage near the couch where she sleeps. She's heard that each class gets to name it something new, and she thinks that's dumb because it'll never know its name if it keeps getting new ones. Still, she runs ideas through her mind, *Princess, Tinkerbell, Penny*. But then maybe it's a boy, and she's about to switch to boys' names when her ma's voice drifts through the motel room door, deeper than usual, a fake laugh that Lulu hates. She mocks it with her own, but quietly so Maureen can't overhear and get pissed. And she wonders what's so funny anyhow.

Lulu picks up a small rock, one of many spit onto the sidewalk by car tires and dragged by the truckers' thick boots. She considers throwing it at the wasp nest but thinks better of that. Instead, she squints and shoots it across the parking lot where it skips off the fender of a beat-up Dodge. She glances around, but no one has noticed. She picks up another and does the same, though this time it bounces off a tire in a lame thud instead.

If she tries hard, she can make out Eli across the way, slumped behind the cash register at the gas station mart, flipping through a magazine, and she wonders if it's one of those girlie ones that Hank's always buying and hiding under the sofa. Joey crosses over the diner parking lot and she wants to shout out to him to come over, but Maureen has warned her not to fuck around. Instead, she watches him scratch the thick scruff of his messy hair as the diner door swings him away from her. She battles a tug in her belly, a yanking feeling like someone's twisting up bits of her from the inside, and she tries not to think about the last time she ate. It's too easy to fall into wishing she had a burger or a grilled cheese. She picks up another rock and throws it as hard as she can toward the diner, but it falls short and disappears among the other gravely bits in the parking lot. The sun shifts her way, and Lulu steps back into a slice of shade under the motel awning. She watches for the wasp again, but the nest is quiet.

Lulu starts making a list in her head, things that would make her happy. A birthday cake, some money, a dog that's big like Monkey, new sneakers, shorts that don't ride up her butt. She's part way into her list when she notices a lady come outside several doors down. Lulu watches her shirt rise up as she stretches, sees the lines of her ribs, the edges of her boobs, and the scoop of her belly button. She wears jean shorts like Lulu's, but her

legs are sexy like Maureen's. She's got on black boots that Lulu
thinks look cool but must make her feet real sweaty. Lulu looks
down at her own legs, the thin layer of blond hairs that Hank
tells her she'll have to start shaving soon. She switches one leg
over the other, snagging the scab at her knee. She taps her foot,
wondering what the lady is doing and then she can't stand it any
longer.

"Hi," she shouts, and it startles the lady's eyes open, but the
lady smiles wide in a way that makes her cheekbones stick out.
Lulu touches her own face to see if she has those too, but she
does not.

"Hi there." The lady comes down the walkway. "You staying
here?" she asks.

Lulu shakes her head. "My ma cleans here," she says, although the lie makes her feel bad. "I live over there." She
points toward the trailer park and bites her lip, wonders what
the woman is doing here. She's never seen anyone but truckers
and locals in the motel.

"What's your name?"

"Louisa, but people call me Lulu." Lulu twists the ragged
edge of her shorts in her fingers. A long red scratch trails over
a ridge of her lower ribs, noticeable under the bottom of her
favorite tube top that's speckled with faded sunflowers.

"I'm Quinn." She offers her hand, and Lulu takes it, then
giggles because no one's ever shaken her hand before. Quinn's
is soft and firm, and Lulu presses her own palms together afterward to keep the feeling there. "Hey," Quinn says. "I wonder if
I could take your photograph."

Lulu pulls back, unsure why she'd want to do that. "How
come?"

"I think you'd make a great model," Quinn says. "I take photos."

"That's what you do for a job?" Lulu wonders if Quinn is
famous. Then she thinks it's cool that Quinn called her a model.
Maybe she could be a real model someday.

"Well, actually, I work in a bookstore as my job, but I take photos for art."

Lulu likes Quinn's attention and wants to keep it going. "You can take my picture," she says, and Quinn smiles the same wide smile again, and Lulu likes the way it makes her lips thin out before coming back together again in a thick bow.

"Let me grab my camera. I'll be right back." Quinn's shaggy brown hair swoops around her shoulders as she turns.

Alone again, Lulu smiles wide, pressing her lips as far to the sides as she can, so far that it feels like her mouth touches her ears. She flashes the smile in the reflection of the motel window, and it shines back to her from the dull glass, the large front teeth with the gap she hates. She shakes her head to see if her blond hair will flip around the way Quinn's did, but it catches in scrawny knots instead, and she sighs, stops pretending.

Quinn returns and moves them down the walkway, makes some adjustments. "Okay," she says. "All set."

Suddenly, Lulu notices the stains on her shorts and an unraveling bit on the elastic of her tube top. But there's nothing she can do about that now. So, she nods and poses like she's seen in the magazines, her hand on her hip and her head tilted. She hopes Quinn will call her a model again, but instead, Quinn tells her to just act natural. She's not sure what that means so she stands as straight as she can, shifts her weight from hip to hip.

"What were you doing before we met out here?" Quinn asks. Lulu glances at the motel, thinks about Maureen and the trucker and for a split second she wonders what would happen if she told, if she broke the secret she promised to keep.

But instead, she shrugs. "Just hanging out." She gestures halfheartedly at the motel, its constant revolving truckers and the others like her ma who come to be with them.

"How old are you, Lulu?"

Lulu says she'll be ten soon.

"Ma and Hank's taking me to McDonald's. Hank says they give you presents in your food." She's been excited for months, since Hank first had the idea of the party because turning ten is a big fucking deal.

Quinn smiles. "Yeah, right on, a Happy Meal. It's a special box with a toy in it. I used to love them."

Lulu asks what the thing around Quinn's neck is, and Quinn tells her it's a Polaroid camera and that it makes instant pictures. She asks Lulu if she wants to see, and Lulu nods, excited, wondering how it could make a picture inside itself. She holds still as Quinn pulls the box up to her face, adjusts and clicks. There's a noise, like a hum, and then the photo starts to come out the front, and Lulu is stunned. Quinn gently pulls it out and hands it to her, tells her to hold it at the edges. Lulu carefully takes it, pinching it in her fingers. She thinks maybe something didn't work because it's just a muddy looking thing, but Quinn tells her it needs to process still, and then Lulu starts to see the image coming up, line by line, so sneaky that suddenly there's her face and her hair and her shoulders and then she accidentally blinks and now the entire thing is there and it's like how she feels when she misses the second the sun sets.

Quinn watches over Lulu's shoulder, says, "Yep, there you are. You want to keep it?"

Lulu's never had a picture of herself. "I can?" she asks, holding it even more carefully now that it's hers.

"Absolutely," Quinn says. "Hey, I've got like an hour to kill while my friend runs an errand. You want to show me around?"

Lulu nods, but she worries her ma'll say no because it could definitely seem like Lulu is fucking around. She decides not to tell Maureen, which feels risky but worth it. They walk on a path of mashed grass, a shortcut everyone's feet have made. Lulu points out the church, abandoned a long time ago. Its doors are boarded, and the windows are splintered around rock holes. She doesn't tell Quinn she's made some of those herself. There's a playground behind it, but it's not much, a couple of swings and a rusty slide. Lulu does tell Quinn that sometimes the older kids hang out there, drinking beers and smoking pot. The trailers look like Tic Tacs lined up in even rows. Lulu's is a narrow white one with a dented aluminum porch where Maureen drove the car right up into it. The door swings open, and BB comes out. With everything going on, Lulu forgot they were supposed to play, but BB seems unfazed.

"BB, this is Quinn. She takes pictures. Quinn, this is my cousin, Bumblebee."

"That's a pretty name," Quinn says. Lulu can tell Quinn's not sure what to make of BB's face. That's what usually happens when someone new meets her. It's hard to look at her scarred-up lip, and it sure doesn't help that BB won't talk.

Lulu says, "Her lip got stung by bees when she was a baby. That's why they called her Bumblebee, but now we mostly just call her BB." BB looks nervously at Lulu. She's not used to new people coming around. "Hey, can you do her one of them instant pictures?" She holds hers out to show her cousin, but she doesn't let BB take it.

"Sure," Quinn says. Unlike Lulu, BB doesn't even try to pose. Her face is like a solid surface, and Lulu wants to tell her to at least smile. But it's too late, and Quinn already has that machine up to her face. When the photo comes out, BB holds it less carefully than Lulu did, her thumb making a mark on the side. Lulu's relieved she didn't let BB hold hers.

Lulu wishes she could have tidied up. She steers Quinn away from Maureen's pile of high heels that everyone's always tripping over, and the empty beer cans Hank left from the night before. She wants to show Quinn the planter she won in the school raffle and reaches for its frog-shaped body, minus one hand from when Maureen threw it at Hank, but Quinn's got the camera up again and she's taking pictures of the mess. Lulu is embarrassed by the broken La-Z-Boy, the sagging couch, the overflowing ashtray.

"You live here too, BB?" Quinn asks, but BB isn't going to say anything, so Lulu does it for her. "She lives a few houses over with Papa Don." She touches BB's shoulder because she can tell her cousin is still worried.

Quinn's finally ready to go, and that's a relief. They leave BB at her own trailer, and Lulu waves to neighbors as Quinn takes their photos, but no one is looking any good because it's so hot out now. Sweat trickles down Lulu's spine. Even her head feels hot, prickly at the roots. She asks Quinn where she lives, and Quinn tells her New York City. Lulu's never really been out of Riverdale, but she doesn't tell Quinn that.

Finally, they circle back to the motel. Lulu drags her feet, tries to think of something else to show Quinn to keep her attention. But Quinn says her friend's back and she's got to go now. She thanks Lulu and shakes her hand again but this time it doesn't make Lulu giggle. Lulu watches as Quinn goes back inside the room.

Someone has dragged a chair up by door six. Lulu sits. The wasp is back, and it buzzes above her head, louder then softer, louder then softer, and she thinks about swinging up the chair and knocking the whole thing down, letting out whatever is zippering inside. Quinn comes back out with a cute guy and Lulu watches, wonders if it's her friend or boyfriend. Lulu trails him as he jogs across the parking lot to return the room key. Quinn is tossing things in the car. She doesn't look Lulu's way again. She might as well already be gone.

The motel door swings open, and the fat trucker comes out, the one Lulu hates the most. She bites her lip to stop the tears. She knows it's no big thing, that's what Maureen says at least, and that they need the money, though Lulu wonders how come they always need money. He barks at Lulu to stand up and she does, and he sits and pats his knee, but Lulu doesn't move.

"Sit," he says, in the voice that scares her, the one that tells her what to do and what he'll do to her if she doesn't. She sits. "Good girl," he whispers behind her car. He smells metallic, even worse than Hank after a day of construction work. He holds her tight with one arm, wrapping his scratchy fingers around her belly. He offers her a cigarette and when she says no, he tells her again to take it. And she does. She inhales when he flicks the lighter near her face and does not cough because he gets angry when she coughs. Her shoulders slink together.

She looks over and sees Quinn watching her. And the camera is there, the one that makes the pictures inside itself. Lulu exhales a long stream of smoke.

For a second, it's like time freezes, but then the trucker notices Quinn and grabs the cigarette from Lulu's hand, shifts her up, hefting her by the middle, so tight that it feels like her insides are squishing together. He pushes her into the motel room.

BILLY AT THE DIVE BAR

1980

C-PRINT, 8 x 10 INCHES

Quinn smacks at the off button on the alarm clock, silencing Donna Summer. She's due for a double shift at the bookstore but wishes so much that she could spend the day in bed, or better yet, in the darkroom, surrounded by the sulfuric smells and the rippling washes, the blooming images of her subjects. She's about to reach for the 35 when Ronald Reagan's voice blares next to her head, and she startles, realizing she must have touched *snooze* instead of *off.* She's tired of his voice, tired of seeing the advertisements all over the place—Let's Make America Great Again. She hits the bar hard, several times, but his voice continues to assault her ears, and so she yanks the cord from the outlet.

The Canon rests at the side of her mattress. Quinn lifts it up and rolls onto her back, the strap swinging near her chin as she inspects the lens and brushes off a bit of dust that lingers there, cursing herself for forgetting to put the cap back on before she crashed last night. She pries open the side and brings out the spent film, rolling it into a tube that she accidentally drops onto her chest before placing it into a box next to the bed where it collects with the other rolls she can't yet afford to process.

Outside, an argument breaks out between two men, and she recognizes one of the voices as Jian, the owner of the bodega that cuts into the street corner, attracting locals at all hours of the night who come for forties and rolling papers. And the others, like the old man who lives next door who does his entire grocery shopping there, stocking up on dented cans of spaghetti and nearly expired cartons of milk. She kneels on the mattress and looks out at the scene, leaning on the window ledge and wishing there was a breeze to pull the stale summer air from the apartment. An ambulance goes by, temporarily overpowering the argument. It continues, but Quinn leaves off, makes her way to the kitchenette, and warms up yesterday's coffee on a hot plate. Only the butt end of a loaf of bread remains in a tangled plastic bag on the sliver of countertop. She drops it in the toaster which lights up in a zig zag of red that smells as if its burning. She twirls her finger around a mostly empty butter dish, swiping it on the toast and licking off the residue.

A knock at the door nearly startles her coffee over the cup's edge. Her landlord stares back at her through the peephole. She ticks the dates in her head and curses, realizing how late her rent is. She grabs a cigar box from the kitchen cabinet as he begins pounding.

"One sec," she yells. The cabinet door teeters on its hinge, and she shoves it back into its socket. She pulls the few small bills from the box and counts them out. It's short, which she knew it would be or she would have paid on time in the first place. And she wonders what is wrong with her that she somehow thinks that the money in that little box will miraculously grow even if she doesn't feed it anything. She crosses the room to dig up the jeans she wore the night before and checks the pockets, relieved to find a few dollars there. It's still short, though. When she opens the door, her landlord is propped with an arm on the wall.

"Sorry," she says, handing it over. He counts it out in front of her, and before she can say it herself, he says it for her, "It's short. Again."

"I'm sorry," Quinn says. "I get paid this week."

"I need the rest by tomorrow," he says. "Unless you want to pay me another way." He reaches his other arm to the wall, caging her at the doorway.

Quinn stares at the stains on his shirt, the pelt of hair from the flab of skin sagging over his pants. She straightens, says, "I'll have it tomorrow," and swings the door shut, latching the bolt lock after. He pounds on the next door down, and there's some measure of relief in knowing she's not the only one. She needs to keep looking for a second job, something she's not been able to find in this city where everyone is always looking for something.

The toast is cold, but she stuffs it in her mouth anyway because it's all she's got. Her clothes are strewn on a worn velvet chair, a blush-colored period piece she and Billy snagged off a Greenwich Village street. She picks up the pants she hastily discarded and inspects a mysterious mark on the knee, curses. She had hoped to wear them again, but instead throws them toward a pile that overflows a laundry basket near the bed. The record player is loaded up with The Cramps and she sets the needle, stares at the string of photos that line the wall. And she wonders, Are they any good? Are they worth this? Maybe she should move back to Connecticut, cram into the small house under the bridge with her dad and his two cats, get a job taking photos of weddings or some shit. But even in this dingy apartment with its horrible landlord, the cracked ceiling and precarious cabinets, the windows that constantly stick open or shut, the unreliable hot water, she finally feels at home.

Her eyes rest on a photo of Billy, a cigarette dangling from his lips. His hair is wet from a shower and falls in dark curls around his eyes. He scratches at the back of his neck. It's as if his eyes are fixed on hers, and she tilts her head, watches them watch her. She sips her coffee and stares back at him over the rim of the cup, feels a twinge of something that she pushes away because she's not sure where it's coming from except that ever since they went to Riverdale, it's as if something has shifted between them, and she wonders if it's because of the little girl, Lulu. If it's because they drove away from her. Something about that has made them complicit, beholden to a shared bad decision and that has deepened what was already deep to begin with. Quinn moves closer to the photos, studying the angles, the choices made in shutter speeds, the small mistakes and the lucky shots, the cataloging of her decisions without recognition of them being made. That thing her professors always called *the art*.

She rubs self-consciously at the hollow below her ribs, drinks the rest of the coffee quickly, spitting small grounds back into the cup before setting it down. The acid churns inside her as she picks up the Polaroids from last night and selects a few, clips them to the string of others and they flutter like prayer flags before resting against the wall. She glances at the alarm clock, forgetting that she yanked it dark. She knows she's going to be late because she's been standing around looking at the photos for too long now.

Kate is in the stockroom when she arrives. Quinn punches in then joins her by a box of new hardcovers. The two set in, pulling them out and sticking price tags to their backsides. Kate leans toward her and with an exaggerated whisper says, "Jack noticed you were late today."

Quinn isn't concerned about that. Everyone but Kate is always late, which is bound to happen when you mostly hire poets and artists. But Kate is neither. Kate has a husband and a kid and lives in Queens. She works at the bookstore in the summer and on weekends to supplement her job as a librarian at the public school in Forest Hills. Behind her back, the other staff call her Mom, though Quinn secretly likes how Kate cares about each of them.

Still, Quinn doesn't feel like being lectured. She says, "I'm going to take these up," and steadies a stack of books in her arms. There are summer students and literary types with thick-framed glasses milling about the store. Quinn sets the books to the side of a stand in the front, then arranges them into a small pyramid that she has to redo twice to get even. She's admiring the stack when a man asks her, "This one any good?" He picks up the top copy, flipping it over in his hands.

"I'm sorry, I haven't read it," Quinn admits. She catches his eyes and stops there. They're steel-colored and lined with thick dark lashes. He's handsome, older than her, and dressed nicer than their usual bookstore regular. There's something about him that's familiar but she can't place it. The color creeps into her cheeks. She resists an urge to touch them because she doesn't want to draw attention.

"Well, I'll read it and let you know."

She notes the way he studies her, those dark gray eyes locked on her own hazel ones that are rimmed with tiredness and a reminder of last night's black eyeliner that she couldn't wash off entirely in the shower. She tries to smile, but it comes out in a twist instead because it hits her then, who he is, and she has to take a moment to recover because she's been in his gallery hundreds of times, coveting his artist roster, wishing she was one of them. "I know who you are," she blurts out, and he smiles. "I'm an artist."

"Everyone's an artist. You can thank Andy Warhol for that." He winks, and he's still flipping the book in his hands, and she wonders if it's his own nervous issue, like her flushed cheeks, but then she can't imagine someone like Eric Hoffman ever gets nervous.

"Photographer," she says, and then stalls because she can't think of a single thing to say to him next.

He realizes she's not going to and rescues her with, "What's your name?"

Somehow, she manages, "Quinn."

"Well, Quinn, I like photography. You should come by the gallery sometime."

He stops flipping the book, and she wants to ask him what he means—come by to see the work there or come by to talk about her work or *what? What?* "All right," she says, but even she can hear how weak it sounds. He heads to the register to pay, turns before leaving and waves the book in the air.

Jack puts her at the register next. She rings up several customers before Billy comes in. He hands her a to-go coffee from the nearby deli. It's watery and weak, but she doesn't mind. "Is that powdered sugar on your lip?" she asks. "Did you eat a doughnut without me?" She thumbs at the sugar on his mouth. If Billy knew how hungry she was, he'd rush out to buy her food, and yet she can't find a way to tell him that she's out of groceries, short on rent money.

"I'm a super asshole because I got one for you too and ate them both."

She punches at his arm, playfully, despite feeling real pain over it. "Where'd you go last night?"

Billy shrugs. "Mudd, but it was lame."

"You could have taken me," she says. "I heard Debbie Harry was there."

"She wasn't, and it looked like you were having fun with Liv and Micky. I needed to do some deals. There's that art opening tonight though at Club 57."

Quinn will go because her friends will go, but art shows in clubs is something she's not particularly fond of. All the drinking and drugs and cigarettes so close to the art. It hurts a bit of her soul. "Guess who came in here just before you?" Billy shrugs his shoulders. "Eric Hoffman." He presses up against the counter, and Quinn moves toward him, propping on her elbows. Billy knows who he is too because she's dragged him into the gallery with her at least half of her hundreds of times there. "He talked to me, and I was a complete idiot."

"I doubt you were," Billy says. "But what was he here for?"

Her cheeks redden again thinking about the encounter. "A book, I guess. I don't know, but he told me to come by the gallery sometime."

Billy smacks the countertop with his palm. "That guy's bigtime shit, right?"

She nods. "Next time, I won't make an ass of myself." Quinn shakes her head, and Billy grabs her arm at the elbow.

"Be nice to my best friend," he says, and she smiles. "Hey, I got to go. But I'll see you tonight."

She wants to find something to say to keep him, but "Okay," is all she says.

It's after eleven when they get to the club and push through a thick crowd to the back of the space where a secondary makeshift bar has been set up by placing a wooden door over two garbage cans. Girls, with their hair pulled into tight buns away from their dramatic faces, are painted in gold color and walk among the group in a choreographed movement. They stop at set intervals and pose questions to whomever is closest by. Quinn steers clear of them. A punk band begins to play, and the singer thrashes around in biker shorts, sweat flinging off his torso. His stiff mohawk chops through the air. If there's actually art, it's impossible to see with the number of people pressed up against the walls.

Billy hands her a drink that's the color of fruit punch. She makes a face as she sips. She takes some photos of the gold girls, battling with the shutter speed in a packed room with variable lighting. She wonders if they'll even turn out, tries not to think about the fact that she could be wasting film, because, if she starts to think like that, it could make it all feel completely useless. Billy tries to say something, but Quinn shakes her head and touches her ear. He pulls her by the arm through the gallery and back to the entrance where the summer night is hot but cooler than the sweltering indoors.

"I need a smoke," he says. He pulls two from a pack, and they light up. "What's with the gold ladies? You think they painted that shit all the way up their twats?"

"Hell if I know," she says. She hadn't realized they were naked under the paint, but a quick glance back inside the gallery reveals the perky nipple of one of the performers. "That'll be a bitch to wash off." She exhales, and they both laugh.

"Don't become one of those weird fuckers when you get famous, okay?"

Quinn sighs. "I can't even afford to develop my film right now."

"That's just bullshit, Quinn." Billy looks around and pulls out a wad of cash. "How much do you need?"

"I can't," she says, and she feels the heat creep into her cheeks for the hundredth time today. She's relieved it's too dark out for him to notice. She looks enviously at the thick stack in his hands. And then she thinks about her landlord's flabby stomach, the way he said she could pay him another way. Quinn shifts. "I need about a hundred," she admits. He fingers out a few bills and presses them into her hand, and when she takes it, she knows it's more than that by the bulk in her palm. This is the drug money, no doubt, because just like she doesn't like to take other people's money, Billy doesn't like to take his parent's even though it sits in an account he can tap into anytime he wants. And she's always wondered how that would feel, to have that kind of reassurance. He's never treated her like it, but they both know she's a charity case in his world, given access only because her dad is a janitor in the country day school where they met.

With that settled, Billy says, "So, hey, you want to party? Like really party?" And with Quinn's hesitant nod, he places a small pill in her mouth and closes her lips with his fingertips. She knows these are the magical pills from Riverdale, the ones everyone is desperate for. The pills that will transport you to the moon and back again. And it's true because the pill hits her quickly, and Quinn's body immediately begins to tingle in a way that's both alarming and beautiful. She swallows twice, her mouth filling with saliva. She takes a few deep breaths to calm her racing heart. "Let's go back in," Billy says. "I want you to meet this artist guy I know."

Inside, everything glows with a fuzzy edge. Lights brighten and dim. Billy drags her to the bar and hands her another cringing drink. The punk rocker's performance is over, and a DJ is setting up. The artist is tucked in close to one of the gold performers, his face angled into her slim neck. When Billy taps him on the shoulder, it takes some doing for him to emerge.

"Hey, man," the guy says. A halo of glittery light surrounds him, and Quinn is in awe. It's the pill, she knows, and it is pure joy, how she would paint joy if she was a painter.

"Hey, yourself," Billy says. "Myles, this is my friend, Quinn. She's a photographer."

Quinn breathes deeply against the rising heat in her body as Myles turns to her with another showy flourish. His eyes are intense green; his dark hair flips over one side of his face.

"I see that." Myles points to her camera. "What kind of work?"

Quinn tries to speak but can't. Billy sees and answers for her. "Street shooting. You should check out her stuff." She wonders how Billy can hold himself together when she feels like she's scattered across a galaxy. Myles touches Quinn's bare shoulder, and she shivers. "You want to show me your stuff?"

Her voice is back though it sounds foreign in her ears when she manages to say, "Yeah."

Billy smiles at her, pats her back, and takes the gold performer to the dance floor as a mix of Bowie's "Stay" comes on. Alone, Myles says, "You're pretty cute. What's your name again?"

"Quinn." The pill starts to rear, and Quinn reaches out to touch Myles's chest, a V of hair and skin that's soft under her palm.

"That's a fucking weird name," he says. "I like it." He slips his hand up the inside of Quinn's tank top and her entire torso feels like a million small explosions. "You wanna go somewhere," he says into her hair. She nods, and he leads her through the crowd to the bathroom where he kicks out two girls doing coke. He kisses her neck and licks the groove of her collarbone. Her head tilts back, and she feels the shooting stars.

"Let me see that." He takes the 35 from around Quinn's neck and snaps several photos of them in the bathroom mirror. Her knees disappear as she leans into him. He holds her up, rests her against the sink, and yanks down her jeans.

In the morning, the worn off glory of the pill leaves Quinn in a deep low. Her camera sits next to a pile of clothes she hastily discarded upon arriving home. Her boots are strewn across the room. She vaguely remembers the trouble she had kicking them off. Tears well in the corners of her eyes. The glittery beauty of the pill is not worth the come down. She swipes a hand over her eyes and reaches for the Canon, opening the back to take out the film. She finds it empty.

Quinn sits up, too abruptly, which makes her head swim. She curses as she looks around, grabs her jeans and goes through the pockets, but there's only the cash from Billy and her apartment keys. She rummages through the box where she keeps her unprocessed film, but it's not there either. She bangs her head into her mattress and fights an urge to throw up from the dizziness it brings on. It feels like a little piece of her has been snipped away. She tries to retrace her steps from the night before, but the pill makes piecing it together nearly impossible. She doesn't even remember how she got home.

The door buzzer breaks her out of the moment. Myles is standing below, leaning against her stoop and looking more handsome than she wants him to. "Hey," she shouts out the open window, and he looks up. "How do you know where I live?"

"You told me," he yells back. "Can I come up?"

She buzzes him in and waits for him to climb the two flights to her apartment. He has coffee, she now notices, and she takes one gratefully. "What are you doing here?"

"Bringing you this." He shows her the rolls.

"Where did you find them?" She grabs the film, wondering if they were properly rolled, wondering if any of the shots were even worthwhile.

"In my pocket. I'm pretty sure you put them there and told me that I would have to come see you. It worked, here I am."

"Well, that's embarrassing." Quinn curses the damn pill.

Myles laughs. "Since I'm here, you want to show me your work?"

She nods and says, "Yeah, sorry. I just got up." She grabs her boxes and a few stacks of photos and hands them over to Myles who has cleared off her chair and is sitting in wait. As he flips through them, she tries not to hover, sips her coffee casually, and wonders why she even cares what he thinks when she doesn't even know him. It's impossible to read his impression though. While he's preoccupied, she studies his features, notices things she didn't the night before when the drug and the lighting played with her perceptions. His strong jaw is covered in the shadow of a skipped shave. His large hands have colorful paint under the tips of his fingernails. It reminds her of the painters she dated at the School for Visual Arts, how they always smelled like turpentine.

"Pretty rad," he finally says at the end of the pile. "This one with the kid and the dude, though." He whistles. "What's up with that?" Myles has held back the photo of Lulu and the trucker. Quinn resists the urge to grab it from him. She thinks about the moment the Polaroid emerged in the car as they were nearly on the highway. She had grabbed Billy's arm, made him pull over to see it. And they had both stared at the ghostly image, the shadows and the framing and the little girl there, staring back at them, her eyes dull, almost bored, and that meaty hand around her thin stomach, hooked under her visible ribs. That tilt in her tube top and the way her legs swung above the ground on the man's lap. The cigarette, too expertly perched in her fingers. And the trucker, his face tilted away, his beard catching strands from the back of her hair and connecting to his face like a cobweb. Quinn has memorized the photo, doesn't even need to take it from Myles to know exactly how it looks.

"Kind of an accident?" Quinn says.

"Not staged?" Myles looks more interested.

"No. Billy and I got stuck at this shitty motel in Pennsylvania, and I met that kid. I caught that as we were leaving."

"Well, shit." Myles holds the photo carefully at its edges. "This is your golden ticket. Lulu and the trucker."

She takes the Polaroid from him and carefully sets it in the box with the others. "But, like, how do I get someone to check these out? I've had a couple of group shows, but no luck with galleries."

He looks sideways at her. "Well, I work with Patty Arnet. She's pretty cool. Likes emerging artists." He waves a hand, meaning Quinn. "I can introduce you."

"That would be amazing." She looks at him, and then says, "Is one of those gold performers your girlfriend?" It's not what she meant to say.

"I don't believe in girlfriends," he replies.

"You know, they aren't like Santa Claus," Quinn says, feeling bolder.

"And Billy? Is he your boyfriend?"

"Hardly. We've known each other since we were kids."

"I was joking." Myles pushes at Quinn's hip, and she steps back. He stands too and pulls her close. "Last night was fun though."

"Yeah?" she asks as he's walking her backward, toward her bed. She reaches for the Canon as she passes by it. Myles lets go of her to pull off his shirt, and Quinn catches a photo as it's coming off. The motion has coaxed his hair in a messy pile. His jeans sit low on his hips, exposing the curve of muscle that dips into the seam. She sees this through the lens in the second it takes to capture it.

⁂

It's clear when Quinn meets Patty Arnet that she's the kind of woman who looks younger than she is and makes a game out of sleeping with artists. And Myles is no exception. It's the way she says his name, rolling out the *i* sound in exaggeration like a secret purr. It has taken a month to get this meeting because Patty has been vacationing in the South of France. Quinn has never known anyone who has vacationed in the South of France, but Billy says that's just what wealthy women say when they're recovering from plastic surgery.

The woman sizes up Quinn from behind round, black-framed glasses that reflect Quinn's image back at her. Quinn tugs at her ripped T-shirt that has twisted out of place, smooths the stray hairs that she can feel clinging around her chin. Patty's hair is dyed a glossy tar and cut with severe bangs. Her lips are lined in a blood red. Her lashes are most definitely fake. They make a spider-like crawl toward her thin eyebrows. She's head to toe in black clothes that seem draped and wrapped on her thin body. Quinn can't find the beginning or end of any garment. While Patty looks as if she's never once pulled a shirt over her perfect hair, Quinn realizes she herself looks like she just got out of bed.

They sit at a thick table with a polished top as smooth as ice. Quinn glances around the gallery at the stripped walls on summer hiatus, the swirls of concrete floor. The space is larger than she imagined, configured as a white cube but with two quarter partitions for more hanging space. It's like the other SoHo galleries Quinn has frequented, but with her sitting here, like this, it seems more spectacular somehow.

Quinn clutches her hands, kneading her locked fingers, as Patty begins flipping through the portfolio that Quinn and Billy spent hours putting together the day before. "Have you had any shows?" Patty asks and she smiles, and Quinn notes her perfectly straight teeth, *money teeth*, and thinks about her own small twists and gaps. She bites on the edge of her thumb.

"I've had a few photos in a couple of group shows."

"Why people?" Patty studies the photographs. Her eyes are on one of Billy and Liv outside a hot dog stand at Coney Island.

"Well, I used to love looking at old photos when I was a kid," Quinn says. "Wondering how the people in them felt, what their lives were like. My dad has a photo of my mom from a beach party when they were twenty something. I love that photo. I used beg him to let me hold it, and I'd just stare at it." Quinn doesn't say that it's also the only way she really knew her mom, as an image, as a trick of paper, emulsion, and silver salts.

Patty takes off her glasses and sets them next to the portfolio. She's younger looking without them. "You have a lot of talent," she says as she flips backward, faster now, through the portfolio. Little waves of air puff at Quinn from each page slapping against the last. "But I will tell you that this isn't just about talent, it's about business too. Not all talented artists are able to sell their work. So, how about we do a show and see what kind of artist you are?" Before Quinn can respond, Patty continues, "I had an exhibition slated for the season opener in

September, but I think we'll bump that and do yours instead. I'm eager to see the reaction we get."

Quinn is stunned, manages to blurt out a thank you but then asks, "How does it work?" thinking about the few dollars she has, the amount of darkroom work needed.

Patty smiles in a way that makes Quinn feel foolish. "We'll select about thirty of your photos, frame them, install them, and throw a big party. And hopefully people will buy them. It's pretty simple really."

Quinn tries to smile back. "I don't have much money for framing," she admits.

Patty waves her hand and says, "I pay for that."

"Oh, thanks." Quinn feels even more foolish.

"We'll split the sales sixty forty, me at sixty. You understand why that is?" Quinn nods then also says *yes*, but she doesn't ask what happens if nothing sells. She hopes she won't have to find out. "All right, we have a month to prepare. I want to go through these again with a fresh eye and make the selection. Can you leave these with me?" Quinn nods, though moments later when she leaves the gallery without her work in her arms, she feels as if she's just handed over her life to someone else. It's simultaneously a relief and a horror.

Billy is waiting outside. "I'm dying here!" he says as he links an arm around her shoulder. "I figured it was a good sign that it was taking so long. What did she say?"

Quinn grabs his hand and squeezes. "She's showing my work," she says. "I'll be the opening show in September. Can you believe it?" Her heart races again at the retelling.

"Holy shit, Q!" He pulls her into a tight hug. "We should get a drink." And it's a good suggestion because Quinn feels electrified, currents of excitement and anxiety surging simultaneously inside her.

"Yes," she says as they peel apart. "I definitely need a drink. That was super intense. I mean, holy shit intense."

They veer into a dive bar a few corners down, exchanging the breezy outdoors for the scent of stale booze and rotting wood, the slight undertones of vomit and bleach. The place is dark, and it takes a minute to adjust as they take seats at the bar. The bartender scoffs when Billy asks him if they have champagne and pours them two tall shots of tequila instead. The bar top is sticky black lacquer with initials cut here and there, crude hearts, an anarchy sign. Quinn runs her fingertip over a heart, and it deposits grime under her nail.

The Jam's "Going Underground" is on the jukebox, and Billy sings along to the *I'm so happy* parts. She smiles, welcoming this change from being next to Patty with all her dark intensity to being next to Billy with all his simple charm. The alcohol burns but then smooths out Quinn's nervousness. Their knees touch on the barstools, and Billy grabs hers, squeezes. She links her boot onto the metal spindle of his stool, says, "Oh my god, the whole time my knee was like." She frantically moves her knee up and down under his hand, and he laughs.

"What's she like?" he asks.

Quinn shakes her head. "Like, all in black, super cool, gorgeous in a creepy vampire kind of way. Probably sleeping with Myles." Billy's eyebrows raise. "It's cool, who cares." Quinn doesn't mean it, and she's pretty sure Billy knows that, but she's already put that part of the day away in her brain, into the little orbit she imagines to be somewhere behind her ears, the repository for all things she just does not want to have to deal with.

Billy makes a twirling motion with his hand, and their shot glasses are refilled. He bites into a scrawny wedge of lime. There are a few other patrons, seasoned day drinkers slumped in the recesses of the bar. Billy puts his hand on the side of her head, and she presses into his palm. "Thanks, you know, for always being in my corner," she says.

"It's a good corner to be in." He moves his hand and for a moment her head feels like it's floating away.

"Patty asked me why people. It made me think about my mom." Quinn hiccups and presses her hand to her chest. "Sometimes, I remember her on the beach with her friends and then I realize that I wasn't born yet and that it's this photo my

dad has of her that I'm thinking of. Not my own memories. I
don't have my own memories."

When she thinks about her mom, something changes in
Quinn. She feels the shift, the welling darkness that she thinks
might actually change her composition. It has always felt like a
hardening from the inside out. "I think that's why I'm making
this work, well, like this," she says. "Someday it'll become the
memory of right now." Quinn hiccups again and curses. She
holds her breath for a moment, willing away the contractions.
"I think it'll be like time traveling," she says. "When we're older.
We'll look at these photos, and it'll bring us back here." She raises the Canon and takes a photo of Billy, the shot glass wavering
between the bar and his lips.

"Shit," he says, checking the clock above the bar. "I have to
go in a sec." The words sting the moment. "You'll be okay?"

"Yeah, yeah. I have to meet Liv at Ernesto's anyway." Quinn
disengages her boot from his stool, and he pushes out of his
seat, tosses several bills on the bar. When he kisses her goodbye,
she can smell the tequila from his breath and feel the wetness
of his lips for a little bit longer.

Liv's waiting for Quinn outside the tiny taco shop. Her hip
leans on a graffitied wall scrawled with a faded *SAMO© is dead*.
She hands Quinn a half-smoked joint. Quinn takes a hit and
hands it back. Liv gently taps it against the rounded edge of the
© on the wall, putting it out. She drops the roach in her cigarette pack and steps around a sparkling fan of broken window
glass on the sidewalk from a car no longer there.

"Let's get food and then I want to hear everything." Liv
claps her arm around Quinn's shoulder. A string of bells on the
door clangs as it closes behind them and they squeeze into the
compact space. The air is rich with the smell of hustle, a food-
and-sweat combination. They make their order, and Quinn
takes a photo of the cooks tossing the taco fillings over a siz-
zling sheet of metal that wafts grease and meat. They're handed
foil-wrapped tacos and a beer, then find a seat outside to eat.

"So?" Liv asks.

"I'm going to have a show," Quinn says, and Liv knocks her shins against Quinn's under the rickety table.

"That's fucking fantastic. When?"

"September, season opener. But listen, I'm nervous." It's what she didn't say to Billy but does to Liv because Liv has done this, a few times now, and she knows.

"What are you nervous about?" Liv takes a wide bite of her carnitas, her golden eyes glancing away for a second to watch a man halfway down the block pissing on a relay letterbox.

Quinn pauses to think it through, but it's so many things, too many things. "I don't know," she says. "I just am. Like, what if everyone hates the work?"

Liv shakes her head, swallows. "This isn't your first rodeo. People love your work. It's good, and you know it's good."

"Yeah, but this isn't drunk people at the Palladium. I mean, this needs to go well."

Liv touches Quinn's knee. "It's going to go well," she says. "You'll have to trust me on that, okay?"

"Patty said it doesn't matter if I have talent, it matters if my work will sell, or something like that." She eyes Liv over her own taco, not yet ready to eat it with the acid churning in her belly from her nerves and the tequila shots.

Liv makes a face, shakes her head. "These gallerists can be such assholes," she says. "What did she think of your little girl pic?"

"I didn't take that one," Quinn admits. "It doesn't fit with the others, you know?" She didn't take any of the Riverdale photos. Liv tilts her head but then simply nods.

"Let's talk opening night," Liv says, changing the subject. "We'll find something rad for you to wear."

Quinn hasn't even thought that far ahead, stuck as she's been on the content, the idea of the show. This adds another sliver to her anxiety. "I forgot that I actually have to go to the opening." She's never liked being the center of attention, as if people will figure things out about her, will know she doesn't belong.

Liv laughs and slurps the fizz off the top of the can she just opened. "It's like losing your virginity. Seems like a big deal, but afterward you'll be like, oh okay, so that's that."

Quinn laughs. "Well, I lost my virginity to Billy." She raises her eyebrows.

"Wait, how did I never know that? How old were you two?"

"Fifteen, but I wasn't his first." Quinn thinks of the photo from that day—Billy with a cigarette between his lips, the washboard ribs in his thin chest, his wiry arms wrapped around her while they lay on a lounge chair pad pulled into his parents' pool house. Her Kmart bathing suit slung on the indoor-outdoor carpeting.

"Hilarious." Liv takes a long drink. "Where's he tonight?"

"He's going to meet us at the party." Quinn finally eats a bite of her taco. She licks at a drip of hot sauce that slinks down the side of her hand. Liv hands over the beer, and she takes a long sip. It reignites the slight buzz carried from the dive bar. When they're done, they toss the trash and head the few blocks to La MaMa for Micky.

They catch the end of Micky's rehearsal, sitting in the nearly empty theater with their elbows resting on the back of the seats in front of them. The space is dim and warm, and Quinn relaxes her head on her arms to watch.

"Fuck, she's good," Liv says.

"For real." Quinn sits back up, shoots several photos of Micky and the dancers, huddled on stage, then breaking apart into trial movements, then reuniting again to discuss. Though Quinn has never been fond of performance art of the recent gold-painted girls' variety, she loves performance, the way a body can tell a story, each muscle and movement like a string of adjectives and metaphors.

Micky slings a duffle bag over her shoulder as she comes off the stage to meet them. She high-fives Liv and hugs Quinn, and Quinn inhales the musky sweat from her neck that smells like incense and something sweeter. The underside of Micky's curly hair is damp and a deeper dark. Quinn pats the beads under her eyes and on her forehead, noting the perfect arch of her friend's thick eyebrows and the crests of her brown cheeks.

"I'm super gross," Micky says. "It's so hot in here tonight."

"You're not gross," Quinn says. "You're glistening."

"You're a little gross," Liv says, grabbing Micky around the shoulders. "But we love you anyway."

"Ha, ha," Micky says, and she turns out of the hold. They follow her out of the theater. "You guys mind if we walk? It feels good out here." They don't have far to go anyway. At Micky's apartment, Quinn and Liv rummage through her clothes while she showers. Liv changes out of her shirt and into one of Micky's. Quinn draws dark lines under her eyes, sweeps purple shadow over her lids. She sprays her hair into a teased version of itself.

Outside, the streets are filling with nightlife. They step around a group of guys throwing dice near the shelter as they pass over Bowery. Houston Street is a car lot of taxis honking aggressive moves, vying to make it through the light.

The party is thrown by an artist they don't know and it's in an old factory space that leads them deep under the foul smell of Canal Street where they trek through the dark, dirty alleys, past a buzzing Mudd Club to where the other pedestrians have thinned out. The night feels thicker here, condensed in the abandoned buildings and worn-out streets. Quinn stumbles on a cobblestone and is relieved when her next step feels all right. They spot Myles outside smoking.

Liv eyes her. "This guy still? You know he fucks everyone, Quinn."

Quinn sighs. "I've heard. But he hooked me up with Patty, so." Her friends have shared plenty of stories about Myles and his exploits, and those too have gone into that little orbit of *not now* in her brain.

"I mean, he's hot as hell," Micky adds. "Who cares if he's a slut?"

Liv shakes her head. "Don't say you weren't warned."

Liv and Micky go into the party, while Quinn strolls up to Myles. Her steps are like little sways, because now she's almost

all excitement about the show and only part anxiety. She owes
it to him for setting up the meeting with Patty in the first place.
He tosses the cigarette down. It smokes near his shoes. "Hey,"
he says. "How'd it go?"

"Really good," Quinn says. "I'm going to be the first show
of the season." She expects him to smile, but his mouth drops
instead.

"September?" he asks, and she nods. "That bitch promised
me a show in September." Now, there's space between them,
and Quinn isn't sure what to say. He must be the show Patty
mentioned bumping, and she wonders if there was more to the
timing than the woman let on. "I need to talk to her," Myles
says. He starts to walk away, and Quinn rushes to catch up to
him, grabs his arm. "Right now?" she asks. "What about the
party?"

Myles spins to look at her. "Fuck the party, Quinn."

Quinn bites her lip and lets him leave. She pulls up the 35,
takes a picture of the back of him, slouched under the haze of
a streetlamp as he crosses Church. It spends the film, and she
rolls it up, shoves it in her pocket where it bulges from her hip.
She lights a cigarette and leans against the building near the
door Liv and Micky disappeared into, not quite ready to join
them now. Her shirt snags on the bricks and she curses, steps
away, and tosses the cigarette to the ground. She's about to go
inside when she sees the man approaching, rapidly, too rapidly.
He's her height, but thick, and she thinks, *Why is he rushing?* and
then she sees the ski hat that, in the darkness, looked like hair,
and before she can wonder how he can stand to wear a hat in
this heat, he's grabbing her, yanking her backward into the alley.

Quinn doesn't think to scream. Instead, she grunts as the air
is knocked out of her when he pushes her face-first against a
dirty brick wall. The edges of mortar cut into her cheekbone.
The rotting stench of fat trash bags down the way are only
momentarily distracting. His hands dip into her front pockets,
tossing her things as they swim around her crotch and come
up empty of cash because she used her only dollar on tacos.

He curses. His knee digs into her as he presses his body against hers and, for a moment, his sweat mixes on her skin. Quinn squeezes her eyes shut, her mind racing at options. But then she hears the thick sound like a slump and feels the severed camera strap whip away as he pushes off her and runs with it out of the alley. And now, she realizes he had a knife and that it must have been a damn sharp one to cut that easily through the leather strap. Quinn turns her back to the wall, presses against it, glancing nervously around at the shadows and slim lines of light. She tries to catch her breath against a deepening pain in her ribcage. She touches the wetness on her cheek and winces, wipes the blood on her shirt. The saltiness of her tears burns in the wound.

A rat scuttles from the trash bags as Quinn picks up her film and cigarettes from the ground, along with her apartment keys which splay further away. She does a quick step though the rodent is nowhere near her, has already fled the scene. She feels the loss of her camera like the loss of a limb. She rubs her shoulder where the strap has set a permanent indentation in her muscle. It's only then that she sees that she's wet herself. She stares at the soaked crotch of her shorts, swipes her legs against one another where the piss has dripped down her thigh, and a rumble of ache comes over her, and it erupts everything inside, covering the earlier excitement of the day. She thinks to find her friends, but she can't go inside now, not like this, and so she walks, her back to the wall, her eyes darting, to the corner, to the streetlamp that burns out at her approach like a too late warning, and then she runs back toward her apartment, her breath catching painfully in her injured ribs, counting each block as she goes, whispering each street name until she's at her own and she does not stop until she's inside, with the door locked and the bolt locked and the chain locked behind her.

"I brought you a book I *have* read," Quinn says when Eric Hoffman ushers her into his office. She's pleased he remembered her from the bookstore when she arrived, unexpectedly, to the gallery, asking for him by name, a new boldness that she knows has something to do with what happened in the alley that night.

She hands it over, and he says, "*Zen and the Art of Motorcycle Maintenance*. This is a great book."

"Okay, I didn't actually read it," she admits. Eric laughs, and she likes his laugh. It's rich and comes from somewhere in the back of his throat.

Quinn touches her cheek where the wound has finally healed to a muted pink that could be any small irritation. It no longer draws attention the way it had, and she's grateful for that. The bruising on her ribs is a golden green, easily hidden under clothes and a careful wrapping of her arm like a broken bird wing. She is almost whole again, minus one big missing piece of her. There is no camera around her neck, and though Billy has offered to buy her a new one, she can't let him do that. For now, it's only the Polaroid, which is too cumbersome to carry for hours on end. All her money has gone to darkroom costs for the show. She needs to sell a photo so she can finally replace the 35. She sends her once again late rent into the *not now* orbit in the back of her mind.

"I have a show opening tomorrow," she says. "At Patty Arnet Gallery." She has practiced these words over the past month on friends and coworkers, on her dad, and each time she says them, they still feel a bit unreal, like a little fib, as if someone might not believe it.

Eric says, "I've seen the promo materials." He gestures for her to sit with him on a couch. The book is still in his hand. She leaves a person-wide space between them, even though she has an urge to be as close as possible. The couch is soft, comfortable, and Quinn could sink into it, sleep on it. For a minute, she imagines kicking off her shoes, tucking her feet up under her and leaning an arm casually on the back of it. Like she belongs here.

"You should open that," she tells him, nodding to the book.

He flips it open, and the Polaroid of Lulu and the trucker

sits there somewhere in the middle pages. "What's this?" Eric takes it out and squints at it. "You took this?" Quinn nods and tugs self-consciously at her hair, looping its ends in her finger. "Did you show it to Patty?" Quinn shakes her head. "Well, well. You just became even more interesting, Quinn Bradford. Pos/ neg film?" He studies the photo. She shakes her head. "Just that print."

He inhales deeply. "Shit. You have to be careful with this then." Which, of course, she already knows. "Tell me about it."

She switches her crossed legs. "I was just passing through this truck stop town in Pennsylvania and met the girl, Lulu. I think her mom is a prostitute who uses that motel in the background. That guy is a trucker I met in a diner there. When I saw them together, I snapped this so fast, before I really knew what I was seeing, you know?"

"For a quick shot, it's really incredible. A little blurring here on the right edge, and the left corner is dark, but hell."

Quinn knows it's nearly a miracle that the photo came out as well as it did. She wasn't kidding when she told Billy that the Polaroid is all about luck. Seeing it in his hands, she feels relief, like someone else is carrying her burden as well.

"You could think there's something innocent to it, but there's enough of a question mark," he says. "I mean, her ease with that cigarette. Where his hand is on her."

"Will you come to the show?" she asks him, even though she meant to respond about the photo.

"Yeah, I planned to." He smiles and checks his watch, and she inches to the edge of the couch because she's sure he's about to tell her that he needs to be somewhere or that she needs to go. But instead, he says, "Hey, can I take you to lunch?"

She's so surprised that she doesn't respond for a second and then she realizes he's watching her. "Oh, yeah," she says. "Like, right now?"

"Yeah, if you're hungry?"

He's smiling, looking maybe a bit confused, and she shakes her head, says, "I am, that's great."

She tries to ignore the pulsing in her belly that she's sure is going to creep up her body to blush her face. Eric sets the book and the photo on his desk, *for safe keeping*. He grabs a wallet and sunglasses and motions for her to go ahead of him out of the office. The gallery walls are being prepped by painters in white coveralls. Eric stops briefly to confer with them, then they exit out into a bright day, and Quinn takes a deep breath of the September air, relishing in the simultaneous warmth and chill of it. He leads her several blocks to a tiny Italian restaurant on Ninth Street that's tucked between curvaceous brownstones, and immediately she's conscious of her appearance.

They sit, and Eric orders a bottle of champagne by name without the need to consult a list. She's careful with the thin-stemmed glass that's handed to her, worried that in her anxious grip she'll snap it in half. It doesn't seem real, this restaurant in a brownstone with only a few tables that seems more like a film set than a place you might go for a casual lunch on a September afternoon. She thinks about Fred's in Milford, the family go-to for celebrations with its five-dollar mostaccioli night and red wine that stains the stemware. And she pictures her dad sitting there, alone, while she sits here in this fancy place. It makes her sad again that he'll miss the opening. He has to work a school event. He doesn't like driving to the city. The crowds, they're a lot for him. But he's proud. Very proud. She knows all of this.

"What are we celebrating?" she asks as she glances around, catches the eyes of other patrons who openly stare at her, sizing her up, making her feel as if she doesn't belong here.

"You," he says, casually tipping his glass to hers, and she gently, barely, touches his back. They sip. "And that photo."

Quinn sets down her glass and leans in toward him. "The problem with that photo is that I don't want anyone to see it."

Eric leans in as well. Their faces are just inches apart. And he's so handsome that she holds her breath without meaning to. "And why is that?"

She thinks how to phrase what she wants to say, how much of herself to give up, because even though, somehow, he doesn't feel like a stranger to her, she reminds herself that he very much is. "I'm ashamed of it, I think," she says. "Or not of it, but of the fact that I didn't do anything about it. I like literally just took off after taking it."

"What would you have done differently?"

Quinn scratches her forehead. "I don't know. I have these daydreams where I knock down the door and rescue her, or I kick the shit out of the trucker."

"And then what?" She likes that he doesn't look amused, more concerned instead.

"I don't get further than that. I mean, she'd have to go somewhere. But maybe she has family to take her in or something. She has a cousin. I know that for sure. I met her." Quinn thinks about the ragged trailer park, BB with her scarred face and no adult supervision.

Eric sits back and drinks from the flute. "I don't think hiding the photo away is going to solve something. It's been taken, whether people see it or not. Do you know what I mean?"

"I think so." It's not that she doesn't know what he means, but she's not sure she agrees. He's left a scent of something musk and spicy in the air between them. She realizes she's still intensely leaning in, so she sits back and takes another sip of champagne. The bubbles twinkle down her throat. And then she pauses to think about the fact that she's sipping champagne with Eric Hoffman and the incredulousness of it is almost overwhelming. A forming buzz pushes away the other patrons.

Eric taps his glass. "If you don't want anyone to see it, why did you show me? Maybe you want permission to show it?"

Quinn makes a sound of *hmm*. She knows he's probably right because she wouldn't have brought it to him otherwise.

"So, here's the thing," he says. "You need to decide what kind of photographer you're going to be. If you're going to push yourself, you're going to have more experiences like that little girl. Things that are uncomfortable, out of your control, painful, emotional. That's the stuff of good art, in my opinion. Especially with photography, that's what brings it into the realm of art."

"I don't know if I can handle it, that kind of work. I mean, honestly, I can't stop thinking about her." She wonders if this makes her incapable of being an artist, a real artist.

Eric nods. "Think of it like this, these are important stories and you're helping to tell them. Once these kinds of photos are taken, they become part of our collective consciousness. Hopefully, they force people to take notice. And hopefully, that starts to change something. It's the difference between looking and listening, you know? This work, when done well, will make people listen, not just look." He refills their glasses, and Quinn sips more champagne, tries to smile, but his intensity has left her feeling jarred.

They order from menus that have no prices, and Quinn has a moment of panic wondering if she'll have to kick in for the lunch bill, but Eric casually says "my treat" as he watches her studying the options, and she knows he knows, and she appreciates that he said something. He tells her about the gallery as they eat, and Quinn likes this change of subject, likes learning about his dual degrees in art history and business, his artist aunt who inspired the gallery and the money she left him to get it started. She likes him, she realizes at the end of lunch. She likes him a lot. They finish and head back to the gallery where Eric hands *Zen and the Art of Motorcycle Maintenance* back to her with the photo tucked carefully inside, and says, "This is actually a really good book. You should read it."

Quinn fusses with the tie on her shirt and tries to ignore the sweat running down the small of her back. The black leather pants Liv picked out at the resale shop hold in all her heat. She knows they were a bad idea, but Liv insisted they looked hot, and they were only two dollars because part of the inseam is shredded. It rubs awkwardly at her thighs.

Patty is moving her around like she's on a ride. They don't spend more than a few minutes talking to any one person, and it's a barrage of kisses and hands reaching out to take hers. She tries to focus outside these circles Patty creates, like a dancer spotting so as not to keel over in dizzy rotation. In one such moment, she sees Liv and Micky pointing at photos of themselves. In another, there's Billy and Myles at the bar, their backs to her. She wants desperately to break out of Patty's grip and go to her friends, but she stays because she knows that's what she needs to do. And then they're moving again, and when she sees who is next, she's both relieved and worried at the same time.

"Eric, this is Quinn, the star of the night." Patty squeezes Quinn's shoulder as she ushers her toward Eric Hoffman. Quinn smiles and nods her head.

"Nice to see you, Quinn," Eric says. "This is exciting work." Patty is hovering so close that Quinn swears she can feel the woman's blood surging in her veins.

"Isn't it?" Patty says. "Such talent and so young and sexy, am I right?" Patty grabs on to Quinn's waist, just missing her sore ribs, which forces Quinn to buckle in the side.

"You are right," he says. "And how did you find one another?"

"Myles Wainright. Quinn's his girlfriend." Quinn winces at the word, starts to object, but Eric tilts his head and studies her face.

"What a talented couple," he says.

She realizes she hasn't said a word for herself, turns to Eric and says, "I'm thrilled you came." A look remains on his face, the one that set there when Patty called Myles her boyfriend, a term Quinn wouldn't use herself.

But then it shifts, and he smiles. "How could I not?" Quinn wants to stay here with him, but Patty ushers her on. She looks over her shoulder, but he's back to the photos, studying them closely.

When they're out of earshot, Patty leans in and says, "Watch out for that one. You're just his type."

"Warning received." Quinn hides the small nod of pleasure the words bring her.

Patty peels off to talk business with the gallery assistant, and

Quinn winds back to where Eric is studying one of her photos of Billy at a party. "Really, thanks for coming," she says.

"I wouldn't miss it." He rests a hand on her shoulder and the slight pressure, the bulk of his hand, is a reassurance she realizes she's needed all night. It grounds her. "I have to run, but I hope you keep thinking about what we talked about yesterday. In the meantime, keep that photo safe." He kisses her cheeks before heading for the door.

In an act of contrition, Myles has offered to host an after-party at his penthouse loft, and he has already left when Quinn makes her way to Billy. "Hey, you." He loops his arm carefully around her. He knows of her tender spots. "How's it going?"

"Kind of surreal," she admits. She enjoys the moment of peace, watches people looking at her work. "I wonder what they think of it."

"Let's just wonder what Eric Hoffman thinks about it. Myles was losing his shit over that." Before Quinn can respond, Patty is upon them, ushering them out the door with swooping crow-like arms.

In the coolness of the night, Quinn's leather pants finally separate from her skin. Patty swerves her away while Billy hails a taxi, angles her head in and says, "We got a lot of feedback, though I wish something would have sold. I have two collectors stopping in tomorrow. With any luck, we'll get some interest." Quinn feels a knot form in her shoulders, a swelling of tension from what seems to be a mixed review. She wants to ask her if it's normal for nothing to sell, if the feedback is good or bad, who the collectors are. But she stays quiet.

On the ride across town, Billy fills the car with boisterous stories about nothing at all. Quinn watches out the window at the blur of lights, the people rushing to cross over intersections, the swarms outside of bars and restaurants. Her own reflection in the window is like a haunting, another version of her that moves when she moves, one she doesn't fully recognize. She has felt this split all day.

There's already a crowd at Myles's when they arrive, including

Liv and Micky who are flipping through cassette tapes at the stereo. They put on X-Ray Specs and the singer's voice screams into the space. When Quinn finds Myles, there's lipstick on his cheek, and he rubs at it when she tells him. He's been taking something, and while she wants to talk to him about Eric Hoffman and to ask what he thinks about Patty's response, he's not in the right state of mind. There are several girls hanging around, and Quinn recognizes the gold performer from the very first night they met. The girl leans close to Myles.

Quinn goes to the bathroom, locks the door, and the muted party is a welcome relief to her pounding ears. She leans against the vanity, stares at herself, trying to see the part that has blurred, but there is nothing unusual in the reflection. Dark semicircles crest above her cheekbones. She worked three doubles in a row to have off today and tomorrow and her back aches from lifting books. She sinks to the floor, leans against the wall, and listens to the laughter and the music and the sounds of lightness from the loft. She should rejoin the party, it's her party, but she stays where she is until someone pounds on the door.

Things have become messy in her absence. Her friends are doing shots at the concrete bar. There are many unfamiliar faces. The elevator door opens next to her, and she swaps places with the people in it. No one notices her leave.

Instead of home, she goes to a diner with a dollar special after midnight, realizing she hasn't eaten since the morning. She sits at the counter and looks around at the other patrons. A punk rocker with a chain from his nose to his earlobe is sipping coffee; a couple—her black eye makeup smeared, and his hair disheveled—slouch in a booth. Quinn stretches out the tension in her spine. Away from the party, a rush of emotions course through her. She feels a stab of guilt for leaving without telling anyone. The leaden exhaustion of preparing for the exhibition finally hits her. She reaches to cradle her camera, something that has always soothed her, but forgets that it's gone.

The waitress leans across the counter, asks, "What can I get you, hon?"

"What's the dollar deal?"

The woman smiles. "Pancakes and a beer."

"Pancakes and a beer it is." Quinn quickly double-checks the few dollars in her pocket. The diner door clangs, and she looks up. Eric Hoffman stands there and for a moment they stare at each other in equal surprise before he comes over to sit with her at the counter.

"Why aren't you at a party somewhere?"

"I was," Quinn says. "But now I'm not."

He shifts to face her. "Well, now you know my dirty secret."

"What's that?" She likes how casual he's being with her, as if they're old friends.

"Pancakes and beer." He winks at the waitress, and Quinn realizes he's not joking.

"You come here a lot?" she asks.

"I want to answer no, but yes, yes, I do. I live near here," he adds.

"Me too," she says, but she knows they aren't talking about the same neighborhood.

"Are you pleased with the show?" He leans on the counter, and she likes the way it brings him closer to her.

"I don't know," she admits. "Patty is pretty intense, and nothing sold tonight, and I can't tell if that's normal or a really bad thing."

Eric moves his head around in an ambiguous way. "It depends on what her goal for this opening was," he says. "But don't let that get you down. Your work is great. I would have put the content together differently, but that's on Patty, not you."

Quinn feels the frustration of being new to this rear. It's a sensation she's felt many times over the past few weeks when realizing what an absolute tourist she is in this process. She wants to ask him if she's going to have to pay Patty back for the frames—she's still so nervous about that—but it's such a dumb question that she almost blushes just thinking about it. She's kept a tally of costs though, including what she'll need for a new camera, and the amount is staggering, a sum that she's added up over and over again hoping for a different outcome.

"I guess we'll see how the rest of the show goes." She shifts her shoulders. "I had an idea, you know, about what to do next." An idea from a conversation with the bartender in Riverdale who only came to New York City once to see Times Square.

Eric's eyebrows raise. "That was fast."

"Well, I've been thinking about it for a bit now, but our talk pushed it back up in my mind. I'm thinking about doing a Times Square series. You know, like photos of the prostitutes and the addicts. The Deuce is like this mythical thing, but underneath all the lights and excitement is a real struggle. I want to get inside of it and see what's there."

"I like that," he says. "How do you plan to get started?" Quinn doesn't know that part yet, and she tells him so. Their food comes, and she watches in awe as he pours a puddle's worth of syrup on his pancakes. She smears a thin layer of butter on hers.

"Where's your boyfriend?" Eric asks between mouthfuls.

"Myles?" Quinn says. "He's not really my boyfriend, I don't think. And right now, he's probably screwing some gold performer." Eric looks confused, but she doesn't explain what she means.

"And you're not jealous about that?" he asks.

"It's just sex, right?" But she doesn't even sound convincing to herself.

Eric considers it, says, "I guess so. I don't know. I've been divorced twice already. I'm not good at that stuff."

"You aren't good at sex?" Quinn sets down her fork in mock exasperation.

"Don't put words in my mouth," Eric says, smirking at her. "I'm really good at sex. I'm not good at knowing what women want."

"Well, it might be because women don't know what they want."

"You seem to know what you want," he says.

"I don't know shit." Quinn looks at him, and they both laugh. She knocks her shoulder against his as she would with Billy. Eric lets his knee sway to touch hers. Quinn drinks and feels the night's adrenaline coming down. She thinks how this is the second meal she's shared with Eric Hoffman in two days and that thought makes her smile.

"But really," Eric says. "Not many people walk into my gallery like that. It was bold."

Quinn waves her bottle in the air between them. "You invited me, in case you forgot."

"I know I did, but you actually showed up. I didn't think you would."

Quinn wonders if most people do not. She swallows, not sure if she wants to share what compelled her to go there. Not sure how to explain the way she felt sitting in the scrawny bathtub the night of the attack, letting the water rush down her spine, washing the abrasion on her cheek, flushing away the shaking feeling. The feeling she could break into a million tiny pieces and flow down the drain and away, that she was that inconsequential. She had gotten dressed and packed a bag, checked an outdated schedule for the first morning train to Connecticut, but when the sun came up just hours later, she couldn't do it. She couldn't give up like that.

When they finish eating, she asks him if he wants to come to her place to see more of her photos. She's so sure he'll say no that when he agrees, she's almost confused about what to do next, but she gets it together to lead them down to Wooster. The moon is full and starting to dip down the horizon. Quinn has lost all track of time, because walking with Eric, leading him back to her apartment, feels like walking into a black hole, time expanding from what would normally be several minutes to light years.

Quinn's self-conscious about her shabby apartment with Eric in it. She has nothing to offer him but water, which he takes. His clothes are too nice for the gritty hardwood floors and cramped space. The cracks in the plaster seem more prominent now. The blooming brown stain on the kitchen ceiling has appeared to spread, darken. If he notices, he says nothing. He sits on the floor with his back against her chair as she pulls out the box of photos and contact sheets. He flips through them, setting several aside as he does so. Quinn bites her lip. She shifts how she sits, hiding the ripped inseam in her pants. The intensity of her anxiousness about his thoughts is well beyond what she felt when Myles sat here doing the same, and yards above what she felt with each *poof* of Patty's rapid page flipping.

When he's finished, Quinn waits for him to say something, but he's quiet, contemplative. Finally, she asks, "Well, what do you think?"

Eric picks up the pile that he's made and flips through them again. "There's a show right there," he says, and Quinn notices they're almost entirely the photos from Riverdale, including those of Billy in the car, blowing smoke rings. "Do you have a contract with Patty?"

"No, not yet," Quinn says. "The show was a test run." That ripple of worry returns, the one that Patty won't want to work with her again. That no one will.

Eric nods, and Quinn wonders what he's thinking, but he says nothing, instead he stands up, so she stands too. "Let's talk again soon," he says, and Quinn is confused but says okay. She leads him to the door, and he kisses her cheeks yet again and leaves. She slides over the bolt lock and links the chain, tries to watch him out the peephole, but he's already too far down the hall to spy.

Tourists stumble by in groups of bachelor parties and business executives with equal enthusiasm. It's a playground, these blocks around the nonstop buzz of Broadway marquees and the ticker-tape chaos of The Deuce. But that's what makes this great for business, as Tisha told Quinn months ago upon their first meeting.

Tisha is originally from Minnesota and is prone to dropping her *A*s in a way that will forever label her a midwesterner. She

takes Quinn by surprise as Quinn is watching in the other direction for her. She laughs when Quinn startles. "Scared you?"
she asks, and Quinn shakes her head.

"Surprised me," Quinn says. "There's a big difference."

Tisha sits down next to Quinn, squeezing tightly against
her. "How you been?" she asks, and Quinn considers how to
answer because her own problems seem like nothing compared
to Tisha's.

"I'm all right," she says, and Tisha calls her out on it, saying,
"Everyone's always all right." Quinn tilts her head. "Well, I got
a second job last week, bartending, which is kind of hilarious
since I can't make anything, but it's helping. How about you?"

Tisha whistles. "I'm all right too." And they lean against each
other which says more than they ever really need to. Quinn pulls
away first and twists to shoot a photo of Tisha, whose heavy
breasts hang thick in her slight slump forward on the stoop.

"When do I get to see all these pictures of myself finally?"
she asks.

Quinn sighs. "Hopefully soon." She doesn't want to get into
the details, how Patty decided not to represent her when nothing sold during the three-month exhibition and how Eric hasn't
yet offered despite many conversations, countless lunches, and
late-night pancakes. The ticking months have felt painfully re-
dundant. Quinn's in limbo, a frustrating seasons-long one where
she wonders if it's even worth continuing, but every time she
thinks about quitting, the pressure comes back, the dull ache
in her brain, the compulsion to create, and she's back out here
with her camera again, the one that she finally let Billy pay for.

It's summer solstice, and the night is warm and humid. A
halo-like haze rings each streetlamp and even on this, the longest day of the year, the sun has finally agreed to set, sinking
all its color under the horizon, letting the unbridled revelry of
The Deuce begin. Quinn pats the sweat on her forehead with
the back of her hand. It didn't take her long to decide to focus
on the women here, and there are plenty of them. Sex always
on sale. Female flesh always in season. Prostitutes, peep shows,

massage parlors. The demand is relentless. Tisha unweaves a soft pack from her bra strap, taps out two and hands one to Quinn.

"You want to get some food?" Quinn asks as she blows a long stream of smoke into the sky above her. It trails in the thick air. Tisha nods, and they push off the steps, swiping a thin layer of dirt from their butts. They decide on a diner around the corner where they know the manager won't hassle Tisha and where there are fifty-cent burgers and fries. They settle into a worn booth with a cracked tabletop that traps grime. Quinn shifts a sticky carafe of syrup to the side and snaps a few photos of Tisha in the booth.

"It's a weird thought though, you know? Someone wanting a photo of me." Tisha presses on a fake lash that slips from the side of her lid. As Quinn captures it, she thinks about something Patty told her before the exhibition, about how talent is only part of it. She doesn't want to think about the other things Patty said, after the exhibition closed, the woman's disappointment in having no sales despite a good write-up in the *Village Voice*, how Patty told her she was too much of a risk to represent. That she needed to learn to promote herself better, try harder, think like a businessperson as well as an artist. Quinn still feels shame over the invoice that Billy paid to transport the framed works from the gallery to his apartment because Quinn's was too small to house them. The humiliation she felt watching the art handlers empty the gallery walls, watching the assistant dump a stack of price lists into the garbage, Quinn secreting one for her archives, something to push her to try harder, to do better, even though she feels like she's already trying her hardest, doing her best. And yet, it's not enough.

Their food comes quickly because flipping customers is the only way to make a fifty-cent menu work. Quinn pushes a fry into ketchup, swings it toward her mouth. "This series is new for me, you know? It'll be a guess how it goes over." She doesn't say more, about how it needs to go well. "But what about you? What's going on with you?"

Tisha shakes her head. "Nothing good out here."

"You ever thought of going back home?"

"Not possible. I made a big show coming out here. There's no place for me back there." It's the same thing Quinn's heard from the other girls as well. There are three in her series, and over the past months, she's gotten to know them intimately, but Tisha is the only one she might call a friend. The two are the same age, and Quinn wonders if she has it in her too, if she was pushed hard enough, if she was desperate enough. She knows it's about survival.

"But look," Tisha says. "I gotta a surprise for you. Was gonna wait until we finished eating but looks like you need a pick me up."

"Oh yeah?" Quinn asks. "What's that?" She shoves a french fry in her mouth.

"Hooked up with this guy last night who likes people watching. I told him about you, and he booked again for tonight. You ready for this?" Quinn swallows hard to get the fry down. They've been trying for weeks with no luck to find someone willing to be in the shoot with Tisha. It's the missing piece in her series, the other half of the equation the girls face night to night. Quinn's mind begins to race through shutter speeds and angles. She wonders what the room will look like, the lighting, the skin tones. It's easier for her to get technical than to think about what's about to happen.

"So, like, you're definitely okay with this?" she asks.

"Yeah," Tisha says. "Listen, the guy paid extra for it even."

"When? Where is it happening?" Quinn's knee bounces in excitement.

"Half hour. Around the corner." The details make it real. They're quiet for a moment. "It's okay, Quinn," Tisha finally says. "I feel like you're wondering how I'm feeling. I'm trying to say, don't worry about me when we're in there. Okay? Just get what you need from it."

Tisha hums as they saunter down the block and even through the sounds of laughter and revelry on the street corners, Quinn can make out "Pale Blue Eyes." She follows Tisha to the side entrance of Taboo II, through a plain gray door that smacks shut behind them with a rusty wheeze. The hallway is dimly lit, and the stairs are carpeted in worn shag brown. Tisha catches her heel halfway up, trips forward and curses. Her round ass squeezes her leather miniskirt to its seams, and Quinn notes the plump trace of red lace panty between her legs and the splattering of bruises on the inside of her thigh.

They stop midway down the hall in the crosshairs of murmurs, laughter, and shouting from nearby rooms. Quinn takes a deep breath and follows Tisha inside. The man is already there. He introduces himself as Jeffrey, and Quinn wonders if that's his real name. He's younger than she imagined he would be. "I'll be taking photos if you're cool with that?"

He nods and touches her hip, and she moves slightly away so that his hand drops. "You want to join us?" he asks.

Quinn holds up the Canon. "Just here for this."

Tisha sits on the bed, one leg tucked underneath her. She smiles and tells Jeffrey to come sit too. Quinn moves to the side of the room and catches the light from a covered lamp. She adjusts her shutter speed.

He's paid for thirty minutes, but they finish with a bit of time to spare, and Jeffrey asks Tisha if she wants to get high. Quinn shoots this new exchange, the intimacy in how he sprinkles the white powder into the weed, rolls it up and lights it for her, holding back her hair and touching her chin when she smiles as the smoke slinks down inside her. They turn to Quinn and their offering breaks a spell she didn't realize she had been under.

Outside, Quinn slides into the moving body of people, the adrenaline intensifying the bright billboards. It's like she's seeing things for the first time. She stops to shoot photos of a group of prostitutes outside the HoJo. The women catcall passing men, lean into cars that stop on the busy corner. She captures the seedy Follies Burlesk sign, illuminated by glowing red arrows and the surrounding streetlamps, and then dips the lens to shoot the advertisement for a peep show below it, a faded brunette with her fingers between her legs. Surely, this was here before today, this has been here all along, but somehow in the shattering scenes of this busy intersection, she is only realizing it now. Across the street, the GLOBE marquee promises the Filthiest Show in Town. Quinn marvels at the lights and the gawkers and the shifty drug deals. The Canon clicks, etching image after image onto the film, making every second a new memory of itself.

The downtown train platform is packed with groups of people, laughing and loudly talking. She fingers the mace in her pocket, something that now sits among her keys and the tiny bits of cash she carries. She holds tightly to her camera, pressing it to the ribs that took months to finally heal. The film feels extra precious, like she will never get the chance she just got again. The train slinks through stations, turning over passengers at each stop, and Quinn exits at West 4th, checks the number on a slip of paper Billy gave her. She walks down a few blocks until she finds the building and stands outside for a moment, confused by its brownstone facade. A bulky man sits outside the door, watching her. His flashlight sweeps her face, and she holds up a hand to deflect the light. "Where you hoping to go?" he asks.

"To this party," Quinn says. "Or whatever this is. I'm Billy's friend? He mentioned I should come by." In the past, dropping Billy's name has worked at many a club door, and it does so again now. The man moves out of the way and swings the door open for her. "Through the hallway and make a right."

Quinn follows his instructions, tentatively walking into the dark space. She tries to reconcile the outside of the building with the inside, but it seems incongruous. And then she realizes she's treading through what once was the entry hall and toward the back where she follows the pumping sound of music. Her eyes begin to adjust as she passes by coupled-off guys who are intertwined in the dark corridor, mouths on necks, hands between legs. She tries not to stare as she searches out the party, and then she's upon it with a quick turn to her right into what must have been the living room but is now fully a dance club.

It's past one and the party is already well underway. Men move against men on the dance floor, pulsing to the music. Quinn resists the urge to take photos. Billy's warned her not to do that here unless she asks first. She spots him in a corner holding court on a winding black sofa. The club's lighting is amber and red, making everyone look simultaneously glowing and sinister. The color catches in the crevices of muscles and cheekbones, sweeps over armpits and foreheads and for a moment, she just watches the dancing, the simultaneous undulations like a trance.

Billy makes room for her, and she snuggles in next to him, inhaling the earthy scent of weed and cigarettes. "What is this place?" she asks.

"They have to be careful, you know? The police and all that shit." He leans closer, so that his lips are near her ear, and she shivers a bit at the feeling, despite the heat in the room. "Gay guys love drugs."

Quinn accepts a drink that's handed to her by a bar back in hot pants and is relieved by the cold gin and tonic that cuts down her throat. The club is growing hotter and humid, and sweat soaks the small of her back, clings to her collarbone. The glowing red lights intensify the heat. Locks of Billy's hair catch and cling, and she tugs on one of them before tucking it behind his ear. He turns his face to her so that his chin cuts sideways into the space between them, and she resists an urge to kiss the crest there. She only thinks briefly of Myles when she thinks she sees him at the bar, but it's not him, just a semblance of him. It's been many weeks since anything has happened between them because he still doesn't believe in girlfriends, and every time they start back up again, he finds a way to remind her of that by going off with someone else.

She accepts another drink and slumps back into the sofa, watching the dance floor, all the beautiful men there. The drinks loosen up some tight spots in her shoulders. She feels relaxed for the first time in a while. Billy goes to dance, but she's too hot to join him. She takes a third drink and finds herself in conversation with one of his new friends, Alex, a short, thin guy with curly dark hair that topples over to one side against a hard razor cut on the other. Billy has talked about him, and she knows he's a writer, though she's not sure what he writes. His eyes shine brightly in the darkness, set against warm brown skin, and Quinn can't stop looking at them, loses track of what they're chatting about and realizes she's drunk. It's getting harder for her to hear in the club. Alex is waiting for her to reply to something he said and when she doesn't, he leans close to her, so close she can smell the cologne on his neck.

"How long have you known Billy?" he asks again, and this time she catches the words, and they make her smile as she thinks about Billy as a kid.

"Since we were little. We had the same third-grade teacher. She hated him because he was such a troublemaker."

"I like him," Alex says, and she smiles. "Are you guys together?"

Quinn shakes her head. "Just friends." She sips her drink, and it drips condensation onto her knee. Alex watches her but doesn't reply. He lights a cigarette and hands it to her for a hit, which she takes.

"Why aren't you dancing?" she asks, and he shrugs. Even in the darkness of the club, she can see that something sad has set itself inside him. And she's always thought about grief like that, like a parasitic thing that climbs in, entwines inside and peeks out. Her own rears in response, but she pushes it back down. She knows her monster well, has lived with it since she was a child. Quinn grabs his hand and holds it tightly in hers, and his head tilts toward her as he crushes out the cigarette. And then he sinks into her, his head on her shoulder, his arm around her, and she holds him because she knows that's just what he needs.

❧

Quinn watches Eric's expression as he studies the contact

sheets. She bites at the edge of her thumb and then stops herself, takes a calming breath.

"If I didn't know any better, I'd think they were a couple,
and then you see the money sitting there on the nightstand." He
points to the photos where Tisha and Jeffrey cuddle after taking
the drugs. In one, her leg bends over his and the purple and
yellow blossom of a heart-shaped bruise strays above her knee
on the meaty part of her thigh. Her lacy panties are trapped
halfway down her leg where they never quite made it off.

Quinn nods as she looks over his shoulder through the
loupe at them. She knows they're good. She lets a rare feeling
of pride swell through her instead of pushing it away. Tisha has
given her an incredible gift in these images. The vulnerability
in her eyes contrasting with the confident arches of her body.
Her gestures are both commanding and conceding. Quinn will
find a way to thank her. She shuffles the contact sheets into
her portfolio and sits back in her seat. She waits for Eric to say
more about the work, about the shoot, but he just smiles at her
and instead says, "You want some breakfast?"

"It's two in the afternoon, but why the hell not?" She tries
to hide the exasperation that rings her words. There's a small
voice in her head that says if they have another meal together
and nothing comes of it, she's officially walking away from him.
But then she knows that's not true. Something has bound them
together, even if it's not technically official.

Eric stands and grabs her hand to pull her up. Quinn keeps
ahold of it as they walk out of his office and through the gallery. He rubs his thumb on hers, and she likes the way his hand
feels nestled in her palm. He steers her to the outdoor seating
of a café she's never been to and never would have been able to.

"This place serves breakfast?" she asks, her chair scraping
against the concrete.

"This place serves whatever we want." Eric sits, and Quinn
smirks. "I know the owner," he adds. "He lives in my building. I
don't complain about his loud dog, and he makes me breakfast
whenever I come in."

Sure enough, a man comes from inside and clamps his hand on Eric's shoulder. "Andy, this is Quinn."

Andy takes Quinn's hand and kisses the top of it. "Pleasure to meet you. Menus or your usual?"

"You want a menu, Quinn?" Eric asks.

"What's your usual?"

"Fried chicken and waffles," Andy says. "Can you believe this guy eats that at least once a week and still looks like this?"

Quinn smiles. "I'll have that," she says. "And a Bloody Mary."

"Same for me," Eric adds, and Andy nods, feints a bow and leaves.

"I wouldn't have pegged you for a chicken and waffles kind of guy." She leans into the table. It rocks the surface on the unsteady ground, sending a glass saltshaker skidding. Eric steadies it.

"What can I say? My mom was from the South. Fried food is in my genes."

"So, do you bring a lot of women here?" Quinn's joking, but realizes she's very interested in the answer.

Now it's Eric who smirks. "No, I'm usually here alone. Most of the women I date won't eat fried chicken and waffles."

"Oh, is that so?" Quinn sits back. "I've never had fried chicken and waffles. I hope it's good."

"Wait, what? Never?" Eric leans forward now, and the saltshaker rushes his way. She steadies it. "Quinn, you have no idea what you've been missing. It's a good thing you met me."

"So I can try fried chicken and waffles?" She laughs.

"Don't joke. You have no idea what you're about to experience."

"Wait, go back. So, do you have a girlfriend?"

Eric looks sideways at her and squints. "I do."

"You do?" She has too much surprise in her voice. But of course Eric would have a girlfriend. Why wouldn't she have thought so. "How come I didn't know that?"

"You never asked."

"Huh." She shifts in her seat. "I'm a bit jealous."

Her comment's in jest, but even to her own ears she can hear the truth behind it.

"Oh, the girl with two boyfriends is jealous?" Their drinks arrive, and Eric takes a sip of his, winces at the spiciness.

"No boyfriend," Quinn says, eating the olive from hers. "I don't think Myles and I were ever really together. And Billy is just a friend." Though she wonders if she's telling the truth. *Friend* really isn't the right word for it. Maybe there's no word for what she and Billy are. "Do you believe in soulmates?" she asks, testing that out.

Eric looks her in the eyes. "No, I don't."

"Not the romantic type?"

"I can be very romantic. But I don't think there's just one perfect person for each of us."

"Says the man who's been married twice." Quinn holds up her glass in a toast. "Maybe you just choose the wrong women."

"I definitely choose the wrong women." He watches her.

"Well, maybe that'll change some day." She watches him back, and they stay that way for longer than they probably should. The food arrives, breaking their locked eyes.

"This looks intense," she says, surveying the stacked plate.

"Just go straight into it." Eric pours a lake of syrup on his before carving through it and shoving a large bite in his mouth. She chuckles at his bulging cheeks.

It takes him several swallows to get it all down, but when his mouth is clear again, he sets his fork down and says, "I want to talk business."

"Okay." Quinn's own bite is only midway to her mouth. She rests it back on her plate.

"I think we're ready, Quinn." She's waited for a version of these words for so long that when she hears them, they are so simple that it's almost comical.

"Ready, ready?" she asks. "As in, ready for a show?" The Bloody Mary churns in her belly.

"I'm ready to represent you, if you'll have me." Quinn nods repeatedly because she can't actually make words form yet.

"This business is all about timing," he adds, and she knows it's his way of explaining why it's taken this long for things to move forward. And she doesn't care about that now because she's ready. She's never been more ready.

"Yes," she finally says. "Yes, yes, yes!" Eric smiles, and they grab hands. Quinn needs his grip because her excitement is propulsive, and he seems to be the only thing keeping her from flying up and away.

"I can get paperwork drawn up today," he says. "I want to start with Riverdale, debut *Lulu and the Trucker*, and then do the Times Square series shortly after. It's important that you have enough content for what's about to come."

"What's about to come?" she asks.

Eric waves his fork, and his nonchalance is almost alarming. "Attention."

She tries to smile, but it twists instead. A weight has come over her since she started this series, and she knows it has to do with Lulu and the trucker. She thinks about her constantly, wonders if she's okay, thinks about Tisha's own stories about her childhood, the abusive father, the alcoholic mother, the longing to escape to New York City only to be trapped in the same cycle again. And Quinn knows, as sure as she knows anything else, that she should have helped Lulu that day. That even if she didn't have a plan, just showing up for the kid could have changed something. It would have been worth a try at least. She wonders, as she has many times, if it's not too late.

THE RIVERDALE SERIES

1980

"Here," Maureen says, pushing a few bills into Lulu's hand. "Get me the Virginia Slims."

Lulu doesn't need to be told; she knows the kind her ma likes. She takes the money and shoves it down in her pocket.

"You can get a candy with the change but get right back here. I got work." The word *candy* lingers in Lulu's mind, and she repeats it to herself, *Candy, candy, candy,* almost like a cheer. She forgets to say thanks, but Maureen is already busy doing her hair anyway.

Lulu drags her feet as she walks, relishing in the scuffing sound it makes. Like tap dancing, kind of. She saw that on TV once, this lady scuffing her feet on the stage, but she had some kind of special shoes that made all kinds of great sounds. Lulu wishes she had those shoes. She'd tap dance all the way to the gas station and back. Out on the gravely walkway though, her flip-flop catches and she stubs her toe, walks normally again, and ignores the pulsing pain around her nail. She winds her way out of the trailer park and swats at a fly that's following along, making attempts to land on her shoulder. It finally swoops away as she grabs at the air for it. She passes the church where a few kids from her grade are throwing stones, trying to smash out the remaining glass in the top level. They hit with the sound of hail on a trailer top, a *pitter pitter scatter.* They wave to her to come over, and she starts their way before remembering how pissed that'd make Maureen. But she really wants to throw some rocks too. She hesitates then continues walking toward the gas station.

She passes the bar and the diner and walks through a mess

of trucks and a few cars perched at pumps. She steps around the splotches of oil on the cement and inhales the strong smell of gas, which she loves. There's a fan propping open the door, and she steps around that too. While she waits for a trucker to pay for his Slim Jims and Cheetos, she walks slowly up and down the aisles of grab-and-go snacks. Her mouth waters over the goodies. She picks up a package of soft-baked chocolate chip cookies and considers putting it in her back pocket, but she knows they'll get smashed, and she thinks Eli might notice, and she likes Eli.

He greets her when she gets to the register and offers his large black hand for a high five that she jumps up to give him. She asks him for a pack of Virginia Slims. "For my ma," she adds.

"I hope so," he says, tossing the pack on the countertop and taking the money from her. There's only a nickel in change, not enough for a candy, but Eli says, "You want a candy?" and she nods, eagerly. He grabs a huge jawbreaker that's normally a quarter and tosses that on the countertop too. It's blue, Lulu's favorite color. It's the kind that'll take her hours to suck through.

"Thanks, Eli," she says as she puts both into separate back pockets of her shorts.

"Tell your ma hi for me, all right?"

She knows they went to school together; her ma once told her that. But Maureen doesn't like to come into the store herself, so Eli's always telling Lulu to say hi for him instead. "She said to tell you hi too," she adds, even though it's not true.

Lulu waves as she leaves and makes her way back along the same course. The kids are done throwing stones. The top window of the church is now a jagged ridge of glass, and Lulu has a moment of regret that she didn't at least throw one or two while she had the chance. There's no one at the playground, and Lulu walks through it, steps around the empty bottles and crumpled cigarette packs. The swings tempt her but only for a second.

At the trailer, Maureen is putting on lipstick, getting ready for work. "Light one up for me," she says. Lulu unwraps the pack, smacks it against her palm the way Hank does. She pulls out a smoke and finds the matches, lighting up the cigarette and handing it to her ma.

"Eli says hi," Lulu tells her. Maureen doesn't respond. She takes a drag from the smoke, hands it back to Lulu to hold for her. She dabs some makeup on the spots that crack under her lip and on her chin from where, Lulu overheard her telling Hank, she walked into the cupboard. The makeup's a little too dark, but Lulu doesn't tell her that because she knows it'll make her angry. It's Lulu's fault anyway. She pocketed the wrong one.

"You want to make sure you smooth this in, so it looks natural." Maureen dabs a bit on Lulu's nose, runs the tip of her finger around in a small circle. Lulu holds very still, and even though she has the urge to scratch her nose, she doesn't. Even after her ma moves her finger away, Lulu can feel her swirly touch.

"Can you put that green on me?" Lulu asks, and Maureen tilts Lulu's head back, tells her to close her eyes. The eyeshadow brush sweeps her eyelids. The cigarette smokes in her fingers.

"Open," Maureen says, and Lulu does. Her ma dabs at the corner of Lulu's eyes, evening out the color. "You're a pretty little thing, you know that?" Maureen smiles at her, and Lulu's heart soars. "I'm gonna be at the motel pretty late tonight." Now, Maureen runs her hands through her thick blond hair and uses her fingernails to rake some volume into it. "You go over to Papa Don's and ask about supper, okay?" She takes the Virginia Slim from Lulu, inhales deeply.

"Okay," Lulu says.

Maureen shoves a few things into her back pocket. She twists the pack of cigarettes into the arm of her shirt. Lulu watches her, thinking how glamorous her ma looks with all that makeup on and the way she blows smoke into the air, her thin wrist with the small cross tattoo holding the long cigarette. Even in her jeans and T-shirt, Lulu thinks she looks very nice. Hank calls it being *all dolled up*. The aluminum door clangs behind her when she goes, and Lulu feels a pang of missing her.

She watches the backside of her ma walking out toward the road, the cigarette flicking to the side of the pathway. Lulu rubs the makeup off with a tissue. She opens the small refrigerator in the kitchenette, but there's only beer inside. She picks one up, thinks about drinking it, but knows Hank'll be pissed because it's his. The door clangs again, and she almost drops the can, quickly pushes it back inside. But Hank is there, and he's seen her. He's holding a bag of chips, crunching them in his mouth around his bad teeth that he's always complaining about. "What're you doing?" he asks, but he's smiling.

"I'm hungry," she says. He tosses the chips toward her, and she catches them, puts a few in her mouth.

"You want a beer?" She shakes her head because she knows he's only teasing her. "Aw, come on now," he says. "I saw you with that." He reaches around her and opens the fridge, takes one out and cracks it open with a loud hiss. He swigs it, and Lulu watches the ball in his throat bob up and down. "Here." He hands it to her.

She takes a tiny sip, but almost gags. It tastes like smelly socks. "Gross," she says, and Hank laughs.

"You got to work up to it." He takes it back and has another long drink.

"How come you ain't at work?" Lulu asks.

"Jesus, you sound like your ma," Hank says. "We finished early. I'm going down to the bar in case you need to know that too." Lulu blushes. "You ready for your birthday?"

"I can't wait," she says. Ever since the photographer told her about Happy Meals, it's all she can think about. That and the small square photo of herself that she keeps in a box under her bed with her other important things—a unicorn pendant she found outside the motel, a lucky clover BB gave her, a dollar bill Hank handed her once when he was drunk.

"You know, you ain't gonna be a kid anymore, Lulu," Hank

says. "Turning ten is a big fucking deal. You're a lady at ten."

"Okay," Lulu says, but she doesn't know what Hank means.

"You're gonna start getting some boobs, like your ma." Lulu presses her arms over her chest. "Aw, don't be like that," Hank says, coming closer to her. "Let me see what you got now."

"No." She hates when Hank does this kind of thing.

"Come on, now." He pushes her arms down and yanks at her tube top. "Look at them itty-bitty things." Hank pulls her top back up. It's crooked, but Lulu doesn't fix it. He laughs, and grabs another beer from the fridge, leaves.

Lulu watches him walk away, moves her top back in place. She reaches into the fridge and pulls out one of the beers, cracks it open in the same way Hank did and takes a long sip, trying not to gag over the taste. She burps then giggles and then drinks more. She's drunk half the can when BB shows up at the door. Her cousin stands outside, peering in.

Lulu waves her inside, and BB pushes through the door. "Ma says I'm supposed to come to your place and ask Papa Don about supper." BB shakes her head, and Lulu knows it's because Papa Don's at the bar. "Well, I guess we'll just have to make our own supper then. You got some stuff at your house?" BB nods yes. "You want some beer?" BB's eyes widen, and she shakes her head. "It's not bad once you get going on it." Lulu tips the can back and takes a long, fuzzy drink. "It's like dirt, kind of, and soda pop all mixed together." BB shakes her head again. "Fine, I'll drink it myself." Lulu finishes the can and takes it with her as she motions for BB to follow her out. She stashes it in a neighbor's garbage. Hopefully, Hank'll forget he didn't drink it himself.

"Hey, guys," Joey yells from outside his trailer. "Where you going?" They walk over to where he's dumping a big bag of dog food in a dented metal bowl. Monkey jumps around them, then stops to lick BB's leg.

"To hang out at BB's," Lulu says. "My ma's working tonight."

"Mine too," he says. He sets down the dog food and scratches a patch of dry skin on his arm. "Can I come over?"

Lulu shrugs. "Sure. We're gonna fix some supper. You eat yet?" Joey shakes his head, and Lulu motions for him to come along. He tosses the bag of food under the edge of the trailer, leashes Monkey to the post, and runs to catch up.

BB's trailer is tidy inside. Papa Don's is a double and she has her own room. Even though it's small, Lulu is jealous of the single mattress and the pleated pink curtain that hangs over a slice of window next to it. BB leaves them to go to the bathroom, and Joey sits on the brown flowered couch, crosses his legs under him. His knees are chalked up, and the knobby bones jut out wider than his skinny legs. Lulu is a little dizzy. She stands in front of him and says quietly, "You want to see my boobies? Hank says they're gonna get real big soon." She glances toward the bathroom but hears nothing from inside.

Joey looks in that direction too, hesitates, then says, "Yeah, all right."

Lulu pulls her tube top down so the pink bits show. "You can touch them if you want." He touches the left one, carefully, almost like it might hurt him. The bathroom door creaks and they both startle. Lulu pulls her top back in place. If BB's seen anything, she doesn't let on.

"Let's make supper," Lulu says, but it comes out louder than she meant. Joey looks away.

They rummage in the cupboard and find a few cans of tuna and some crackers. Lulu squints at one of the tins, says, "Al... ber...al...ber...core tuna. This is the good shit." She pulls back the tops and forks the tuna into a bowl. The smell is pungent and dense in the small kitchen. They scoop it up with the crackers, cursing when they break and fishing out the bits with their fingers. BB gets three bottles of Coke from the fridge, and they pry off the tops, slurp it. Joey burps and they giggle. Lulu wishes Maureen would buy her Cokes too, but her ma says it'll rot her teeth right out of her head. Lulu doesn't care about that though, and she's surprised her ma does. She holds a mouthful on her next sip, feels the bubbles tingle and burn on her tongue.

After eating, they go back outside where the summer air

has cooled some. Joey drags a stick in the dirt and writes their initials and then what seems to be a skull next to it. He looks up, and Lulu catches his eyes, feels bad about what she did earlier. But he just looks back at her with the same soft look and little bit of grin that he always has, and she thinks maybe she's making too much of it.

"You want to come over to my place?" he asks. "I don't want to leave Monkey alone too long." They follow him back around the pathway. Monkey barks excitedly at their approach. His leg is healed now from the wound it had when Joey found him on the side of the road, but the fur hasn't yet come back. Lulu gently touches the bald spot and tells him it's all okay now. He's a mix of chocolate lab and something else huge, and Lulu thinks how nice it would be to curl up with him on the couch. She wishes they could get a dog too and thinks someday when she has her own house, she's going to have as many dogs as she can fit.

"You can come over and see Monkey whenever you want," Joey says, like he's heard her thinking. She's about to tell him thanks, but the look on his face stops her and she turns to see what he sees. Barb's coming their way with a man following her, and Lulu knows that man. She holds her breath as her heart begins to race. Monkey spots them too and starts up barking something terrible, but Joey has caught his collar, so he stays put.

"Ma," Joey says.

"Put that dog in the house," she tells him. The man kicks at the small pieces of gravel that make up the walkway. They bounce off Barb's calves. "Fuck, man," she says, giving him a dirty look. Joey pulls a now growling Monkey into the trailer, and Lulu and BB go with them. They watch out the window as Barb and the man stop in front.

"You really have to drag me back here to do this?" she asks.

"What the fuck was that?" he says.

"I told you, I'm not into it. I don't care what he's paying."

"When did you get a choice about it?" The man grabs Barb's shoulders roughly, and Joey moves quickly out the door.

"Don't touch her," he says, coming to stand by Barb.

"Or what, little man?" The guy turns to Joey, and Joey's hands are in fists.

"Shit," Lulu says quietly. She glances around for anything she could use to defend Joey. BB stares, big eyes.

"Or I'll kill you," Joey says, and this makes Barb laugh. Joey kicks gravel at the man now. "You best be going." The man puts his hands up like he's getting arrested and starts to walk backward. Lulu knows he's just making fun of Joey, but Joey stands there all puffed up like he's made it happen.

"I expect you back at work," the man says, pointing to Barb.

Barb nods, turns to Joey and says, "What a man you are. My protector." She messes his hair, and Joey swats away her hand. He turns his back to her and comes inside the trailer. His cheeks are flushed, and his breath is ragged. Lulu and BB are quiet. Barb lights a cigarette and sits on the cement-block stair outside.

Joey flops down onto the couch. "Who was that asshole anyway?" he asks.

Lulu knows all too well. "Roy," she says. "The new boss."

"I fucking hate him."

Me too, she thinks. She tries to push the thoughts of the man out of her mind. She's seen him at the motel, taking the money and ushering over the truckers. And she's seen what he's done to Maureen too, knows her ma didn't walk into the cupboard like she told Hank. Barb tosses her cigarette butt into a coffee can that's full of others. She heads out again the way she came.

"I'll kill that asshole, for real," Joey says.

"Then you'd go to jail forever," Lulu replies but thinks that's not a bad idea because she really wants Roy gone and can't imagine how else to make it happen.

"I don't care." Joey buries his head in Monkey's scruff. Lulu sees his shoulders heave up and down in quiet crying. She motions to BB, and they leave.

Lulu wakes up at BB's when Papa Don comes home. "Your ma's gonna wonder where you at," he says. She wipes her eyes and tells him goodnight. Passing Joey's trailer, she sees Barb clear as day in the lit-up window. She's pressing a bag of frozen food on her eye and smoking a cigarette. Her head is tilted down and to the side, and her hair covers the uninjured part of her face in a cascade of thick, dark curls.

Monkey wakes up as Lulu passes by, growls until he sees it's her. She bends to scratch his hiney. "You're a good boy, Monkey. You're a good sweetie." She wonders why he's outside, thinks it's maybe to protect Barb from whoever busted up the side of her face. She thinks about her own ma's cuts and how maybe she can convince Maureen and Hank to get a dog if it can stay outside and protect them like Monkey does. She watches Barb crush out the cigarette and the gesture seems like something a movie star might do; the way Barb gingerly holds the butt and blows a stream of smoke as she twists the lit part into the ashtray.

Maureen isn't home when Lulu gets there. She finds a crumpled pack of smokes in the kitchen drawer and lights one up. She holds it near the top of her fingertips like Barb does, because she finds that much more attractive than how Maureen holds it low near the webbing of her fingers. She blows a long trail of smoke as she sits down on the couch. It makes her head feel floaty, but she takes another drag all the same. She coughs a little, which is definitely not like a movie star would do. The trailer is stuffy, and Lulu goes back outside, sits on the front stair. She thinks about the Happy Meal and wonders what kind of toy she'll get inside it. She hopes it's a doll or a stuffed animal. She thinks about the photo of her that's sitting in the tin box in her hiding spot and wonders if the photographer will come back again. Quinn, such a cool name. That's a name a movie star could have. Lulu imagines being a famous photographer in New York City. She'd go to parties and eat really good food.

Maureen comes up out of nowhere and scares the Jesus out of Lulu, grabs the cigarette from her and puts it in her own mouth. Lulu waits for the shouting, but instead Maureen dances in a circle and giggles, drops to a knee. The cigarette falls to the ground next to her, and Lulu presses it into the dirt with her flip-flop so her ma doesn't get burned on it.

"You okay, Ma?" Lulu watches her, trying to gauge which direction her mood might take, but she remains all smiles and laughter.

"I'm on top of the fucking world." Maureen sighs out the words, and Lulu wonders if she's been having the needle again. The pills make her happy, but the needle makes her laugh.

"You should come on in," Lulu says, getting up and taking a few steps toward her. Maureen tips over and lands on her butt, laughs. "Come on, Ma. Come on, now." Lulu tries to get under Maureen's arm, but her ma keeps slipping. She finally grabs her hand and simply pulls until Maureen gets up and follows her inside. Lulu helps her into the bed, takes off her ma's pink jelly shoes, and slips off her own flip-flops.

"You're pretty as an angel," Maureen says and even though Lulu hates when she has the needle, she likes it too because Maureen is so nice to her. "My pretty, pretty baby girl." Maureen runs her hand over Lulu's cheek, but her eyes begin to cloud in confusion and their lids fall heavily down so that her eyelashes are pressed against the tops of her cheekbones.

Lulu clicks on a small box fan that's propped in the window and lays down next to her. She wiggles under Maureen's arm and curls up around it. When Hank comes home, she'll have to go, but for now, she loves the feeling of her ma's hot breath on her neck. Maureen smells like something familiar, bread maybe, and body, and a hint of spicy perfume.

"I love you, Mama," Lulu says, quietly even though she knows it'd be almost impossible to wake Maureen now, but the arm around her tightens up and pulls her closer, and Lulu can feel her ma's lungs fill and deflate and fill and deflate against her back. Like a baby being rocked, that constant motion lulls Lulu into her own sleep.

❧

There're glasses smashing and plates breaking, and the ashtray that's always overflowing is swept to the ground where the burned butt ends of cigarettes scatter across the carpet. The ash is like a poof of rain cloud. Lulu trains her eyes to a stub that lands near her; it holds Maureen's ghostly pink lipstick print. Her ma is on a rampage, and Lulu tries to make the smallest version of herself that she can because there's nowhere to hide in the trailer that's already bursting at the seams with the three of them. Hank's done something that Lulu can't make out in the slur of words and whizzing of hands. But it's bad. He tries to grab for Maureen's wrist, but she frees herself and backhands him across the face.

"Fuck, Maureen," he shouts, pulling away bloody fingers. His nose gushes down to his upper lip. Lulu crouches near the couch, in the corner, her back pressed to the wall. She fingers a scrap of faded flowery wallpaper, nervously rolls it down. It leaves a yellowy scar of dried glue on the wall. Maureen is between her and the door. There's no way to leave without putting herself right in the crosshairs. So, she stays as small as possible, pulling her knees to her chest and tucking her chin. Her hair drops around her in a dirty blond curtain. Willie Nelson is somehow still singing from the small radio that's now on its side. "Someone to Watch Over Me" plays into the carpet.

"There wasn't nothing going on," Hank says, coming at Maureen again, trying to slow down her flailing arms that continue to sweep everything in their path to the floor.

"Liar," she shouts, and they circle each other like caged animals. "I saw you with my own damn eyes."

"You're fucked up. You got no idea what you seen."

"I let you live here, you son of a bitch." Maureen's cheeks are red with the effort. Her forehead and neck are covered in a thin glaze of sweat. "I can't believe you'd bring her to the bar. My bar. My *fucking bar*."

"It was *nothing*. And you're really one to talk," Hank says, pouring fuel on the fight. Lulu shakes her head, sighs quietly, but it's not like either could hear her anyway. The energy of their anger is like a sound, like the buzzy wasp's nest that Lulu's always wanted to smash to the ground.

"It's my *job*," Maureen yells. "I don't see you complain none when you spend my money."

Lulu's foot starts to fall asleep, but if she moves to wiggle it awake now, she's sure to end up smack dab in the middle of it all. She clenches her teeth through the pins and needles. Hank had been making pancakes on the griddle before all this mess, before Maureen came barging in the door in a mood, and they sit there still, the half-cooked rounds now cold and congealed.

"I don't touch your money."

Maureen seems near out of steam. She finally sits, her elbows on her knees, her head hung. Hank stomps past her, to the bedroom, where he opens and closes the drawers with extra emphasis. He returns with a garbage bag under his arm. His bloody nose has dripped down his lips, over his chin. Lulu wishes he'd clean it up.

"Where the fuck you going?" Maureen asks, but Hank doesn't answer. He blows right by her, out the door. Maureen curses and stomps into shoes, follows after him. Lulu waits, just long enough to be sure they're gone, until the car door slams and her ma's muffler-less Dodge growls away.

Alone, Lulu stands, shakes the blood back into her foot, cringing at the prickly pain. She rights the overturned coffee table, picks up the ashtray and the planter that has now lost its shriveled vine. The station has moved on from Willie to Johnny Cash. Lulu shuts it off. She carefully collects the broken pieces of plates and the shards from the glasses. Maureen's done in their entire cupboard. The smallest pieces stay stuck in the carpet, but the vacuum hasn't worked in a long time, so Lulu lays on her belly and plucks each shiny bit. And then she finds every cigarette butt and beer can and high heel and kitchen utensil that Maureen has strewn across the trailer. She thinks she's cleaned it all, until she finds a coffee cup in the hall and a tube of lipstick on the bathroom floor.

The pancakes are burned on one side and raw on the other.

She starts up the griddle again, scrapes the wasted ones into the garbage. The batter is split, but she whips it again. She pours two circles of it onto the hot plate and the grease spits sideways at her, catching her bare arm with a hot little zap that makes her curse to high hell.

She does what Hank does, watches the bubbling top to know when to flip, but when it's time, she isn't quick enough and the pancake folds in half in a wet mess. The second goes better, and when they're done, Lulu flips them both off the griddle, onto a napkin. She dribbles syrup across the top. She doesn't realize she's forgotten to turn off the griddle until the smoke starts filling the air. It clouds in black whorls as she rushes around the trailer, opening the small windows, propping the door. Even after the smoke clears, the smell of burned butter lingers for hours still.

Hank has been gone for a week, long enough that the wrecked air in the trailer is gone, long enough that somehow Maureen has forgotten what Lulu did. But Lulu wakes to the sound of a man snoring and thinks, *Happy birthday to me!* He must finally be home. She knew he wouldn't miss her birthday, not after promising her a party, not after getting her so excited about the Happy Meals. But, in the bedroom, the hair next to her ma's isn't the dirty blond of Hank's. It's black and thick, and Lulu is confused. She tiptoes closer to the bed so she can get a look at his face, but there's a feeling in her belly that she's had before. It's like rocks and bad orange juice. She knows who it is. She just knows. His snoring stops as he shifts over to his back and it's him, Roy.

Lulu rushes out of the bedroom and quickly pulls shorts over her undies. She grabs her flip-flops and tries to bend into them as she's hurrying out of the trailer. She nearly falls twice and curses. Her face is red hot, and she pushes the heels of her hands into her eyes to keep the tears in.

BB takes a while to open the door. Her hair is wet and she's in her good shorts. Lulu knows she's dressed up for the birthday party. She touches her cousin's shoulder, says, "I don't think we get to go to McDonald's. Hank's gone still, and Ma brought home Roy." BB sinks in a chair and touches her wet hair. "I know, I'm sorry," Lulu says. She knows BB was as excited as she was. "I guess we could go to my place and see what they say? Maybe Ma'll want to take us still." But Lulu knows in her heart that it's not going to happen.

At the trailer, Lulu makes noise on purpose to wake them up. It's almost noon now. Maureen comes out first, pulling a shirt over her loose tits. Lulu looks away.

"What's she doing here?" Maureen points at BB.

"We're ready for McDonald's," Lulu tries.

"Oh shit, that's today?" Maureen lights a cigarette. "I got to work now, Lulu."

"But Hank promised." Lulu hates the way she sounds whiney, but she can't help it.

"Hank can go fuck himself."

BB looks down at the ground as Roy comes out of the bedroom in his underwear. The dark hair on his chest draws a fuzzy line into the band. Lulu feels uncomfortable looking at it.

"Gimme a smoke," Roy says to BB, who sits closest to the table. She stares at him, wide-eyed, not moving. "Can you hear?" he asks, pushing toward her.

Lulu stands, steps between them. "She can hear just fine," she says.

"She a retard?" he asks. "Look at that fucking mouth, Jesus."

"She's not a retard," Lulu says. "And she got stung by bees on her mouth."

Roy scoffs. "Ain't no bee stings. Looks like cigarette burns to me."

"All right, you get some shit on," Maureen says. "I'll bring you a cigarette."

Lulu squats by BB's side, her hand on her cousin's knees, and whispers, "Don't listen to that man, BB. You okay?" BB nods, but Lulu can see her back heave and knows she's holding in a sob. "Let's go outside." She leads BB to the porch, and they sit. Lulu puts her arm around her cousin and dabs her fingers at the small lines of wetness that come down from her eyes.

Lulu says, "Maybe we can get a gun and shoot him." BB looks up at her. "Can you picture that? Roy's head popping off and his eyes falling out?" Lulu giggles at the thought of it, and BB smiles. "We could shoot him right in his own mouth." And for the first time, she starts to really think about it. Roy's head exploding. Roy's hairy chest with bullet holes in it. And it's an amazing thought.

BB gestures down, and Lulu laughs. "In the penis? You want to shoot up his dick?" BB nods, and they both lean over laughing. "Okay, now we just got to get us a gun." And even though it's all just jokes and no one's going to be shooting Roy's dick, Lulu feels better for some reason.

Maureen and Roy come out of the trailer a few minutes later. "I'll see you tonight," she tells Lulu.

"Ma, what about McDonald's?" Lulu tries not to beg, but it's her birthday.

"Come on, Lulu, you're too old for that shit anyway. Here." She hands Lulu a five-dollar bill. "Go to the diner and get some lunch. Tell them it's your birthday, and they'll give you a free shake."

Lulu stares at the money in her hand long after Maureen is gone. BB sits silently beside her. "Should we go to the diner?" Lulu finally asks, and BB nods. They start walking that way. At the street, a car horn blows as it pulls to a stop next to them, gravel flying at their bare legs.

"Lulu!" Hank leans out the car window. Lulu has never been happy to see him until now. She rushes over, and BB follows. "Happy birthday," he says. "You think I forgot about you?" Lulu nods and tries not to cry. "Your ma around?"

She shakes her head. "Work." She knows better than to mention Roy.

"Get in, girls. Unless you don't want McDonald's no more?"

"We do!" Lulu nearly jumps in happiness. She pulls open

the passenger door and gets in, BB follows. They crowd across the cracked vinyl of the front seat. Hank smells like rubbing alcohol. Lulu's sure he's been drinking the hard stuff, but she doesn't care because he's here just like he promised.

At McDonald's, Hank gets them both Happy Meals and a Big Mac and fries for himself. Lulu tucks the five dollars from Maureen into her pocket, doesn't tell him about it. She carefully takes the tented box from the plastic tray and sets it in front of her. BB watches and does the same. Lulu tries to hide her disappointment at the size of it. It definitely can't fit a doll or a stuffed animal, she now realizes. But maybe it'll have stickers or markers or something like that, and that would be all right too. She wiggles the box around a bit to try to hear what might be inside and taps her toes in anticipation.

"Maybe we should open them at the same time, BB? Case we get the same toy?" BB nods. Lulu counts to three and they pry open the cardboard closure and fish their hands around inside. Lulu pulls out the cheeseburger and fries and sets them aside. BB is already bringing out a plastic-wrapped toy so Lulu hurries to get hers too, tilting the box.

Lulu pulls apart the wrapping to find a small toy shaped like a hamburger person driving a car. She flips it around in her hand. It's the kind of thing she might have liked when she was five, but definitely not now that she's ten. BB's is the exact same.

Hank shoves a bunch of fries in his mouth all at once and chews them up. "What you think about them prizes?" he asks. Chunks of food flip around in his mouth.

Lulu shrugs. "It's okay," she says. BB seems completely pleased with hers, which makes Lulu feel even worse.

"Shit, just okay? Let me see that." Hank takes her toy and holds it up. "This is some cheap-ass little kid's shit, that's the problem. Hang on." Hank gets up and takes the toy to the ordering area. Lulu watches him talking to the woman working who is shaking her head. He's moving his arms around like he does when him and Maureen fight.

"Hank's gonna get us in trouble," Lulu says. BB's eyes are

wide. She puts her burger and fries back inside the Happy Meal and Lulu does the same as Hank's voice starts to rise. A man comes out from around the counter and tries to put a hand on Hank's arm, which makes Hank yell even more. They look over to where Lulu and BB sit, and Lulu grabs her Happy Meal in one hand and Hank's food in the other. "Come on, BB, we better go."

Hank is walking toward them now, furious, and Lulu says, "Come on, Hank, let's just go home."

They walk out together in a hurry, but Hank stops to kick a life-sized Ronald McDonald in the leg on their way out. The plastic figure tilts but doesn't topple over. At the car, he takes his food from Lulu. They stand around the rusty Buick, propping the food on the trunk, and eat.

"I appreciate that you brought us here, Hank," Lulu says.

"I suppose your ma forgot it was your birthday again?" He bites into his burger and the ketchup squishes out the side of his mouth, lingers there until he catches it with his tongue.

Lulu scratches her shin with her other foot. "Kind of, I guess."

"She alone while I was gone?"

Lulu swallows hard and looks over at BB, who looks away as she shoves a french fry into her mouth. "I haven't seen her much," Lulu tries, but she knows Hank can see right through her.

He cusses. "Was it Roy?" Lulu stares at her burger. "Fuck, Lulu, just tell me, dammit."

Lulu nods. "Just last night, though." Her mouth has gone dry as she struggles to swallow a piece of bun. They forgot to bring their Cokes. She looks at BB who continues to chew quietly by the side of the car.

Hank doesn't say anything, but his jaw is hard as he finishes eating. "Get in the car," he tells them, and they wrap up what's left of their food and put it into the Happy Meal boxes. Now Lulu and BB sit in the backseat instead of next to Hank. The torn-up seat scratches into Lulu's bare legs, but she doesn't move. Hank swerves out of the parking lot, just missing some-one coming from the drive-thru, and flushes them into traffic, making horns go wild. Lulu grips on the door handle with one hand and BB with the other. Her cousin holds on back, her chewed-up fingernails digging into Lulu's skin.

"The problem with your ma," Hank says, "is that bitch has zero loyalty. She'll fuck anything. And I get that, it's her job, it's what she does, and I always known that. But she likes it, Lulu. She likes it."

Lulu doesn't say a thing about it. She doesn't remind Hank that Maureen just caught him cheating too. Her lunch unsettles in her stomach, lingers too close to her throat, threatening like a small volcano to come back up. "What are you going to do?" she asks, and she's not sure he hears because the wind is whipping in the car windows now that they're speeding on the highway.

But Hank says, "You know what I'm going to do? I'm going to gut that motherfucker Roy."

Hank swerves up the exit ramp, chewing up the side of the road, and speeds through the intersection, once again just miss-ing another car that's coming from the gas station. He stops in a slide and tells Lulu and BB to get out. When they do, Lulu realizes they forgot their Happy Meals in the backseat. Hank parks by the motel and yells at them to go home.

"Come on, BB." Lulu touches her cousin's arm and leads them toward the trailer park. She looks over her shoulder once to see Hank pacing outside the motel doors. And she wonders if he really will kill Roy, because that would be the best birthday gift she could ever hope for.

"Are you proud of yourself?" Maureen comes in shouting an hour later. The girls are sitting on the couch playing Go Fish, but the game is swiped to the floor as Maureen grabs for Lulu, yanking her up by her arm. "They're both in jail now. What were you thinking telling Hank that Roy was here? What is wrong with you?" Maureen shakes Lulu, and Lulu accidentally bites her tongue, feels the rush of blood that tastes like metal.

BB stands and takes a protective step forward, but Maureen is already pulling Lulu toward the trailer door. She kicks it open with her heel and pushes Lulu out and down the cement steps. Lulu tries to keep her balance but falls onto her knees on the hard-packed dirt. She presses her lips tight, so she won't cry out. Maureen makes a move to hit her, but now BB is standing between them and Maureen's arm drops.

"You stay away until I tell you otherwise," Maureen says to Lulu, then turns and goes back into the trailer.

Lulu stays on the ground for a few minutes, her knees aching with prickles of blood where the ground broke through her skin. *I'm ten,* she thinks. *I'm not a little girl anymore.* And even so, that's not enough to keep the tears from welling up in her eyes.

Maureen has forgotten how angry she was. She heats up a frozen steak dinner to celebrate her and Hank being back together. The smell of it makes Lulu's stomach growl, but there's only two plates set, and she knows it's not for her too. Maureen scrapes the wilted broccoli side into a small bowl for her instead. Lulu eats it in a few bites. Hank glances at Lulu out of the corner of his eye as she pretends not to watch them eating. She shuffles a deck of cards, quietly, so as not to piss off Maureen.

"How about a little bit of steak for Lulu?" he tries, but Maureen slams down her fork. He holds up a hand to stop the fight from coming. Maureen shakes her head but doesn't say anything. Lulu keeps her eyes trained on the cards, but they clip each other's sides and flip out of her hands. She scrambles to collect them from her lap. And she thinks, maybe she could be one of those card dealers she's seen on the TV, the ladies that wear bow ties and suits like men but lots of makeup like women. She needs to get good at shuffling, though, and she tries again to get the cards to slip through each other, but again they dump in her lap.

"That's annoying me," Maureen tells her. "Go in the bedroom." Lulu makes a messy stack of the cards and drags her feet as she walks to the bedroom. The back part of the trailer is warm and stuffy. The smell of dinner has collected there, making Lulu's stomach growl once again. The broccoli has left her even hungrier somehow. She lays down on the bed, leaves the cards in a pool at her side, and closes her eyes. Her mind flashes to the truckers, to the motel owner and the diner ladies and the bartenders and the gas station attendants. To Maureen, Hank, Eli, Papa Don, Roy, Barb. It's like being on the merry-go-round at school, one face flashing after another after another after another. And she opens her eyes and sits up, dizzy but not moving at all.

Hank leans in to tell her they're going to the bar, and Lulu waits a few minutes until she's sure they're gone before she comes back out. She makes a jelly sandwich with the last of two butt ends of bread and sets it on the coffee table as she plays a round of solitaire with the deck that, it turns out, is missing a king of diamonds. It keeps messing up her game, so she makes a card house instead that falls over every time she tries to add a second level.

Finally, she's tired. She changes into one of Maureen's old shirts that hangs to her knees. She lays on her back on the couch, stares at the cracked plastic ceiling and tries to imagine what it's like to live in another place, maybe a big city like the photographer, Quinn. She thinks about all those photographs and wonders, as she has many times since the woman came through, if anyone has bought the pictures of her. Maybe her face is hanging on some fancy person's wall right now. Lulu smiles, thinking maybe she'll meet the person one day and they'll recognize her. They'll get excited that she's the kid in their pictures and maybe they'll give her some money too so she can get her own trailer. Then she can leave Maureen, and maybe her ma will finally feel bad about how mean she is.

She's falling asleep when the trailer door bounces open and the voice that calls out for Maureen is not one she knows well, but she does know it. And then suddenly Roy is in front of her and he's shouting. "Where's Maureen?" But Lulu is too scared to reply. He grabs her arm and pulls her up. "Where's your ma?"

Lulu shakes her head. "I don't know," she lies.

Roy keeps a strong hold on her forearm and shakes her. "Is that piece of shit living here again?" Lulu doesn't reply. She tells her tears to stay away. "Tell me."

Lulu looks down at where his grip has tightened on her arm. "She's at the bar," she says. "Hank moved back today." Lulu prays he's going to leave now that he knows. The tears bust through and trickle down her face. She swipes at them with her free hand.

"How old are you?" he asks, finally loosening his grip on her arm.

"Ten." Her throat is dry, and she swallows hard.

"Them men like you a lot." Roy grins at her, and she hates the way it looks. "I get a good price for you." She squirms, shame coloring her cheeks. "I never understood that shit myself," he says. "Little kids." Lulu's tears are coming hard now, down her face, dripping off her chin. She tries to remind herself that she's *ten. I am not a little kid*, she says over and over in her mind. Roy yanks on her T-shirt, and Lulu tries to jerk away from him, but he pulls it up and over her face so she can't see. Her breath clenches in her lungs. She tightens her legs together, but they're too thin to clench in place. He pulls down her underwear and pushes her legs apart. And her tears sink into her shirt. She gasps for air, but it won't come. And she thinks maybe she's going to die. Maybe this is going to kill her. "It's like looking at a baby," Roy says. And she waits for him to touch her like they touch her, but he doesn't. He shoves her instead, and Lulu falls backward against the edge of the couch, unable to see with the shirt still over her head. She lands partway on the couch and sinks to the floor. She yanks the shirt down and pulls up her underwear. And finally, the air comes back into her lungs. She gulps for it. She can't stop the sobbing now, and he watches her for a minute, shaking his head. "Tell your ma that Hank is dead."

When he finally leaves the trailer, Lulu curls into the smallest ball she can make, squeezing her knees to her chest, putting her arms around them, and grabbing her feet so that she is as tiny as she can possibly be. So that she can almost pretend she's nothing at all. She lays like that, not sleeping, staring straight ahead into the darkness of the trailer. And in that darkness, she sees shapes that float in her eyes, dark cloudy globs of things that pull her forward and push her away. The ghosts, her ghosts, they swoop and dive and land in her head where they pound their fists in her skull and split her mind sideways.

When Hank and Maureen come home later on, they don't notice that Lulu is still lying in a ball and that she is wide awake. They pass her and head into the bedroom. She pretends she can't hear them moaning.

Lulu does not sleep, and when the day breaks wide enough open, she goes to the gas station mart, to the only grown-up she trusts. To her relief, Eli is working. He grins when she comes in. "My favorite customer," he says. "Pack of smokes for your ma?" He starts to reach behind him in the rack, but Lulu stops him.

"I come to talk to you, Eli," Lulu says. "I need your help."

"Well, that sounds serious." Eli chuckles, but stops when he sees her look. "What do you need?" He leans down and across the counter so he's at her height.

Lulu looks around to be sure no one else is in the store. "I need a gun."

Eli watches her, and Lulu bites her lip because she's nervous this isn't going to work, and this is the only option she's got. "Are you in danger?" he asks. She sighs because she was hoping he wouldn't ask any questions. "Lulu, if you need help, I can help you, but a gun won't solve any problems. It'll just make more."

Lulu frowns because a gun is the only way to solve the problem. She needs Eli to understand that too. "You know Roy? From the motel?" she asks.

Eli looks away. "That's what this is about? You want to get rid of Roy?" Lulu nods, and his eyes come back to hers and she keeps them locked because he needs to know how serious she is. But before she can say more, he says instead, "The best way to get rid of Roy is to tell the cops what he's doing." And those simple words are crushing. Because she can't talk to the cops. Because Maureen has always told her to never talk to the cops. Because the truckers have always told her to never talk to the cops. Because the fat trucker Curtis who she hates the most has told her he will kill her if she ever talks to the cops. And so, Lulu is about to tell Eli she cannot talk to the cops, but a customer comes in, and Eli puts his hand on Lulu's hand before he stands up tall again. While Eli helps the customer, Lulu steps away and looks at the rack of magazines. As usual, they're all hunting and naked women. Alone again, he waves her back over.

"I can't talk to the cops," Lulu finally says. "I just can't."

"How about you tell me what you know, and I talk to the cops and then you don't have to?" Lulu considers this, and it sounds okay to her because she's not actually doing the talking. And so, she tells him about Roy and Maureen and Barb, but then she stops. He watches her. "Is there more?" he asks, and Lulu wants to tell him about all of it, but she can't figure out how to make the words come out of her mouth and so she simply shakes her head no. Eli asks her if she can go to Papa Don's now, and Lulu nods because there's no way she can face her ma right now anyway.

Lulu has said nothing to BB, so it comes as an extra surprise for her cousin when Papa Don rushes into the trailer a little while later and blurts out, "Lulu, your ma just got arrested." He's out of breath, and she knows he must've run home from the bar. It's not what Lulu expected to hear, and she thinks, *But, what about Roy?* Her panic rises, wondering if Eli got it wrong.

"The police are all over the motel," he says. "They picked up Barb too." And now Lulu's heart is thumping hard in her chest, and she has to press her hand over it because it feels like it could pop right out.

"We need to get Joey," she says, but Papa Don stops her.

"Lulu, you need to stay here where they can't find you."

"But why shouldn't they find me?" Lulu is confused about what's happening, thinks about how Eli told her to come here. "Did Joey get arrested?" But that doesn't seem right because he's just a kid. *We're just kids,* she thinks.

Papa Don shakes his head. "They got to take him since he's got no one to look after him."

Lulu realizes then what she's done. BB's eyes are large and full of tears. The knock comes just seconds later, and Lulu knows it's the cops, coming for her too.

BB presses her palm to the back window of the cop car, and Lulu presses hers back. The glass holds them apart. Tears and snot are running down her cousin's face, and Lulu wishes Papa Don would give her a tissue to clean it up. She shouts, "I'll be okay," but it's weak because she doesn't believe it herself. Papa Don's head bends in toward one of the cops and they look her way. He shakes his head, and she wonders what they're saying. The cop takes notes on a small notepad that he tucks into his pocket. Papa Don comes to the window now too, and he levels his head with Lulu's, says loud enough for her to hear, "Hang in there, Lulu."

The cops get in the car, and one turns to her. "You okay back there?"

Lulu nods but her eyes fill, and she asks, tearfully, "Am I getting arrested?"

"No, no," the cop says. "You understand your mom was arrested though?" Lulu nods. "So, we're going to take you into temporary custody. It just means we need some time to sort out who's the best person to watch you."

"I have Hank," she says, trying to be helpful. "And Papa Don." But her voice trails as they drive away from Papa Don, and she wonders where Hank might be. "Or maybe Eli could watch me."

"We'll look into all them, okay?"

Lulu nods, and she can tell that they're done talking about it. She watches out the window as they pass by the church and

diner and then the motel, where there are still two other police
cars, and Lulu worries about who's going to take care of Monkey now and about school starting in a week and about how
mad Maureen is going to be. And the black spots start to come
again, forming at the sides of her eyes and clouding her vision
before the pounding, pounding, pounding headache returns.

Lulu huddles by the guinea pig's cage. It's a shaggy little animal
with blotches of white and brown fur. She sticks her finger
through the metal, touches its pink nose. It twitches in response.
Even though she offered up some really good names, the class
voted on Pebbles, but Lulu secretly calls her Penny instead.
There's a bundle of carrots that they're allowed to feed, and
Lulu sticks one out, watches as Penny's tiny front teeth work it
into nothing. Lulu has asked every Friday since school started if
she can bring Penny home, but Miss Jeanie always has an excuse
to give and sends her with someone else instead. Sometimes
though, Lulu's allowed to hold her in class and when she does,
Penny leaves pellet-like turds in her hands, but Lulu doesn't
care. She's the one who cleans her cage the most, the one who
feeds her and pets her.

Lulu's thinking how soft Penny is when there's a sickly plunk
on the back of her head and she twists around, looks to see
who threw something at her, but the other kids are looking
away, trying to contain their giggles. She touches the back of
her head, brings the mess of wadded tissue and spit out of her
hair. It catches in the long strands. Miss Jeanie doesn't notice.
She never seems to notice when the kids do these things, not
when they trip Lulu or throw things at her or call her names.
It's not worth asking who did it. They'll just pretend she's crazy
or tell her it's always been there because, as they say, she's *gross*
and *dirty*.

The bell rings and Lulu takes her seat, and because she's
a Belnap and it's alphabetical order, she sits front and center.
Miss Jeanie calls roll and then comes to pick up homework.

The other kids have backpacks and Trapper Keepers, but Lulu pulls hers from her pocket where she's folded it over and over so many times that it takes some doing to smooth it out. She scrawls her name at the top and tries to hide the way that some places have worn thin from too much erasing.

The teacher looks it over when she takes it from Lulu, says, "You didn't finish."

Lulu doesn't know how to explain that she couldn't figure out what to do, that there was no one at home to ask for help, that even when she went to BB's, Papa Don was at the bar and so she had stared at the questions for hours, wrote and then erased and then rewrote what she thought was right and then erased again.

"I'm sorry," Lulu tries, but Miss Jeanie just shakes her head. It'll be another bad grade in the gathering bad grades Lulu has had this year. The days of crafts and easy math are long gone, and Lulu feels like she's the only one who has been left behind with it. The other kids raise their hands, know the answers, while she sits, hoping she doesn't get called on.

She shifts in her seat. Her pants are too tight and cut into her legs. It feels like she inched up overnight and nothing fits right now. It makes sitting in class uncomfortable. Her Micky Mouse shirt that Hank got her last year from Kmart is too short too, and she's already been told if her belly button shows again, she's getting sent home. Lulu tries to put it out of her mind. She stares at Penny, out the dirty window behind her through which she can see the older kids playing kickball on the over-grown field. Lulu has been skipping gym, and it's not because she doesn't like kickball. It's not even because she gets picked last. It's because the other kids make fun of the way her boobies jiggle when she runs. Maureen's bras are all too large for her. She crosses her arms self-consciously over her chest.

Miss Jeanie leaves their homework in a pile on her desk and tells them to get out their science books. Lulu props open the top of her desk and takes hers out. Someone has written SLUT in marker across the front. She glances around, but her classmates are busy cracking their books, finding the page the teacher has told them to turn to. Lulu quickly opens hers too, hiding the cover.

"Lulu," Miss Jeanie says, and Lulu's heart races. "Start reading on page sixty-eight."

Lulu takes a deep breath, runs her finger under the line in the book. "Cells are div-div-div-i-ded to, I mean, into, two main classes. Prok, prok-a-ri, prok-a-ri-itic and e u kay-otic." The kid next to her snickers, mimics her under his breath with a fake stutter. Miss Jeanie holds up a hand to stop Lulu, calls on someone else. Lulu's face is as hot as a sunburn. She keeps her eyes on the desk, tries to even out her breathing. She follows along as the other student reads without issue, tracing the words with her fingertip as he says each with confidence. When Miss Jeanie turns her back to write on the chalkboard, a note is slipped into Lulu's lap, so quickly that she can't determine the sender. She leans back and opens it under the desk. The lettering is bold and in all caps. It simply says MORON, and she can read well enough to know that. The minutes tick by even slower than usual. Lulu wishes she could hold Penny. Outside, the kickball game is over, and the kids are running laps on the dirt path. The sun is high in the sky, makes it seem warmer than it is.

When the bell finally rings for lunch, Miss Jeanie asks her to stay behind, and for a split second Lulu thinks that maybe she's changed her mind about Penny and is going to let Lulu take her after all. Instead, the teacher looks her over, says, "Who's taking care of you?"

"What do you mean?" Lulu asks.

"I know your mom is in prison, so who is responsible for you when you aren't at school?"

Lulu bites her lip. "My ma's boyfriend."

"And what's his name?"

Lulu whispers, "Hank."

"Well, you tell Hank he needs to start helping you with your homework and working on your reading skills or I'm going to

recommend you go back to fourth grade." She gathers the pile
of homework and shoves it into the wide mouth of a bag.

Lulu doesn't nod; she doesn't say anything at all because
there's nothing she can say. She sniffles a bit as the tears threat-
en to come, and Miss Jeanie hands her a tissue without looking
at her. It's the same kind the kids used to make the spitball,
yellow with baby blue flowers.

At home, Lulu lays on the couch with her hand over her
eyes. The heater sputters and hisses and then turns itself off
entirely. She does not have the energy to see what's wrong with
it, isn't even sure what she can do about it anyway. She goes into
the bedroom and finds one of Maureen's wool sweaters, pulls
it over her head. It drags to her knees. In the kitchen, she toasts
bread and presses a slice of American cheese between it. She
pours herself a glass of milk that tastes sour and spits it back
in the sink. The weekend stretches long before her, but she
doesn't mind. It means two days of not having to deal with the
other kids. No name-calling, no spitballs, no tripping or being
mean. She'd take being alone any day over that. She places her
homework in the trash.

Maureen's getting out early thanks to parole, but Lulu doesn't
know what parole means. Barb's already been released, long
enough for Joey to come back to school and get Monkey from
BB's place. Hank has been in and out for weeks and every time
he comes and goes, he leaves a mess of cigarette butts, food
wrappers, and cans behind, but sometimes some cash too. Lulu
sighs as she dumps the junk into a trash bag. He was supposed
to be watching her all this time, but she won't say a word that he
wasn't because she doesn't want to get anyone else in trouble.
The spot she cleared for Penny remains empty.

The heat still hasn't been working, and Hank says that's because the gas company is run by *fashits*, but Lulu doesn't know
what that means either. She wears her jacket inside, layered over
Maureen's sweaters. Her stomach is in knots, both from hunger

and nervousness. She hasn't seen her ma in months because Hank hates jail visits and no one else would take her to the prison. Lulu shakes out a blanket and refolds it as nicely as she can.

She hears the spit of gravel and hurries outside to see Hank pulling up. Maureen stares straight ahead in the seat next to him, and Lulu waves to catch her attention. She now realizes how much she missed her ma. And she never thought she could have missed Maureen like this but seeing her in the car makes Lulu's eyes fill up and her heart ache. She wants to tell her about the first few months of school, about Penny and how hard fractions are, that they did a fake election in class and Reagan won that one too. She will not tell her that Miss Jeanie threatened to put her back in fourth grade. She will not tell her that on Christmas, Hank gave her hot dogs and beer and then left for the night.

Maureen finally looks her way and raises her hand, but it's not really a wave and there's no smile. In Lulu's dream the night before, her ma rushed from the car to pick her up in her arms and twirl her around. But when Maureen gets out of the car, she looks smaller than normal, skinny to the bones. Lulu runs to her, but Maureen just touches the top of her head, and Lulu knows this skinny ma doesn't have the strength to lift her up. Not that normal Maureen would do that anyway. A little bloom of purple lines Maureen's right eye. She notices Lulu looking, says, "The guards," as she touches it. And Lulu tries not to imagine how that happened, instead she thinks they can put that makeup on it, and no one will ever know.

Maureen lets Lulu lead her into the trailer. But Lulu is worried because this hollow ma is not like Maureen at all, and Lulu thinks it's almost like Hank brought the wrong ma back. She catches his eye as he follows them inside, and he shrugs.

Maureen looks around and Lulu hopes she notices how clean it is, the folded blanket, the shoes lined up by the door. But instead, she says, "Why's it so cold in here?" and though her voice is angry, Lulu's relieved because it sounds like something normal ma would say.

"Well, it *is* winter," Hank says, and Maureen turns on him.

"Is that a joke? You didn't think to pay the bill?" Maureen storms into the back of the trailer and emerges with a thick sweater. That angry motion would normally upset Lulu, but now she's relieved because it seems Maureen is fully back. Her ma pulls the sweater over her head. It's one Lulu likes because it has a reindeer on it, but there's a large hole in the arm that Maureen's elbow sticks out from. "Or were you too busy drinking away my money, as usual?" And yes, Lulu almost smiles because for sure this is the ma she knows. Hank sighs and runs a hand through his hair.

"And you." Maureen turns on Lulu now. "You realize now I have no place to work? Thanks to your big mouth." It didn't take long at the station for Lulu to admit she was the one who told Eli the details of what was happening at the motel.

Lulu isn't sure what to say back, but Hank interjects anyway, says, "It's not her fault." Maureen shakes her head with a half-smile that's not really a smile, which Lulu knows means she's about to get real angry. But as soon as that storm comes, it's already gone, and she plops down on the couch instead.

Maureen lights a cigarette and sighs deeply. "It's good to be home," she says, and Lulu's chest fills with lightness. She blows smoke up at the ceiling and closes her eyes, and Lulu stares at the purple ring around her eye, the deeper color in the corner and lighter greenish tint toward her nose.

Hank takes a drag from Maureen's cigarette. "What do you want to do tonight?" he asks, his hand on her knee.

"Drink," Maureen says. "Let's go down to the diner, get some food, and then the bar. It's too cold to stay in here anyway." Maureen stands. Lulu gets up too. "Where are you going?" Maureen asks her.

Lulu has misunderstood. Because she hasn't realized how angry her ma is with her. And then she sees that hollow ma was really angry ma. Maureen shakes her head, and Lulu sits back down.

"Sorry, kiddo," Hank says over his shoulder as he follows

Maureen out. The door clangs behind them, sending in a rush of cold air with it. Lulu takes a beer from the fridge and even though it makes the inside of her as cold as the outside, she drinks it all the way to the bottom. She puts the hood up on her jacket, pulling the strings tight so that only a small circle exists for her to look out from. She tucks her knees to her chest, ignores the rumble of hunger in her stomach, and makes the smallest ball of herself that she can. She thinks about going to BB's where the heat works and where she can wedge into the small bed next to her cousin, but now that Maureen's back, she knows she should be at home. The beer has left her with a little buzz that she somehow finds a way inside of to sleep.

The earliest bits of sunlight creep through the trailer windows at daybreak, finding their way to Lulu's cheeks. The light is like a warm kiss, and she almost smiles before she opens her eyes and remembers where she is. Maureen and Hank have not come home, and Lulu fights a sliver of panic. This isn't the first time and won't be the last, but she wonders where they might be. She unwraps from a blanket and takes off her jacket, pleased that the trailer finally feels less frigid, thanks to the sun. She doesn't bother to look for breakfast because she already knows there's nothing.

In the bathroom, Lulu brushes away the fuzzy feeling from her teeth, then changes her clothes and returns to the front of the trailer to slip into shoes. BB is eating oatmeal from a roughly torn package when Lulu arrives. The grains are barely soaked, and Lulu says, "Here, let me make that right," as she heats up a kettle of water on a hot plate. It whistles and she pours it carefully over the grains. "You got to get the heat right on these," she tells BB and then stops her cousin before she digs right in. "Give it a second to cool some." Lulu makes her own bowl and tries not to think about how much yummier it would be if it was the flavored kind.

"Papa Don come home last night?" she asks, and BB shakes her head. "Ma and Hank neither." Now, Lulu wishes she had come over. She doesn't like the idea of BB alone all night.

Papa Don startles them when he comes banging into the trailer. He smells like cigarettes and booze and walks right by them without a word on the way to his bedroom. They eat their oatmeal in silence, their eyes not meeting. Lulu's in no hurry to get home where she's sure to find her ma and Hank in the same condition.

After breakfast, Lulu and BB watch TV, laughing to *Three's Company* and *Brady Bunch* reruns, until Papa Don wakes up awhile later and tells Lulu she should go home. At the trailer, Lulu finds Maureen and Hank asleep. She stands near them, watching the rise of their chests, the puff of air in their cheeks. The hole in Maureen's reindeer sweater has gotten longer and Lulu stares at her ma's skin, the pale switch of marks like long scratches that cover the tender spots near the crook in her elbow. They've healed while she's been away.

"What's parole?" Lulu asks when Hank finally opens his eyes.

"What?" he replies, yawning and swiping at his eyes.

"You said Ma's on parole, but I don't know what that means."

"Let me get up," he tells her as he slowly disentangles from Maureen who still sleeps soundly. Hanks takes a loud piss in the bathroom before he comes to sit on the couch where Lulu now is.

"You don't know what parole is?" Lulu shakes her head. "Means, your ma is technically still on her jail sentence but since they don't want to waste no more taxpayers' money on her, they put her back out here, and she's got to check in once a week with the police."

Lulu's not sure she really understands. "So, it's like she's still in jail?"

"Yep, but without the lovely accommodations." He lights a cigarette, takes a long drag.

"But as long as she doesn't do bad things, then she won't go back to jail?"

"Yeah, that's the gist of it." Lulu nods because she gets it now. "But listen up, that means you don't go running your mouth about nothing to nobody, all right? She's got another six months, and if you mess that up, she'll go away for a long time. You don't want that?"

Lulu shakes her head. She wonders what the cops consider to be good behavior and if leaving her to go drinking all night would make Maureen go back to jail. She swears to herself that she'll never tell anyone anything again.

"Good," Hanks says, but Lulu has lost track of what it's in response to.

෨

Joey gets on the school bus just before the doors close, and Lulu moves to make room for him to sit next to her. "I thought I was going to miss it," he says, out of breath. "That asshole Mr. Canning held me after to talk about my homework. Where's BB?"

"Stayed home sick again today," Lulu says.

"You want to come over and play with Monkey?"

Lulu shakes her head. "I can't. Hank says I have to go with my ma to her parole."

"She still working?" Joey asks, and Lulu nods, thinks about how all she used to want was McDonald's and now that Maureen brings it home from work every day, she can't stand it.

The bus pulls up the hill, swerves to the shoulder, and Joey and Lulu exit. At her trailer, Joey lifts a hand in goodbye, and Lulu does the same. Hank isn't home yet, even though he's supposed to be, and so Lulu quickly rummages around in the drawer where she's seen Maureen slip the bottle of pills. She finds it and brings it out, looking over her shoulder even though she knows no one's there. The label has been stripped from the prescription bottle, and Lulu wonders where the pills come from. She slips out four and tucks them into her pocket. Hank arrives as she's returning to the front of the trailer.

"Let's go," he says, and Lulu follows him out to his car. He snorts into the back of his throat and spits a long stream into the dirt before he gets in. Lulu tucks her knees up and circles her arms around them on the seat.

"Your ma tell you what's gonna happen today?" Lulu shakes

her head. "Why doesn't that surprise me? The police want to talk to you. They'll ask you all kinds of stuff about what your ma's been doing since she got out. Just tell them everything's good, okay?" Lulu nods. "And don't go telling them nothing they don't need to know. Yeah?" Lulu nods again.

"Why do the police want to ask me?" she asks.

Hank shakes his head. "Because they're thinking of ending her parole early. They want to make sure that shit at the motel ain't still going on."

Lulu thinks that sounds like good news, but Hank doesn't seem as excited as she thinks he should be. She stays quiet for the rest of the ride to McDonald's and then waits in the car while Hank goes in for Maureen. Inside, Hank leans on the counter with the funny look he gets when he's talking to women. If anyone is still working here from the first time they came and Hank threw a fit, they've either forgotten or don't care anymore. The woman behind the register moves her hair behind her ear, and Lulu does that with her own. She can't see that Maureen has come out but can tell by the way both Hank and the woman stand up straighter. Maureen yanks Hank's hand, and he trails behind her out of the place, around the Ronald McDonald he once kicked. Maureen's eyes look dark. Lulu knows she's in a mood before she even reaches the car.

"Can you believe that asshole?" Maureen says as she gets in. "Why do I get all the weekends? I told him, I got a kid. I can't work every weekend."

Lulu quickly scooches over to make room for her and relishes in the feeling of Maureen's shoulder pressing into the car and brushing against her. She waits to be told to get into the backseat, but Maureen is going on and on about her manager and let's Lulu sit up front with them. Lulu moves her leg over so that it just touches Maureen's. She wonders if her ma will put her arm around her, but Maureen uses both hands to light a cigarette instead.

"I told Lulu what to expect," Hank says, cutting into Maureen's complaining. "You didn't let her know?"

Maureen finally looks at Lulu and brushes the hair from Lulu's eyes. Lulu's entire body feels like it glows for a moment. "She knows better than to say nothing after what happened, that right?" Her ma looks down at her, and Lulu nods.

"You going to pass the piss test?" Hank asks, his eyes on the road.

"Yes, Jesus Christ, Hank." Maureen misses the window when she blows out her smoke. It fills the car momentarily before sucking through the open space. "They aren't looking for that. They don't even know to."

"The headache pills?" Lulu asks and then knows she should have kept her mouth shut.

Her ma shakes her head. "Mind your own fucking business," she says. "And stop listening to us talk." Lulu's cheeks burn. It's not like she can just not hear. She wants to say that, to stick up for herself, but sitting there between her ma and Hank is nowhere for that kind of mouthing off.

Maureen goes first at the police station. Lulu's knee bounces with anxiousness. "Stop fidgeting," Hank says, setting his hand on her leg though she sees that his foot twitches as well.

"What if I say the wrong thing?" Lulu asks. Her heart is pounding in her chest. She puts her hand there to see if she can actually feel it from the outside. She can. "What if I mess up and then Ma doesn't get her parole done early or they put her back in jail or something?"

"Just don't say nothing, if you don't know what to say to something." Before she can ask what he means exactly, a door swings open and a cop comes to get Lulu. They take her to the back of the station, to a room with a small couch and a table. The officer calls herself Richards, and Lulu takes a seat on the couch as told. Richards offers her pop and a cookie, both of which Lulu immediately says yes to and then worries they're a test of some sort. The officer motions to someone Lulu can't see and, shortly after, she has both a Coke and a chocolate chip cookie in her hands. She tries not to look too excited about it.

"How are you doing, Lulu?" Richards asks.

"Good," Lulu replies, wiping crumbs from her lip. The cookie is the good kind, chewy in the middle. She wonders if she can ask for another one.

"School's okay?"

Lulu nods and tries to push back on the nervousness, wonders if somehow the cop knows about Miss Jeanie and how the kids pick on her. She wonders if Richards can read her mind, if she can tell that Lulu pocketed the pills.

"Good, good," Richards says. "And how about with your mom home? Is that going good?" Lulu nods. "She taking care of you? Home at night?" Lulu nods again. "She been at the motel at all?" Lulu shakes her head. Richards writes stuff in a little notebook. "She getting along with her boyfriend? No fights?" Lulu hesitates a moment, thinking about just this morning when Maureen nearly clocked Hank over the last cigarette. But she recovers quickly, shakes her head, says, "They're okay." Richards looks long and hard at Lulu and finally stands up, tells her she did a great job and that she's done. They walk back out to the waiting room where Maureen is now with Hank.

In the car, Maureen puts her arm around Lulu in the front seat, and Lulu's heart feels ready to burst in happiness. "You did good, sweet thing." She pulls Lulu closer to her, and they stay that way, snuggled together for the entire car ride home. And it feels like gold to Lulu, like holding something very special. And even though the Coke made her have to pee, she holds it in. She does not wiggle because she does not want to give her ma any reason to move away.

"Let's go to the diner," Maureen suggests when they get out of the car. Lulu starts toward the trailer, but Maureen catches her arm. "You, too." Lulu quietly follows them, staying a few steps back so neither changes their mind about her coming along. She squeezes her legs on every other step to keep from peeing. At the diner, she rushes to the bathroom, then slides into a booth just as Barb is coming by with menus. "Hey," she says with a nod.

"How's it going around here?" Maureen asks, tapping out

a cigarette. Barb reaches for an ashtray at an empty table and slides it onto theirs.

"Boring as hell. Making pennies." Barb rests an elbow on her bony hip. With her hair in a ponytail, Lulu can see the ways she looks like Joey. She wants to ask where he's at, if maybe he can come over to the diner too, but she doesn't want to piss off Maureen by interrupting. "How're you doing?"

Maureen picks a bit of tobacco from her tongue. "Shit. Don't really see the point." Lulu wonders what her ma means, but Barb seems to understand because she says, "I have some thoughts on that," and Maureen perks up. "I'm off at ten. Come by."

Lulu's stomach drops as she keeps her eyes on the menu. Maureen says, "She'll have a grilled cheese and fries and a chocolate milk. I'll take a fish sandwich and a Coors. Hank?" Hank orders a French dip and another beer.

"What's she cooking up?" Hank asks after Barb leaves, and Lulu leans a bit closer in because she wants to hear too, but Maureen just shrugs.

"I'll go by," she says. Then she looks at Lulu. "You didn't hear none of that, right?" Lulu shakes her head. "Good girl." Maureen briefly touches Lulu's hand where it rests on the table. "You got a headache pill for me?" She turns to Hank now and he shifts up, pulls it from his back pocket and hands it to her. Maureen slips the fat white pill into her mouth and takes a long drink. She stomps her cigarette into the ashtray, but a small part stays alive, creates a thin stream of smoke that Lulu blows at to watch it break and flatten into the air.

Barb brings the food plate by plate from the counter, and Hank pushes up his sleeves to grab the roast beef sandwich with both hands, dips it into a gravy boat of sauce until the end turns soggy brown and squishes when he bites it. Lulu blows bubbles in her chocolate milk, watching it rise to the top of the glass before blowing it back down again.

"Eat your food," Maureen tells her. Lulu takes a bite of the grilled cheese, scrapes the sticky processed cheese from the roof of her mouth with her tongue.

Hank and Maureen are on their second beers when a trucker comes in and sits at the counter, greets Barb by name. They lean over the countertop, quietly chatting. Maureen watches curiously, but Lulu looks down at her plate. The pile of fat fries she wants to eat sit stacked in waiting, but she's suddenly lost her appetite. The man says something that makes Barb laugh, then cover her mouth. She swats at him and comes around to their table.

"Finished?" she asks, taking Hank and Maureen's plates. "You want them fries to go?" Lulu nods. They sit for a while longer, Hank smoking. More truckers come in, join the others at the counter. Lulu recognizes them. This constant parade of scruffy men through their town. She wonders if they have kids and wives. She hopes they don't. And she realizes, for the first time, and this awareness trickles down her spine and makes her eyes open wider, that it wasn't just Roy that was the problem.

"What are these?" Principal Dan asks, shaking the pills in his hand at Lulu.

"Tylenols," Lulu says.

"I never saw Tylenols that look like that. Lulu, we have a zero-tolerance policy about drugs here. I called your parents, and I have half a mind to call the police too." Lulu's stomach drops, thinking about how much trouble she's about to get into. But it's Hank who comes for her, not Maureen. In the car, he's so angry he can barely breathe right.

"What were you thinking?" he asks. "And that fucking school, threatening to call the cops. Lulu, why? Why?" Hank shakes his head.

Lulu looks down at her knees. "I was getting five dollars for each one," she says. "I been putting that money in a box to help Ma with the trailer rent." She can feel Hank watching her out of the corner of his eye.

"It's good that you want to help, but this ain't the way to do it." Hank sighs.

"But Ma says she's not making shit since she went to jail. And that's all because of me." Lulu pinches her nose to stop the tears that are welling in her eyes. "And I don't know what Barb is up to, but I don't want Ma doing that stuff anymore."

Hank sighs again. "Well, all right, I get it, but this could have got her in a lot of trouble. You have to get smarter on this." Lulu leans her head against the window and watches the street rushing by. "You're lucky school's almost out for summer or he'd have suspended you." Lulu doesn't care. She was only ever interested in Penny, the guinea pig, and all year Miss Jeanie made excuses to keep it from her.

Hank taps a cigarette over his knee and flips it between his lips. "You want one?" he asks, and Lulu nods, takes a cigarette. "Light mine then too." She takes Hank's and lights up both. "Calms my nerves," Hank says. "I been smoking since I was a kid too. You know, Lulu, my ma was kind of like Maureen. And I didn't know my pa neither. Not sure how well my ma even did. I get it, okay? I get it." He looks over at Lulu, and she plays with the lit cigarette, rolling it between her fingertips. "You okay?"

Lulu nods. "Thanks for coming for me," she says, and Hank nods.

Maureen comes home a short time after them, and she doesn't yell at Lulu, just looks at her and shakes her head. "Get me a beer," she says, and Hank passes her one he just opened, reaches into the fridge for another. The night is stale, and she pulls her long hair into a pile, holding it above her neck with one arm. "How many of them pills did you take?" she asks.

Lulu swallows. "Ten."

"Where's the money?"

Lulu stands, reaches behind the couch, and pulls out a dented shoe box. She flips open the top and takes out the cash, hands it to Maureen. "I was saving it for the bills."

Maureen grabs it from her and tucks it into her pocket. "The hell you were."

"I was," Lulu says, and she hates the whining sound in her voice.

Maureen holds up her hand. "I don't give a shit."

"Maureen," Hank starts to say, but she turns on him with a glare and he stops.

She finishes her beer and stands. "Let's go out," she says, but Hank says he's not going. Maureen slams the door on her way out.

"You hungry?" Hank asks, and Lulu nods.

At the diner, he takes a long drink of a beer, and Lulu's bare legs stick to the vinyl. She takes a laminated menu with a big round cigarette burn in it, even though she knows what she wants. She pretends to consider the options.

The waitress comes back with a chocolate milkshake. "On the house," she says, and Hank winks at her while Lulu pretends not to see. They order food, and Lulu secretly loves that Hank lets her get whatever she wants. If Maureen was here, it would be the kid's grilled cheese.

Hank is quiet, and Lulu doesn't run her mouth because she doesn't want to spoil things by getting on his nerves. She checks out the other diners, recognizing a few of them. There's a ding and then the waitress sets down their plates. Lulu dumps too much ketchup on her fries when the blocked bottle lets go. She scrapes some on her burger bun. As she's taking her first bite, the trucker comes. She watches as he takes a seat at the counter and leans toward another man, clamps his hand on the guy's shoulder and laughs. Hank looks too. He stares at them, then glances at Lulu, and then looks down at his plate, and then back at them. His jaw grinds against his food, and Lulu is going to ask him if he's okay, but she thinks maybe that's not a good idea.

After they eat, Hank leaves her to go to the bar. Lulu wanders because she doesn't want to go home. She spots BB sitting alone outside her trailer and so she brings her along to the old playground near the church. There are several kids already there, huddled around the slide, so they go over to the swings where they can be alone. Lulu eyes them while she sways and recognizes two of the boys from her class.

She sighs and kicks at the dirt. "You remember that photographer lady?" BB nods. "I keep thinking maybe she'll get famous and then someone'll see my pictures and come to make me a model or something." BB looks away. "I don't know. Maybe not..." Lulu's voice trails. Maybe those pictures didn't even turn out. And really, who would be interested in buying pictures of people they don't even know? Then she thinks, maybe she can go to New York City and try to find Quinn. If she could just get the bus fare, she could go first then come back for BB and Joey. Quinn's probably got a big apartment with a puffy couch with the bits that come out for your feet to rest on. Lulu could have her own bed with a soft blanket and a soft pillow and Quinn would give her a kiss on her forehead before bedtime, and if she got scared in the night, Quinn would come and sit by her until she fell back asleep, and when she woke up in the morning, Quinn would tell her to remember to brush her teeth and she would take her to school and pick her up when she was done and take her for ice cream and to see movies and to birthday parties and maybe even on vacations.

BB pumps her legs but doesn't get far in the air. Lulu says, "You ever think about what you want to do, you know, when we're older?" BB looks off in the distance and shrugs. "I was thinking maybe a hair stylist. I like doing my hair. You could work with me too. You know they have the girls who wash hair. Or, shit, I don't know. You can do more than be a hair washer, BB. You could be a hair stylist too, maybe." But Lulu knows she doesn't sound convincing. She wonders what BB will be able to do. If only she'd talk, then maybe she'd open up some options. "I don't know how to get into the hair school though."

Lulu's thinking about this when something hard bounces off her shoulder. "Fuck," she shouts. "What was that?" And she hears the laughter coming across the playground. "You throwing rocks at me?" Lulu hops off the swing and, despite BB's anxious gestures, heads over to the boys.

"Which one of you dickheads did that?" She pushes the one closest to her, and he stumbles backward. Two of the others grab her arms. Lulu kicks out, but they're stronger than she is. She spits at them, but it lands on her own arm. "Let me go or I swear I will kill every one of you."

She twists, but it's no use. They have her held tight. She realizes two of the other boys are older, probably in junior high. One of them yanks at her shirt while his friend holds her legs from kicking. He pulls it up to expose her chest and grabs her nipples, twisting hard. Lulu screams out and sees BB running toward them. "No, BB, go!" BB stops but doesn't leave. Lulu can see the tears streaming down her cousin's cheeks.

The boy pulls down Lulu's shorts and her underwear goes with them. He laughs. "I'd have thought you had a dick with that mouth of yours. You ever fucked? Your ma teach you?" He presses his finger on her, and Lulu bites her cheek. The younger boys from her class back away. The older one is unzipping his fly, and Lulu squeezes her eyes shut. She braces for what he's about to do to her, but suddenly she hears him laugh, and she opens her eyes to him zipping his pants back up. His friends let her arms go. Lulu pulls her clothes back in place. She runs toward BB. One of them yells out after her, "Stay away from here, stupid slut."

BB holds Lulu tight in a hug, but it's Lulu who reassures her cousin. "It's okay, BB, it's okay. I'm okay. Those boys just wanted to scare me. It's okay now. Let's go." Lulu keeps her arm around BB as they hurry out of the playground. "We got to get out of this place," Lulu says. "I promise, I'm gonna get us out of here."

Lulu is drifting. She's never been on a boat, but she thinks this is what it might feel like to be on a boat. Her hand drags over the side of the couch. Her fingertips sweep the floor. And she pretends the stiff carpet is water.

The pill has landed somewhere inside her, and she sees it like a little moving thing that's sinking through the pink parts of her, down her throat, churning in her stomach, tumbling along the track inside herself. So, for a minute, it's not surprising the way the red splashes around the trailer like pumping blood. But then Maureen is running from the bedroom, and Hank is pulling on jeans, and Lulu is trying hard to bring herself back down, but the pill she's taken, her ma's pill, keeps yanking her away, to that other place, that drifting place. And Maureen is shaking her, but Lulu only smiles because in this drifting place, she can only smile.

There are cops then, a few cops, enough that the trailer feels smaller than it even is. And Hank is guarding Lulu, and Hank is holding her shoulder so she stays still, and Hank is telling them this is a mistake. Because Hank doesn't know. Hank did not know about the things her ma let the truckers do to her.

But Lulu says, "Yeah, that's right," when the cops ask her if Maureen takes her to the motel. Because even though Maureen hasn't taken her to the motel in a very long time, Maureen used to take her to the motel and right now Lulu doesn't understand the difference. She is lost in time. And even if there was a difference between *does* and *used to*, it doesn't seem to matter to the police anyway.

Now, Hank's arm is around her, and he's kneeling so he's shorter than her and his face is sad and confused and she tells him, "It's all right. It's all right."

Lulu sobers up in a hospital bed to find Hank sitting next to her. She's about to ask what happened, but Hank talks first. "Lulu, why didn't you tell me? You could have told me."

"Where's Ma?" Lulu asks, but then it becomes clear, and she already knows.

Hank's head sinks, looking at the floor. "How long was that going on for?"

Lulu closes her eyes for a minute. "Last summer?" she says and opens them again.

Hank whispers, "Fuck," and he moves like he's going to reach out to her, but then his hand drops. "I'm sorry, kid."

"How did the cops know?" she asks.

"Someone called them," he says. "They have Maureen at the station, questioning her. They got Roy back in there too." And

Lulu almost smiles at that, even though she never wanted to have to think about Roy again.

"Hank, was it bad what I did? Ma said it was just what girls do and that we needed the money." Lulu holds her breath, waiting for him to say something.

Finally, he says, "You didn't do nothing, Lulu. Someone did it to you. Someday you'll understand the difference."

ALEX AND GENE DANCING

1985

C-PRINT, 8 x 10 INCHES

Gene is in a blue and green flowered kimono when Quinn arrives. He tightens the straps, runs a hand over his hair to soothe a crown of mischievous coils. There's a zigzag of glitter pencil drawn from the corner of each eye toward his temples, which calls Quinn's attention to a bolt of blue vein below his left eye, barely noticeable under his dark skin. Alex hands her a cup of coffee. The radiators spew and hiss despite the spring temperature. Daylight streams through the gauzy curtains and brings a feeling of well-being, however feigned.

"How are you feeling today, Gene?" she asks, taking his hands and pressing her palms against their coldness. He is thinner than just a month ago, a gaunt hollow in his cheeks despite her initial sense of optimism. In winter, it felt as if every day might be the last. Spring, as it can, has brought a sense of devious renewal.

"Like a shimmer," he says. "Like sunshine on water. You know how that looks?" Quinn nods, and she can easily feel that feeling too. Gene sits on the couch, almost regal in the way his arm drops over its back. His legs tuck to the side.

Alex says, "New doctor, new pills."

He leads her to a chair by the window, and she takes her camera out of the bag, changes lenses, and checks the light. She shifts focuses, using the parquet floor until she gets the slight fuzziness she's hoping for. As she prepares, she asks, "What do these new pills do?"

"This," Alex says, and his hand flips in motion toward Gene, who is staring in wonder at his own hands. "None of these doctors wants to deal with him too long. They keep shuffling him around. They're all just amazed he's still alive."

I'm sorry, Quinn mouths because Gene has turned his attention back to them.

"Before you came, I was telling Alex a story of a parade I saw when I was a kid," he says. "Quinn, it was the most beautiful thing. There was a mermaid with a gorgeous tail. She spun around and around on the top of the float and her hair was red and thick like rope. All the way down her chest. And it's all I wanted. I wanted to be a mermaid like her."

"That's a beautiful image," Quinn says, taking a photo of Gene in the refracted light from the window. "Was it the Mermaid Parade?"

But he doesn't answer, instead says, "I have new pills," and he cranks open an orange bottle from the coffee table, holding one up for Quinn to see. She shoots a photo. "They make the room glimmer, like a disco ball. Do you want to dance?"

Quinn smiles. "I do," she says. She twists out from the camera strap and hands it to Alex as Gene stands, grasps her hands, and pulls her toward him. He circles them around the room, humming a song Quinn doesn't recognize.

"Quinn, you look like stars," Gene says and squeezes her hand. "So beautiful and full of energy and light."

Quinn closes her eyes to keep the tears from showing in them. It didn't take long upon meeting Gene for her to fall absolutely in love with him. She can't imagine how much Alex must be hurting over what's happening, what's to come. She opens her eyes to find Alex's, and he smiles at her, a deep, generous, grateful smile that she feels throughout her body. She nods to him, "Change places?" He takes her place, and she shoots what she knows will be some of the most beautiful and heartbreaking photos of her series.

Alex leaves with Quinn sometime later as the sky is darkening toward rain. Spring has been warm and wet. Gene has long since gone to sleep.

"What does the new doctor say?" she asks, looping her arm in his.

"It's anyone's guess. It's incredible how little anyone knows about this disease. How little they seem to care to know." Alex presses his head against hers. "The pills will make him comfortable in the meantime. He's holding on longer than most. Last night he said he won't die while I still need him so much." There is a tugging ache to the words.

"Is there anything I can do?" she asks.

"You're doing it, Q." He stops and kisses her temple, and she holds onto him for several seconds until drops of rain start to fall, splashing little thumps on their shoulders and heads, and they part, hold hands as they rush across Hudson Street to the bar. They order drinks, and Quinn looks at a food menu but decides she's not hungry.

"Do you think Gene will live long enough to be part of the series?" Alex takes the cocktail that's been set in front of him. He sips.

Quinn touches his hand. "Oh, Alex, yes, he already is. This is all for him. And for you. And it's not about the duration, it's about getting people to see what's happening. To care about what's happening."

Alex nods, and the grief is there, the darkness she spotted the first night they met. She wishes she could find its edge to help draw it out of him. "My friends are all dying, Quinn." She pulls him to her and rubs circles on his back. And she doesn't know what to say because no one knows what to say about this devastating disease. Her photos are now all that remain of the Greenwich Village gay club, recently shuttered in desperate fear. There are four men in her series, including Gene, but there could be forty or four hundred. The numbers are staggering, and yet fucking Reagan continues to do nothing.

Quinn sits back, shifts on the bar stool. "Listen," she says, "I've had an offer for a show at Cash/Newhouse, to exhibit the pieces I've done so far. I want to focus on Gene." She holds her breath for a moment and watches for Alex's expression. "I think we should do it. Together. I want you to help decide what to select."

Alex sips his drink, holds it in his hand, and pushes down a bobbing ice cube with his fingertip. "This is what I want so why does it sound so scary?"

"I know it does. It scares me too," she says, because it's the truth, because when she mentioned it to Eric, he was so unsure that a huge kernel of doubt grew in her too. "But I really do think if people could see this, intimately, it could change something." And that seems worth the risk, she thinks, but doesn't say.

"They won't be for sale?" Alex confirms, and Quinn shakes her head.

"No, never. Not this series. This is institutional work. I've already told Eric, no collectors. That's why Cash/Newhouse. They don't care about that there." And when Alex nods, she thinks it's in response to her saying this and not to the entire idea and so when he follows it up with, "Let's do it," she feels a bloom of excitement and trepidation unfurl in her chest.

"I'll call them tomorrow," she says. She grips his hand, and he holds hers back, tightly.

"Where's Billy tonight?" he asks, pulling away now. She recognizes the impulse to change a topic.

"In the studio," she says. "He and Myles have a show coming up." She likes this new thing about Billy. How he parlayed his love of video into an artistic collaboration with Myles. He was, after all, the coolest kid in the AV Club in high school, something she loves to taunt him with from time to time. She just wishes he had found someone else to work with. This has embedded Myles in their friend circle, despite Quinn's growing dislike of him. He has the air of the boys she went to school with, the ones with endless cash springing from their parent well, the pretention pooling around them.

"I haven't seen him much," Quinn admits, bringing her thoughts back to Billy. "We've both been so busy."

Alex taps his drink to signal for another. "Well, I feel like this is good for him. Something new to focus on. Now, if only he'd give up the drug dealing."

"Ditto that. And the drug doing," she adds because her worry about his drug doing has morphed with her worry about his drug dealing and developed into a deeper concern about all of it. She can't remember the last time she saw him totally sober. But then she's also only seen him out at night. Their days have been like passing ships. She arrives at the bookstore to find he was just there looking for her. She leaves her shift at the bar and he shows up after. They keep just missing.

I need to make more time for him, she thinks, but she says, "I've been working so much," and out of the context of her thought, it makes it sound like she has now changed the subject.

Because then Alex says, "I've been meaning to tell you, that was a good review in *ARTNews*. I saw it yesterday."

She sighs. "It was okay, but thanks."

"It was good," he says again. "You're too hard on yourself."

But Quinn doesn't want to talk about this, doesn't want to think about the way *Lulu and the Trucker* has been so easily acclaimed upon its showing, and there have been a few now. She imagined there would be some scrutiny, some questioning of her motivation or accountability. But there has only been praise and attention and that's exactly what Eric told her would happen.

Instead, she says, "Why don't we go spring Billy? Do a night out, just the three of us?" Because she doesn't want Myles to come too.

"I'm game," Alex says, and she knew he'd say that. They drain the rest of their drinks. He throws cash onto the bar, and they head out, back into the rain and now into the full darkness of night.

Alex hails a taxi, and they take it to the studio on Houston and Avenue A, where Quinn knows they'll find Billy. The space is on the third floor of an abandoned bank that still boasts ornate architecture under its graffitied walls. Alex is ahead of her, and he slows at the third-floor landing, catches his breath because they've rushed up the stairs in some kind of excitement. They walk side by side down an eerie corridor of what was once offices, now demolished into artist workspace.

Alex goes in first and when he abruptly turns back toward her, they bump straight into each other, Quinn's camera clanking between them. She almost laughs but the look on his face removes any humor. He grabs Quinn's shoulders and is pushing her backward toward the studio doorway, and she wants to protest, to tell him to stop it. But she can see over his shoulder. She can see the huddled bodies, Billy and Myles, the strapped arms and the needle that hovers between them. The confusion is like a scrim that's yanked away and it's as if some small part of her brain understands first and then explains it to the rest of her, the way she can hear herself telling herself what's she's seeing. She lets Alex move her away.

May has sipped the coolness from the breeze and dropped the clouds onto the horizon where they hide the setting sun in diffused pinks and purples. Quinn doesn't take a photo because the color will never match the beauty of nature, and when she's tried in the past, she's been disappointed in the dulled hues, the almost but not quite vibrant tones. There are some things that cannot be captured. She thinks about time like this, like a circular spectrum of tones and focus. She feels like a ghost in the blending edges of heat and light. Her feet reach but don't connect, her hands go straight through things. It's all been slipping since she saw Billy and Myles in the studio and even though her eye only caught edges, pieces, it has constructed the entire scene and played it over enough times to become memorized.

Gene is wrapped like a gift in brightly patterned silk and when Quinn hugs him, she can feel the edges and the bones of his hips and ribs, and she hopes she didn't squeeze him too hard.

"Happy birthday." She kisses his cheek, watching out for a splattering of red glitter on his cheekbones. He's shaved the remaining thin layer of hair from his head, and someone has hennaed the crown with a gold pattern that shines when the light hits him.

"Tell me I don't look tribal? I was trying to bring the Paradise Garage to me, but Alex has no idea what bohemian is. I always forget he's from Brooklyn."

"You look beautiful." Quinn is pleased to see how lucid Gene is. He leads her into the living room where only a few guests are mingling. She's purposefully early so she might compose herself before Billy arrives, find some footing here first. They have barely spoken in the weeks since her intrusion into the studio, a season has almost changed since, each attempt turning into a fight, and she has never before fought with him. They don't know each other that way.

Alex comes up behind her and wraps his arms around her waist, whispers in her ear, "Hello, my love," and gives her a squeeze before letting her go. "Can I get you a drink? A special cocktail?"

"Yes, please." Quinn admires the purple robe he has layered over black underwear. His chest is bare and whoever patterned Gene's head has done the same across his torso. Lanterns cast about in the corners of the room and an intricate splaying of ropes of various colors hang from the ceiling creating a circular space underneath.

Alex brings her a drink and kisses her cheek. "Gene is glowing tonight, isn't he?"

"He really is. He seems so well." Quinn sips her drink and wonders if these moments of lucidity and energy make it even harder for them. She's heard this can happen toward the end.

"I think it's because of me," Alex says. "My test came back negative." Quinn feels the relief like a dam that breaks, a gushing of something that she didn't realize she'd been holding back.

"Oh my god," she says, and she pulls him tightly to her. "Thank fucking god." But when she steps away, she sees on the outer rims of his eyes the sadness there too, circling the glimmering excitement, and she knows it's also hard to be the survivor.

"If you could have known him before, Quinn. He was like this but a thousand times more. Like a shooting star. All light and energy and heat. My heart stopped the first time I saw him. And when he talked to me, I felt like I couldn't breathe. I mean, I literally almost passed out. He's always made my insides crazy."

She wraps her arm around him again and holds him close. "I like that description, like a shooting star. How do you think of me, Alex?"

"You're a fire, Q. A slow-burning, hot as hell fire that could rear up and destroy us all if we're not careful with you." Alex sips his drink and watches her over the rim of it, and she doesn't understand what he means.

"That doesn't sound very good," she says.

"Not good or bad, it's power."

Billy arrives unexpectedly early, before Quinn can respond to Alex, but she wants to say she has no power, not that she's helpless, but that she's powerless, and for a fraction of a moment her thoughts run through the difference as she stares at Billy walking toward her. He loops his arm around her waist in stride and escorts her to the bathroom where he locks the door behind them and leans against it. The room is candle lit and overlooks St. Luke in the Fields Garden where small shimmers catch her eye—fireflies, she realizes, and she wonders what makes them sparkle. She wants Billy to see them too, but when she faces him, his hands are pressed to the sides of his face, and his eyes are closed.

"I'm sorry," he says, opening his eyes and dropping his arms. She steps toward him. "I want things to be normal again with us." He grips her shoulders, and she touches his hands where they land on her frame. "I promise you, no more drugs, none." The pleading widens his eyes and creases his forehead. "I fucked up and I'm sorry." She reaches out to smooth the skin, runs the edge of her thumb above his eyes and around to cup his cheek.

"Do you know how much I care about you?" she asks, and his eyes fill with tears. "Do you know how worried I am about you?" And hers do too.

"Let me come home with you tonight. I need to, Q. For me." He grabs her hand.

"Okay," she says. "Okay."

The relief she sees in his face, in his entire body, shifts something inside herself, and she thinks about Alex describing Gene like a shooting star. Maybe Billy is like air, something she can't live without, something she's taken for granted but needs. Her throat constricts, because she can feel his absence, and the choking panicked sensation lingers too long. She reaches out for him and pulls him to her until she's breathing fully again, deep, greedy breaths of his scent, his skin, his hair and clothes. They hold on to each other like that for several seconds, too tightly, painfully tight so that their bones collide, and their skin blushes red marks, but it restores something between them. And she realizes Alex is right. She is like fire, sucking oxygen in deep and desperate whorls.

The party seems brighter when they emerge from the dark bathroom. The room has filled. Gene is dancing among the hanging silk ropes, twisting them around his thin body where they drape, pull, and part. Alex watches from a leather chair, smoking and sipping a cocktail. The music is foreign and symphonic. Quinn joins Gene's wavering body, their hips sway toward and away, toward and away. Billy sits near Alex, and she watches them watching them, and she breathes as deeply as her lungs will allow. Deeper than usual. Pregnant with air. And in the stars that linger in her sight, she can see Billy's smile like its own constellation. She reaches for it, and he reaches back, closes the space between them.

Day is breaking when they leave the party and they go to Billy's apartment instead of hers, even though hers is closer. She wants to be in his space, in his air, with his things around her. They climb into bed, and she sinks in the comfortable mattress, the smooth sheets. She closes her eyes, and Billy moves over her and into her and she slips into a dream and when she wakes up it's much later in the day and he's asleep next to her. Light cascades through an arched window, glowing strips on their bare skin. She traces the tattoos with her fingers, lightly, so lightly he doesn't rouse, around his side, up his torso, to his chest. He catches her fingertips in his hand, and she nearly startles because she hadn't realized he was awake.

He rolls over and smiles at her, moves the hair behind her ear and gives her lobe a gentle pinch. "I gave you a poem in my dream last night. Do you have it?"

Quinn touches his chin. "I must have lost it on my way back to here." She curls into the slight space between them, and he wraps his arms around her.

The phone rings then, and Quinn knows, somehow, she knows, and as Billy picks it up, as his forehead creases and his hand moves to his brow and the receiver drops slightly in his grip. She knows that Gene is gone.

Lulu watches the others get on the bus and she feels a pain of regret not to be joining them. But with Maureen still in jail, she needs to be making some money now too, and there isn't time for both. Hank's construction job isn't cutting it. The first year or so was fine, but now the electricity has been cut off twice, and they just got an eviction threat for the trailer. She sighs and slinks down to sitting on the curb, waiting for the right moment to go into the lot. Her fourteenth birthday passed a week ago without so much as a call from her ma, though Hank bought her a Walkman and a Madonna tape. A part of her wanted to tell him to put that money to the rent, but then more of her was excited to get a present. She clicks the play button and "Like a Virgin" blares into her headphones. She holds down the Fast Forward button, scrambling the lyrics until it gets to "Material Girl" instead because that's her favorite.

Lulu bends the tops of her flip-flops over, stretches her toes and lets the flap smack back into place. She lip-syncs to the song, waving her head around, and swats at a fly that tries to land on her knee. The bus is finally moving out of sight. She stands and watches its boxy butt end make a final turn away. She stops the tape with a loud click, shoves the Walkman into her back pocket and rings the headphones around her neck. She walks into the lot, weaving between the trucks, feeling tiny next to their bulk.

A trucker immediately spots her and sets down a clipboard. "What're you selling?" he asks as he motions for Lulu to come closer. She wonders how he knows and then wonders if there's other versions of her at other truck stops along the routes these men take. And she could get lost a bit thinking about that, about another Lulu somewhere like Idaho, creeping up to the cabs with pills in her pockets.

She walks over, unfurls her fingers and shows him. "It's like heroin," she says because she once heard Maureen say that. It didn't take her long to figure out her ma's supply had been coming from Digger. "Fifteen a pill." She keeps her eyes steady though there's a surge in her, a ripple of worry that somehow he'll know she's bought them for five a piece herself. The trucker eyes her and Lulu's face flushes, sure now that he's on to her. But instead, he asks, "How old are you, honey?"

She swallows and it clamps in the back of her throat. "Sixteen," she lies.

He looks around. "I'll tell you what. I'll give you twenty dollars if you come up in my cab and give me a hand job. You can keep your pill."

Lulu steps back. "Nah," she says, but he leans toward her.

"Thirty. It'll take five minutes, sweet thing. I'm dying for it."

Lulu looks around, but there are few people in the lot, and no one is watching. It's not that much different from what she used to do, really. And she never got paid for that. Thirty dollars. Thirty dollars could mean a decent lunch, some clothes without holes. Paying the overdue trailer rent and the electricity bill. She takes a deep breath through her nose and nods her head. "Money first."

The trucker hands over a ten and a twenty and she climbs up into his cab, hoisting herself onto the seat. It's stale inside, smelly. But she's never been in a truck like this before and for a minute she's surprised at how high up she is. She looks over the parking lot, sees a dirty Nerf football on top of a nearby shed. And she's about to say something about this feeling, about being up so high in the sky, but remembers why she's here, and he's already grinning with his pants undone next to her. Lulu spits into her palm and moves her hand over him, trying to ignore the stringy bits of hair that catch on her fingers. She looks out at the Nerf ball, imagines how it got up there, pictures the kids trying to get it stuck up there because that's the dumb kind of thing kids around here would do. The windshield is streaked in halfmoons of dirt. She runs her eyes over the arches, slipping as far as she possibly can away from what's happening. Out of her mind. And he's right, it takes just a few minutes for it to be over. The hotness gushes over her fingers and he hands her a Kleenex. She wipes it off. She doesn't stay a second longer than that. She hops back down from the cab and slips the unsold pill into her mouth, swallows and makes her way to the next truck.

She stops leading with the pills at the third truck and goes straight to offering hand jobs first. It's easier with the gliding softness of the drug. It slides away her worry. She gives four more at thirty each and even sells two of the pills along with them, though they'll only pay ten, before heading back out of the lot.

At the trailer, she washes her hands twice with hot water and soap and then pulls the money from her pocket, laying it out on the couch. She buries an excited scream into a pillow. She needs to find a safe place to stow the cash so Hank won't blow it on whatever he blows his money on. She zips it into the couch covering, under the worn foam cushion, keeping out a five to buy lunch.

The diner is quiet because it's just after the rush. Lulu orders a burger and a chocolate milkshake, then does some math with a crayon on the back of the kid's paper placemat menu. If she can get three more truckers today, she can pay off the back rent on the trailer. If she can get four more tomorrow, she can square up the electric bill and get some groceries. She could even go back to school if she can find a way to make this much on the weekends instead. She taps the crayon while she sips the milkshake, does a few more calculations to see how much she could save up in a few months. She'll need a lot to get Joey and BB out of Riverdale too. They'll need bus money and rent money and food money. The burger comes and she takes a large bite, working her jaw as she does more math, and then she has it. She has the amount, the number of months, the goal. She sits back and looks over the scrawled numbers with satisfaction then folds up the paper and shoves it in her pocket.

After lunch, Lulu goes back to the lot. The truckers have turned over and she starts in again. She's hopping down from the first truck when she's surprised by a forceful grip on her arm above her elbow. She yells out and spins to find a cop there. Another has circled the other side of the rig and the trucker is now pinned against the barrel with his arms behind his back.

"You really think nobody's gonna report this?" the cop says, pulling Lulu away and telling her to sit on the curb. And she sits in almost the same spot she sat at this morning, waiting for the bus to leave. She now looks around worried because school is out, and the bus will soon be turning this way. "You want to tell me what you're up to?"

"Nothing," she says, but her eyes fill with tears. The paper placemat in her pocket crinkles in this position.

"You're Maureen's kid, right?" She nods, and the cop sighs. "Give me the money." She looks up at him. "The money you have in your pocket. Give it to me." Lulu shifts and pulls out the thirty dollars, thankful that she already deposited the morning's haul at home. He takes it. She glances to see the trucker flipping through some bills, handing them over as well. "I'm going to have to report something. You want juvie or foster?"

Lulu clutches a brown bag of her things as she walks up the

broken brick pathway that links the gravel driveway with the front of a house that's small but looks pretty nice. She met Rosie, the girl with her, last night when she was hauled into the same detention area. Rosie carries her own matching brown bag. Both have their names in marker on them. Someone has capitalized the second L in Lulu's name and she frowns at it. Libby, the social worker, has told them that this is a nice family who couldn't have their own kids, so they like to help out with others' kids. Lulu isn't sure what a social worker does, but she's heard the word a lot since getting picked up in the truck lot. And she wants to ask now, before Libby is gone, but she can't find the right moment for it. So, she keeps her mouth shut instead. She tries not to think about how upset Hank was when he came to the cop station to find out what was going on. And she can easily hear the words they said to him like it's happening all over again, *You aren't fit to care for her.* And that look Hank gave her, as if he were gutted right there on the floor. She couldn't explain. They didn't give her a chance to. She's not sure what she would have said anyway.

"Kathy, this is Lulu and Rosie." Libby's arm sways out like she's showing off something. And it's that simple, Lulu thinks. It's that simple that now this is going to be her home for the next year, maybe less if Maureen gets paroled again, though they've warned her that's not likely. At least she's not alone. Rosie is biting her fingernails. She smells like the little bar of soap that was pressed into their hands this morning as they were led into the group shower room, where Lulu turned her back to the other girls, ashamed of her swelling bumps and prickles of hair.

"I'll be back next week to check in," Libby says, "but call me if you need me in the meantime." Lulu resists the urge to grab on to her, to beg her to stay. Rosie looks at the ground. And then when Libby is gone, Lulu realizes she doesn't have her phone number and that makes her heart begin to race. It's been a while since the black edges came into her vision, but they threaten her now, clouding up her eyes and making the familiar aches like a little hammer hitting over and over at the back of her skull. She presses her head with the hand not clenching her brown paper bag. She still has two pills in her pocket and eagerly waits for a chance to take one.

Kathy brings them into the house, shows them around. It's nice, Lulu thinks. There are knickknacks around the room, crowded on every surface, mostly owls. She picks one up and Kathy says, "Someone gave me a ceramic owl once and then everyone started giving me owl things. I guess there's worse things to collect." Her face is wide and red. Lulu wants to reassure her because it seems like the woman is nervous or embarrassed or both.

"They're cool," Lulu says and tries a smile, but it only halfway comes. She carefully puts down the owl. Rosie is silent except for the sound of the paper bag clenching in her hand.

They go on through the house to a bedroom in the back that Kathy tells them is theirs to share with a bunk bed and two dressers. And when Lulu sees that, she tries to contain her excitement because she has always wanted a bunk bed. And she does not care that she's probably too old for one now.

"Settle in for a bit then come out when you're ready, and we'll have some snacks." Kathy seems relieved to be leaving them there. Lulu watches her step backward out of the room as if she's unsure about turning her back to them.

Lulu shuts the door and turns to Rosie. "You want the top?" she asks, hoping Rosie will say no. The girl shakes her head, sits on the bottom bunk.

Lulu climbs the three wooden slats to the top and throws herself down, narrowly missing her head on the ceiling. "You know what's funny? I always wanted a bunk bed. What about you?"

Rosie doesn't answer. Lulu hangs her head over the side to look at her. "You okay?" she asks.

Rosie shrugs. "Waiting for the catch," she says.

"What catch?" Lulu swings her legs around and they dangle down now. Rosie stands and leans against the top bunk.

"The catch, Lulu. You think these people just want to help us? People like that get the little kids. She seems scared to even have us here."

Lulu hopes Rosie is wrong but has a feeling she's not. "This your first time?"

"Nah," Rosie says. "Third. My ma is a junkie."

Lulu watches the girl's dark eyes, but they're steady. "Shit," she says. "My ma's a hooker, for what it's worth."

"Lucky us," Rosie says, and for some reason that makes them both laugh.

Lulu touches Rosie's shoulder. "Listen," Lulu says. "I don't know what this lady's problem is, but I swear you're okay with me. I won't let anything bad happen to you." Rosie gives her an appreciative look. "Let's go check out the snacks," Lulu says. "I'm fucking starving." She pushes off the bunk, lands hard on the floor.

They find Kathy in the dining room setting out a spread like nothing Lulu has seen before. There's crackers and cheese, celery with peanut butter stuck in it, potato chips and dip and small sausage links. *Holy shit*, Lulu mouths to Rosie.

"I figured you might be hungry," Kathy says. "And we have a few hours before Doug gets home and we'll have supper. So, dig in." She steps back, and it's like she's admiring the table as much as Lulu is. "I'll go get some Cokes." Kathy goes back to the kitchen, and Lulu grabs Rosie's arm.

"Let's get fat like Kathy," she jokes but Rosie doesn't laugh. Lulu digs into the cheese and crackers and then the potato chips and dip, but Rosie just watches her. "Come on, at least eat something," she says, spraying a light layer of crumbs onto the floor that she pushes into the carpet with her toes.

"It's probably the husband." Rosie looks away toward the kitchen. Lulu stops short of putting a sausage in her mouth. "That's why she's so nervous. Did you see how she looked when she said his name?"

"Hey," Lulu says. "Take one of these. It'll calm you down." She pulls out the pills and hands one to Rosie. "It's like for headaches, but better." They secretly wash them down with the Cokes Kathy brings.

Doug comes home a bit later as Lulu and Rosie are sprawled in front of the television. He sets a large workbag on the floor. Lulu thinks he must fix things for his job. Kathy meets him in the tiny foyer, and there's a whispered exchange that Lulu can see but not hear as he kicks off his boots and straightens them near the door. Lulu nudges Rosie and they stand because that seems like the polite thing to do. Kathy goes back to the kitchen and Doug comes over with a booming voice, asking them how they're doing and telling them how happy he is they're here.

Lulu stares at his face, at his wide hands, and thinks how different he looks from Hank. Hank, with his skinny body and tattoos, shaggy hair and jeans on his hips, is the opposite of this man here who has on a button-up shirt with his name in the corner and a fat body that extends into a potato-shaped head. He reminds her of the truckers. And it's like Rosie's whispering in her ear, the way she hears the girl's words. *It's probably the husband.*

They sit for supper after Doug washes up and Kathy puts heaping servings of pork chops, green bean casserole, and a biscuit on their plates. Lulu is still full up from earlier, but she eats as much as she can and wonders if every supper is like this or just this one because it's their first day.

"You girls are both so skinny. We need to put some meat on your bones." Kathy smiles nervously as she stuffs a forkful of casserole in her mouth. Lulu wonders again what's up with Kathy. She's about to say something about how good the food is, when Doug clears his throat and that stops her. Lulu and Rosie both look his way, and he says, "Rosie, you got interesting coloring." Lulu wonders what Doug is getting at. Rosie stiffens at her side. "Your ma Black?"

Rosie shakes her head and swallows a bit of pork chop. "No, sir." But Doug keeps his eye on her. Lulu moves her knee to touch Rosie's knee, and they press against each other under the table.

"Stop it, Doug." Kathy waves her fork at him. "He's just teasing," she says, but Lulu can see the color creeping back in the lady's cheeks and knows there's more to it than that.

"Well, your daddy must have been then," Doug says, and Kathy stands up so fast that she hits the table, and the plates move. She heads to the kitchen. Doug stares after her, and Rosie stares at her plate, and Lulu thinks how the girl was right to be worried.

After dinner, Lulu and Rosie help clean the dishes and then go to their bedroom where they can hear Doug and Kathy having an argument, but they can't make out what's being said. Lulu sits next to Rosie on the bottom bunk. Lulu doesn't need words; she can read the look on Rosie's face. She's seen that same look so many times on BB's face, on Joey's face, and she's made it with her own.

In the night, while everyone sleeps, Lulu sneaks into the kitchen and finds a steak knife in the drawer. She slips it into the waistband of her pajamas and takes it to their bedroom, shifting it out and into the crack between the mattress and the bedframe. She has a feeling she's going to need it at some point.

Quinn shifts the weight of her camera off her shoulder, cradling it in her hand and stretching her neck against the popping sound there. Her legs ache from hours of shooting, but there's a giddiness in her step still, an excitement over the shots she got today. She rummages for her keys in the pouch around her waist, fishing for them around the rolls of film there. And because her eyes are down, she misses the square Polaroid on the outdoor stoop, only sees it after she's stepped on its corner and it catches some part of her eye. She leans down and snags it from the dirty step. It's the photo of Billy in the car on the drive to Riverdale. She looks around, but there's no other clue as to why it's here, like this, but then she feels a rush of panic and it propels her two stories up where she runs down the hallway, already spotting the taped message on her door.

She struggles to catch her breath as she looks at the eviction notice. Her keys are still in her hand, and she shoves the apartment one in, but it won't twist.

"Fuck!" she shouts, and she pounds the door, the hard wood reverberating through her hand.

The door next to hers opens, and her neighbor is there smoking a cigar. "He came by today, dumped your stuff in the trash outside."

A rush of air leaves Quinn's mouth, and she shakes her head, runs back down the stairs, out to the trash can where she fishes for anything left. But there is nothing.

Jian comes out of the bodega then, and he stops her frantic digging. Only then she realizes the mess she's made on the sidewalk, the discarded cans and twisted food bags.

"I got some of it," he says, and she looks up, hopeful.

"You did? What stuff?" Her heart is pounding.

Jian motions for her to follow him, and she trails him into the bodega where he leans under the counter and pulls out the box of her film and photos. "This," he says. "And one more bag." He rummages around for a fat black trash bag. Inside, Quinn finds some of her clothes.

"You didn't happen to see two cameras?" she asks, and he shakes his head. She's sure her landlord has kept them, and she knows there's nothing to be done about that.

Quinn takes the box and the bag. She tries to walk with both, but stumbles under the bulk.

"I can help you get a cab," Jian says, but Quinn stops and looks around, sets her things back on the floor.

"I don't know where to go," she admits. She runs her hands through her hair, presses her temples. The loss of the two cameras is too overwhelming for her to even consider right now. She exhales a long, jagged breath. She'll go to Billy. He's probably at the studio with Myles. She checks her pockets, but she has only a few coins.

"Can you help me get this to the corner so I can catch the

bus?" she asks, and Jian nods, takes the box while she takes the bag. He flips a BACK IN 5 sign and locks the bodega door.

Quinn slumps midway to the back of the bus. She rests her head against the window, feeling the push and pull of the carriage as it turns corners, stops, and starts again, continually exchanging the other late-night bus riders. She hugs her things closer when a guy sits across the aisle and blatantly eyes her. Her camera is tucked under her jacket. She wills the man not to talk to her, begging in her mind, but he leans toward her. She gets a good look at the crust around his nostrils, the pink scabs on his cheek that cut into his sickly pale skin.

"What's in the bag?" he asks, and Quinn looks around at the others, hoping there's someone who might help her if she needs it.

She considers ignoring him, but he's leaning in and she's not sure how to avoid it. "Clothes," she says, and again she tightens her grip on them as they sit like a passenger next to her.

"Going to the shelter?" he asks, and Quinn shakes her head, but says nothing. "What? You don't want to talk to me? You too good for that?" She looks away, past him, tries to catch the eye of the bus driver in the mirror, but his gaze is straight forward. "You know. I could cut you," the guy says, and he nods at the bulk in his pocket, and she knows it's a knife. "I could cut your pretty little face into pieces so no one would ever recognize you again." He shifts closer, and Quinn's eyes dart again to the other riders, but it's late and there are few. She's on the inside seat, the bag between him and her, which seems both good and bad. She's stuck, but he also would need to get around her things to get to her. He watches her, a mean grin on his face. He's missing teeth. She knows he's a junkie.

"I don't have any money," she tells him, trying to keep her voice calm.

He looks at her stuff, and it must register that she wouldn't be on the bus this late with her stuff if she had money. "Give me the clothes," he says. "I can sell that shit."

Quinn is tempted to close her eyes, to shut out what's happening, to pretend it's not and hope it ends, but she knows that even a second of not seeming alert now will be all he needs to hurt her. She curses the fact that she only recently stopped carrying the mace, something that had started to feel unnecessary. Now, she fantasizes about pulling it from her pocket, spraying his already bloodshot eyes. She shoves the bag at him, and he grabs the top of it with burned fingers—*crack*, she thinks, as he moves it to his lap. He pulls the cord and hops out at The Bowery, and she tries to tell herself that it's only clothes, *it's only clothes*, and while she wants to drop her head into her hands, to sob into them, she remains alert. Three more stops. She eyes the changing riders. Two more stops. She pulls the cord, and when the bus comes to a halt, she pushes out the door and stumbles to the sidewalk, and that's as far as she can go. She sits with her back against the stoop where she hopes Billy and Myles are somewhere inside working, and she finally lets the tears come. They rush out of her, ushering so much frustration with them. Here, in this neighborhood, no one stops to ask why. No one even notices. She's relieved for that.

This is how Billy and Myles find her sometime later, though she's not sure how long she has sat like this. Billy rushes to her side, kneels beside her and pulls her head back to check if she's hurt, but she shakes her head to his questions and wipes the wetness from her face. Her eyeliner is all over her hands in gray streaks. She can't imagine what the rest of her is like. And then she sees that they're both high, the jitter in Billy's hands, the twitch in his neck, the way Myles won't look at her. And she sighs and asks them for a cigarette.

Billy lights one and hands it to her. "What happened?" he asks, and she realizes he's been asking this over and over for minutes now.

"I got evicted and then robbed on the bus. This is all I have." She motions to the box and the tears come again then, and Billy rushes to dry them as they come out.

"Fuck, your cameras?" She shakes her head. "Clothes?" She shakes her head again. "I'm going to fucking kill that guy," Billy says, and she wonders if he means her landlord or the man who robbed her.

"Should you go to the police?" Myles asks, but Quinn shakes her head.

"They won't do shit over a bag of clothes. And they can't do anything about the cameras. I mean, I didn't pay rent."

Billy sighs and looks away, shakes his head. "Why didn't you pay rent?"

Quinn feels her anger rearing and she knows she shouldn't, but she can't stop the words before they come out. "Because I'm not fucking made of money like you two!" She realizes she shouted and then says, "I'm sorry. That wasn't fair."

"Well, you can move in with me," Billy says. "I have room." And she can see Myles shake his head out of the corner of her eye, but she pretends to not have noticed because she's worn out, can't stand the thought of another confrontation with anyone else tonight. "Come on." Billy pulls her up and holds her in a tight hug. She lets her muscles finally loosen.

They take a taxi to his place, and he runs her a hot bath in his ancient tub. "We can get you more clothes, don't even worry about that. What else did you lose?"

"The two cameras, my books, my mattress, chair, toaster." Listing these items makes Quinn realize how meager her worldly belongings were. And she thinks these are the few things that showed she's alive, that proved she exists, and the fact that now she has almost nothing makes her feel like a ghost, unanchored. "At least I had the 35 with me," she says as she steps into the bath. The hot water scolds her briefly before offering comfort.

"It sucks that you just got that other one," Billy says. "I know you were excited about it." He doesn't ask if she couldn't afford to pay her rent because she bought the new camera, and she's sure it's because he already knows the answer to that. He brings her a beer, and he sits on the bathroom floor. The water settles around her, washes like a little shoreline onto her breasts.

"One step forward, ten steps back." Quinn takes a long drink. She rests her head on the back of the tub and sinks lower. She wants to explain to him how it felt, how the knife bulged in the man's pocket, how she could almost feel the cold scrape of the blade on her cheek when he said he'd cut her face into pieces, make her unrecognizable. Those words sit heavy in her chest, making it harder to breathe. But instead, she hooks an already wrinkly toe in the mouth of the tub's faucet and asks, quietly, "Are you high?"

Billy shifts and looks at her. "A little bit." She nods. "I'm sorry, Quinn. I know I said I'd stop, but we're working on a new project and Myles thinks it helps with the creative flow. You know, it opens us up." She doesn't respond because she has no energy left to respond to that. "It's just some meth," he offers, and she closes her eyes.

In the morning, Alex takes Quinn to the Salvation Army, and they pick out a few things. Quinn tries not to think about how the clothes got there. She asks a clerk if they buy them, and when he tells her no, she's immensely relieved. She offers to walk Alex home but when they get close to his building, he nods toward the waterfront, and they continue on.

"It's Gene's birthday today," he says.

"Shit," Quinn says. "I'm sorry. I didn't remember." She presses close to his side, links her arm in his. "How are you doing?"

"I don't know," Alex admits. "Sometimes I go a few days without thinking about him and I feel relieved and then I feel like the shittiest person in the world for feeling relieved. I miss him, Quinn."

She slips her arm around his waist as they walk. "I know you do. I do too."

At the Hudson River, they sit on a bench, look out to New Jersey. Alex knocks a cigarette out of his pack but holds it to shuffle out a joint instead. He pinches it between his lips and lights it, offers it to Quinn and she takes it because she needs the peace it might bring.

"Have you thought about leaving him?" Alex asks as if they've been in conversation about this for some time.

She shakes her head. "Not possible. He's my Gene." She doesn't add that now that they're living together, for however long that will be, it would be even harder to cleave apart.

"Let's hope that's not really the case," Alex says. "That love story didn't end so well."

They watch a barge full of garbage go by on the river and listen to the small waves lick at the steel seawall. A faint breeze tickles Quinn's neck and she leans into it, appreciating the way it cools her. A duck bobs up and down in the wake and calls out, but there are no other birds around to return its cries. She makes a sound like its own and Alex laughs, coughs out a billow of smoke and hands her the nearly finished joint.

"I feel good," he says. "I didn't think I could feel good today. Gene's been on my mind all day long."

She kisses his cheek. "Maybe he's the duck."

Alex squints and looks at it. "Or maybe you're just stoned."

"I'm definitely stoned." Quinn leans back into the wooden bench, sinking into its small slivers. The sun is muted behind a welcome cloud and the humidity has let up with the river's open arms. She closes her eyes and listens to the waves, floats along with them. She almost expects to have moved when she opens her eyes, but she's still in the same spot, the sun now bright again and narrowing her view.

"I feel good too," she says. "And I didn't think I could feel good today either."

They stroll to a grassy patch of lawn under a tree, and Alex surveys for a spot with the least amount of cigarette butts and litter. He lays flat on his back, while Quinn rests on her side, her head on his stomach. Her new bag of used clothes plops next to them, and she puts her hand on it as if someone might rush up and take it away too. Alex links his fingers in the empty belt buckles of her jeans, and she ignores an ant that makes a trip over her hip.

"I have an interview tomorrow," she says. "To teach Intro to Photography at Hunter."

"No shit, that's awesome." His enthusiasm reverberates in his belly making her head bob where it rests on him.

"I mean, it's not much but maybe it could change things." She thinks about the stability the position could eventually lead to. Less menial jobs, hopefully no more borrowing money.

"You've been burning the candle at both ends for a long time, Q."

"We all have," she says.

Alex wraps his arm around her shoulder and squeezes. "Don't worry about Billy, okay? Worry about you."

"I'll try." The weed settles her, lifts away parts of her tension that she doesn't realize she's holding until they're gone. And she sinks deeper into the grass.

"What do you think happens when we die?" Alex asks, and Quinn's mom immediately comes to her mind, and the many, many times Quinn's asked herself the same question.

"Dust, loving dust," she says.

"What do you mean by that?"

"I think we become a million little pieces that go back into the universe. We shed these bodies and blow the fuck away."

Alex makes an *mmmm* sound and runs his fingers over her bare arm. "But we're still us?"

"Yeah, just a million versions of us. A little bit of everything."

His arm trails in the air. "I like the idea of Gene everywhere. I've always been afraid of dying."

She grabs his hand and holds it tightly in hers. "Don't be. It could be way more exciting than being alive."

༶

"Louisa Belnap."

Lulu approaches the counter and takes the mini Dixie cup of

drugs, dumps them into her throat, and takes the regular-sized Dixie cup of water and washes them down. She moves out of the way as another girl is called and returns to the couch to watch a *Brady Bunch* rerun. She checks the clock set high up on the wall where none of the girls can mess with it. Forty-five minutes until group. She slides down on the couch, enjoying the light buzz of the sedative that's given to her twice daily to be sure she behaves. She's never had issues with her anger. Not like her bunkmate who has multiple cracks for various rage issues against other people and who most recently pushed a boy down a flight of stairs, breaking both of his legs and an arm, because he looked at her funny.

But Lulu and Adrian are of the same classification of violent offender and so they are also roommates, which makes no sense to Lulu because it seems they'd be most likely to beat on one another. So far though, the two girls get along perfectly well. Lulu knows when to back off and Adrian proclaims to have respect for anyone who stabs a child molester. Lulu sometimes even overhears Adrian telling new girls what Lulu did. "This perv touched one of the girls in the foster care and Lulu cut his dick off!" It's not totally true. The knife only nicked Doug's dick and landed in his thick thigh instead and, thanks to his fatness, did no lasting harm besides giving him a slight limp. But still, Lulu feels pride when she hears Adrian talk about her. And if she had to, she'd do it all over again.

They start group the same way each time, and it's only these sessions that include the boys from the adjacent wing, who are otherwise cordoned off by a wall-sized gate. Before Patrick, Lulu hated group, the tedious way they sit around in a circle giving their name and how long they're in for, how much time left and, if they want to, for what. But when Patrick came along, that all changed, and now she looks forward to the forty-five-minute sessions where they've slowly rotated seats over the past two months so that they now sit next to each other. She saunters over to the meeting room when the social worker calls them, the sedative masking how excited she is to see him when he comes through a separate door with seven other boys. He finds her eyes and smiles.

When it's Lulu's turn, she mutters out the same thing she does every session—Lulu, one year, four months left of it—and wonders why they bother with this when it's almost always the same people each group. But the social worker explains it's something to do with owning up to what they did and so Lulu does it and does not complain. She stays focused on one thing only. Getting home. It's been almost a year since she was nabbed in the truck lot. Lulu was just settling into foster care when Doug crept into their room. She sat in the courtroom with what Hank called a *shit for brains* court-appointed attorney and got smacked with the max for juvie.

Patrick goes next and his sentencing is shorter, six months for selling drugs, so they'll get out around the same time. When group ends, Patrick's hand sweeps hers, and she shivers. They're not allowed to touch, so they make it look like an accident each time. They exchange a sly smile then he's gone again.

After group is visiting time, and Lulu prepares to plop down in front of the television again, is surprised to hear her name called. She hurries over to the doorway and is patted down by a warden before being allowed into the visitor's room. She pushes around a girl moving too slowly and cranes her neck to see who's come to visit her. Hank is waiting, pressing his hands together and shifting from one foot to another. He's never been comfortable with jail visits and even though this is only juvie, Lulu knows it's a lot for him to be here. It's been a couple of months since she's seen him last.

He smiles big and broad when he sees her, and she lets herself be folded into his arms, squeezed. "You're a sight for sore eyes," he says, and Lulu tells him, "Same." He's her only connection to home now. The only reminder that something else waits for her after this.

"Listen, let's sit." He moves them to plastic chairs at the side of the room, drops his voice and leans toward her. "Maureen's sentence got extended. She got into some shit, and it's going to cost her a lot more time."

"Shit," Lulu says, and it's not just because she misses her ma after all this time, she was also depending on Maureen to be there when she gets out. "What do we do now?" Lulu feels the buzz of the sedative wear thin.

Hanks scratches the back of his head. "Here's the thing. They won't let you come home without a parent there."

Lulu starts to protest, says, "I can't do foster again, Hank. I can't."

"I know that," Hank says, putting up his hand to stop her. "Maureen and I talked about that. We're gonna get married and then I can adopt you and you can come home. But with your age, they're going to ask you if that's okay and you got to say yes." Lulu sees that he looks worried and realizes how much he actually cares about this, about her. Something softens then, and she tilts her head.

"Of course, I'd say yes."

"Good." That part of the conversation seems done. Hank looks around. "What's that scratch on your chin? Someone messing with you?"

Lulu shakes her head. "Caught myself on a cupboard." She doesn't tell him it was because she was high, having bartered cans of Coke for two other girls' sedatives. "How's BB and Joey?" She wishes they would visit her. If she thinks too much about how badly she misses them, she'll have a total breakdown. So, she doesn't. She pushes the thoughts away.

Hank shrugs. "They're fine. BB's been bugging to come up, but Papa Don don't think it's a good idea. Might scare her and all." Lulu nods because she knows Papa Don is right, as much as she wishes he wasn't.

"Hank." Lulu leans closer to him. "There's money. Inside the couch. You'll be able to tell where." Her stomach twinges with regret at giving up the stash, but that hope, that plan, seems far from possible now.

Hank sits back. "You want to tell me where it came from?"

Lulu shakes her head. "Doesn't matter. I should have told you sooner. I'm sorry. I just thought, maybe I could…I don't know. I don't know what I thought."

He watches her for a minute and nods. "I'll try not to use it," he says. "You'll be okay in here another few months?" He squeezes her knee now, and Lulu nods, thinking of Patrick. Hank stands. "I got to get to work now. Picked up some extra shifts on the night crew." She joins him on her feet. He gives her a hug, and it's a big one again, and then Lulu watches him walk away.

"Your dad is hot," Adrian says that night when lights out is called. Lulu is about to correct her that Hank isn't her dad, but then stops because soon he will be. And she thinks how strange it will be to have a pa for the first time in her life.

HEY YOURSELF

1990

Lulu swipes at a line of sweat that perches at her hairline ready to cascade down her forehead. She leaves her hand there, shading her eyes from the blinding sun as she watches for him. The glare off the metal sides of cars combines with the steamy heat seeping up from the asphalt parking lot, and she thinks this is what hell must be like. It's like a mirage the way Patrick suddenly appears across the lot, his outline shimmering in the heat and, more likely, from the pill she just took. He waves his hand, and she waves back, marvels momentarily at the trails that rainbow from her arms. Patrick twists the bottom hem of his Michael Jackson T-shirt and lifts it to swipe his forehead, which is also slick with sweat she can see as he approaches. She thinks to say something like, *It's so fucking hot out*, but he stops her with a kiss to her lips and she takes it, leans toward him. Their hips rattle against each other as he circles her closer, and even though it's hot and they're both sweating through their clothes, she presses into him for as long as they can stand. He runs his palm from the side of her face to the back of her head and presses her close for another kiss.

"I fucking missed you," he says, pulling away to look at her face.

His eyes are like diamonds, so blue they're almost white, and the pill makes them shine like their own small suns.

"I missed you too."

He keeps his arm around her shoulder as they walk away from the building and toward the rusty Ford that Joey loaned her to pick up Patrick from prison. He kisses the top of her head, and Lulu cranks her neck to smile up at him.

They arrive at the car, and Lulu hands over the keys. They slide in, and she curses as the vinyl seat burns the back of her thighs. She adjusts herself onto her hip.

"Where you wanna go? We don't have nowhere to be until tonight. Joey's throwing a party."

Patrick gives her the grin that got her head over heels with him in the first place. It feels so long ago that they shared space in that shitty detention center. Even though it's only been a few years, there are days when Lulu feels ancient. He puts his hand on her thigh and squeezes. "Who's at your place?"

"Ma and Hank, probably." She hates that at age nineteen she still has to live with them, but she hasn't had much choice. Every time it seems like there might be some traction under her feet, something always comes along and slicks the street. This time, Patrick had been nabbed at a park-n-ride.

"Shit, well." Patrick looks around and shakes his head. "We'll find someplace."

He starts the car, and Lulu taps two cigarettes out of a soft pack, lights them and hands one over to him. She studies the lingering circle of blue under his left eye and gently touches it. "It's nothing," he says. "Always some big shot in there, you know?" She leans back and blows smoke out the window, resting her elbow on the frame.

They drive down the highway until Patrick finds an exit he's looking for. He takes several turns on deep country roads. The wind in the window picks up Lulu's hair and tosses it around her cheeks, and she's grateful for the way it pushes the heat out. Patrick finally slows and turns into what appears to be an abandoned farm. What was once a small white house, now tinged gray, sits at the mouth of an overgrown driveway, and behind it, Lulu can see a caving-in barn.

"I used to get high here," Patrick says. "No one's been around here for years now."

He parks behind the house, hidden from the road, and they come out of the car, circle it to reach each other. He slips his hand inside Lulu's shirt as he presses in for a kiss and then grabs her hand. "Come on."

The barn smells like musky hay. Patrick kicks around a pile of it to an even bed on the ground. "Hang on," Lulu says, and she rushes back to the car, fishes around in the backseat until she finds a flannel shirt and brings it back, lays it down over the hay. Patrick's hands are on her, pulling her shirt over her head, pushing down her cut-off shorts. She helps him out of his jeans and T-shirt, and they stand for a moment, naked and smiling at each other. "Hey," Patrick says, reaching for her hip.

"Hey yourself," Lulu says, lacing her fingers in his.

They sink into the straw, trying to stay on the flannel. Lulu tilts her head back as he kisses her neck. She stares at the ceiling beams and groans as he pushes inside her. Her hands circle his head, grab at his thick curls, and she floats somewhere up near those rafters, feels like she can touch the rotting wood if she just reaches out, but her arms are clasped around his shoulders and her back arches as Patrick moves her under him. And Lulu thinks this is the most perfect moment she's ever had.

Afterward, they lay on the flannel, smoking a shared cigarette, careful to not let the ash hit the hay. Lulu rests her head on Patrick's chest, runs her finger over the messy eagle tattoo on his side. A trickle of sweat and cum tickles the inside of her thigh, and she rubs it against the other one. Patrick's fingertips lightly sweep her cheek. "Digger keep the lineup for me?"

Lulu nods. "Says when you're ready, it's yours again. But maybe you should wait a bit, you know? I got some money we can live on."

Patrick lightly pinches her shoulder. "I got to work, Lulu. They'll find someone else if I'm not out there selling it."

Lulu sighs. "It's Digger's fault you went in though."

"Nah," Patrick says. "It was dumb luck. Could have been me or him. I was just in the wrong place at the wrong time."

"We should get going." Lulu makes to sit, but Patrick pulls her back down again.

"I'm ready again," he says, and she smiles, lets him pull her on top of him and start up again. When they're finished, the sun is beginning to dip to the horizon. Lulu reminds him there's a party waiting for him. They dress, and Lulu swats at a fly that lands on her hip as she's adjusting her underwear.

In the car, she lays her head on his shoulder, feels the muscles tense and release as he maneuvers the steering wheel. The pill has long since worn off, but Lulu feels the blissfulness of having Patrick with her again. She won't admit to him how much she missed him, how it felt like a part of her had been cut out and thrown away while he was gone. She has learned to keep that kind of expression to herself, but she looks up in his face and watches lights from passing cars dance in his eyes and feels at peace for the first time since he was picked up months ago.

The party has started without them, and people are spilling out of Joey's trailer and into the dirt pathways around it. Lulu hops out of the car and walks hip to hip with Patrick up to the group, his hand sunk deep into the back pocket of her shorts. She separates from him as someone hands him a beer, and she makes her way to where BB is sitting alone on the trailer's cement steps. Her cousin clumsily handles a red plastic cup. Lulu takes it from her, sips to find it's a combination of booze and something sickly sweet. She hands it back.

"Careful with that," she tells BB, but she can already see the glossy look in the girl's eyes. Soon, she'll walk her to her trailer where she knows BB'll be all right for the night. Lulu hates when the guys see BB drunk; she's sure they'll try something with her as a joke.

Patrick joins them, gives BB a sideways hug and says, "She been looking out for you?" nodding at Lulu. Even in the dark, Lulu can see BB's blush like a little sparkler on her cheeks. She's always been fond of Patrick. BB nods, and Lulu fake punches him in the arm. "Of course, I have."

Digger comes up then and pulls Patrick aside, and Lulu sits down next to BB, watches the two talking. Patrick is shaking his head in the way that says, *It's all right,* and Lulu wishes he'd lay into Digger for putting him up to go inside. But Patrick is too nice, too naive, Lulu sometimes worries, to do that. Digger pumps his flat hand on Patrick's back and walks away, swigging a beer.

"I hate that guy," Lulu says, standing up and pulling Patrick's arm around her. He leans in close. She can smell alcohol on his breath.

"He's all right, Lulu. Don't worry about him no more."

"Don't worry about who?" Joey asks, joining them.

"Hey, JP!" Patrick and Joey bump fists. "Thanks for the party, man."

"Welcome back." Joey sits next to Lulu.

"That Digger asshole," she says as she lights a cigarette. "What do you think of him?"

Joey laughs. "That guy's a prick." Lulu nods and emphasizes Joey's words with a hand gesture. She swats at a hot ash that falls on the back of her hand from it.

Maureen and Hank come up next, and Maureen wraps her arms around Patrick from behind in a way that makes Lulu sure she's high. Hank shakes his hand.

"Back to the free world," Hank says, and Patrick nods. Lulu blows smoke past them. Maureen lets go her grip, takes the cigarette from Lulu, and walks away.

Lulu scoffs. "She's high as a fucking kite, as usual."

Hank watches Maureen, and Lulu wonders if she's right in seeing wistfulness in his face. She thinks about when Maureen was locked up and it was just her and Hank at home. That seems like a world away now, though she sometimes misses his attention.

BB stands and sways. Lulu takes that as her cue to walk her cousin home. She tells the guys she'll be back in a sec. At Papa Don's, Lulu helps BB to bed, then fills a plastic tumbler with water and sets it next to her. She sits on the edge of the bed for a moment and rests her hand on her cousin's arm.

"You'll be all right?" she asks and BB nods, smiles. Lulu

leans down and kisses her forehead. "I'm going back, but I'll check on you in the morning, okay?" BB nods again. Lulu clicks on a fan near the bed and turns it to be sure it'll keep her cousin cool.

She lights a joint on the walk back to the party and takes several deep inhales before putting it out on the bottom of her shoe. Patrick is sitting where BB had been. The party has broken up some and she scavenges leftover pizza boxes for any remaining food, wondering how they forgot to eat. She pulls two slices of sausage pizza from a dented box and rests one on top of the other, carries them on a napkin back to Patrick.

"Shit, I'm starving," he says, and she hands him both slices instead of keeping one for herself. He hands one back. "I know you didn't eat, Lulu." She takes the slice.

"Don't be mad," Patrick says between bites. "I'm starting up again tomorrow."

Lulu swallows hard. The thought of Patrick getting busted again, of going away from her again, is too much. But she only nods. "Why though?"

Patrick wipes his hands on his jeans and moves around so Lulu is between his legs. "We need money, Lulu. I want to get us out of this shithole."

She thinks about the small amount of money she has squirreled away in a locked tin under BB's bed for the same reason.

"I get it," she says. "But that was a fucking long eight months apart."

"I know." He pulls her head onto his shoulder and smooths her hair. "It won't happen again."

The party fully breaks up soon after, and Patrick and Lulu go to her trailer, squeeze onto the couch. She rests her head on his chest. His arms fold around her. A thin film of sweat forms between them. They need their own place, she thinks. They need to get ahead of things. She feels as if she's been running behind all her life, trying to catch up to something. And she imagines what it would be like, coming home to each other every night, having a kid or two, a dog or two. They wouldn't need much space. She likes the idea of them being on top of each other, of bumping hips in a thin kitchen space, pressed up against each other in a stand-up shower. She cuddles in closer to him, nestles. But she can't lose him again. She listens to the wet thumping of his heart like something being tossed down over and over again.

Maureen and Hank come in as the sun is rising. Lulu opens an eye to watch as they try to quietly pass through to their room. Maureen bumps into the coffee table and laughs. She's only been out of prison for a year herself, and Lulu thinks it would be real nice if no one else went in. But it's true, the trailer is too full now with Patrick here. She knows Maureen isn't going to let him stay long. Hank looks back at Lulu and catches her eye before turning to lead her ma down the short hallway. She tries to read his look but can't. She goes back to bed.

Patrick wakes her as he moves an arm out from around her and gently shakes the blood back into it. "Morning," he says, and she leans up to kiss his chin.

"You sleep okay?"

"Like a rock. Can't tell you how good this feels after a prison bunk."

"You want a shower? I'll make some coffee." Lulu gets up and pulls him by the arm, but he yanks her back down and wedges his face in the crook of her neck.

"I love you, Lulu," he says and kisses her there. She giggles at the way his lips tickle that soft spot. He lets her go, and she gets up again and heads to the kitchen to make coffee. Patrick goes into the bathroom and runs the shower. Lulu looks for anything to make for breakfast, but they're clear out of groceries, and she wonders why she hadn't thought to pick up some eggs or at least bread.

Patrick returns in his same clothes, rubbing a threadbare towel over his wet hair. He takes a cup of coffee from Lulu and lights a cigarette. "That felt amazing. No fucking perverts staring at my ass."

"You want to hit up the diner? I got nothing for breakfast."

"Yeah, we can do that. Come sit though." He pats his knee. Lulu comes around the arm of the countertop and sits. He offers her the cigarette, and she takes a drag before passing it back. "I'm gonna have to find some place to stay." Lulu nods. "Digger offered up a room and, before you go getting all upset, I think I should take it. Just until I can get on my feet again."

Lulu shakes her head. "I don't feel good about that."

"It's not my dream place either, but I can stay there rent free for a bit and then we can put something down on a place."

She sighs. "Fine, but I'm not going to that shithole. You'll have to come over here."

Patrick grinds out the cigarette and leaves its curled stump in the ashtray. "Deal." He presses his palm on the inside of her thigh and moves his fingers under the edge of her shorts. "You think they're sleeping?"

"Yeah," she says. She swings around to face him, kisses his mouth and tastes the combination of ash and coffee on her tongue.

His hands trace up her sides. Lulu leans into him. They stand and she slips out of her shorts and him out of his jeans and then they sit back again as he eases into her. The chair creaks and they stop, assess the chance it might give out, and then start up again. She clings to his shoulders, and he presses his hands around her hips. And when they finish, she sinks her head against his neck and he rests his on top of hers, kisses the mess of hair.

And Lulu thinks about the soldier-like ring of birth control pills in the faded flat pink plastic pack from Planned Parenthood that she's let slip by, the days crowding up on one another, lapping weeks, and she smiles.

The hotel room is cold when Quinn arrives back to it that night. She clicks the off button on the thermostat, cutting the air conditioning. She lays on the queen bed, splaying her arms and legs like a starfish and wills her muscles to relax, and they do because she sinks a little bit more. And it's like small excavations how her muscles give out one then another until she's finally fully grounded on the bed, no longer fighting gravity. The show looks good, really good. Worth the months of preparation, the endless darkroom hours and constant meetings. The curator seems pleased. Eric seems pleased. Quinn is pleased. A knock to the door startles her and her body reforms, muscle by muscle, as she stands to answer. An oval of Eric in the peephole. She opens the door, and he has the champagne he promised on the taxi ride back here.

He takes the chair while she perches on the edge of the bed. The cork grazes the curtains when it pops. "To you," he says, tipping a glass to hers.

"To you," she says back, because none of this would have been possible without him. "Thank you for coming down for it."

"I love Philly," he says. "This morning I did the Rocky Run." Quinn laughs. "It's a real thing," he insists, and she shakes her head because she's happy he's here with her.

"I'm exhausted," Quinn says. "And dying for a massage." She clamps a hand on her shoulder, the one that always aches from the weight of her camera.

"Come here." Eric motions, and she slides off the bed, sits between his legs on the floor. He swipes her hair out of the way and pushes on her muscles, gently digging his thumbs in the meaty parts.

"That's pretty good," she says. "I think you found your backup career." Eric scoffs. His thumbs trail up her neck in small rotations, and she resists an urge to moan, but it feels that good. His hands rake through her hair in tiny motions on her scalp. Her head sinks back into his lap, and he catches it with his thighs. He runs his fingers over the newly formed line in her forehead, the crease between her brows.

"You staying or going back tonight?" she asks.

And he's quiet when he says, "I have a car to go back tonight." And she thinks to ask him to stay, but she knows she shouldn't. And she doesn't want to hear him say no anyway. She sits up and his hands drop. She leans for a second against his leg and it sways toward her.

"Refill?" he asks, breaking the moment, and she knows he can tell it needed to be broken too. She kneels a few feet away and slinks sideways to resting against the bed. He comes to the floor as well and he pours them two more glasses. His hand rests on her knee.

"I could take you back tonight too?" he asks. "If you're sick of being in the hotel." She's been gone a week for install and the opening. She shakes her head because she's not sure there's a reason to rush back. Because she's not sure where Billy even is.

"I'll stay tonight. I have a train ticket for the morning anyway." She tries to smile at him, but there's too much seriousness now.

He squeezes her knee. "I'm sorry," he says but neither of them are sure for what.

In the morning, Quinn packs quickly and the hotel hails a taxi on her behalf. The train ride is slow, slogging through station after station and taking twenty minutes longer than scheduled though it's hard to tell where the delay has boarded, more an accumulation of incremental tardiness. Before departing, she tried the apartment again and the studio again but no answers. As the train slides into Penn Station her concern clenches.

Quinn takes a taxi to the apartment, dragging her bag up the flights of stairs and preparing what she'll say to Billy when she sees him, but he is not there. She changes clothes and dials Liv, but Liv has not seen him. And Micky has not seen him. And Alex has not seen him. She walks to the studio, but the door is locked, and someone says no one's been there for a few days. And so, she goes to the only other place she can think to go, and as the ancient elevator creaks up to the penthouse floor, Quinn feels her desperation like it's another passenger. The floor is not locked, and the doors open directly into the space. The dingy light makes the concrete countertops and exposed brick walls look cold and dirty.

No one notices her as she stands, watching. She spends a minute understanding what her eyes are taking in. The bodies, the needles, food wrappers, the funk of a party that's gone on far too long. A rancid, musky smell. And Billy, splayed on a cushion on the floor, his hair like a dark cloud around his head. The band still on his arm. A needle at his side.

"Oh hey, Q." Myles's lazy voice comes from the bathroom. "What are you doing here?" He walks by her, and she wonders if she's as invisible as she feels. The others watch her but say nothing.

"How long have you been here?" she asks.

"I live here," he says.

"You know what I mean." She gestures to Billy's unconscious body.

"He's fine. Just resting."

Quinn resists an urge to smack him. She sits by Billy's side and lifts his head into her lap. She rolls the band down from his bicep, carefully easing it over the pus-filled marks. His nose is crusted shut and his lips are cracked white. It's only the small rise and fall of his chest that keeps her from completely losing herself. She runs her hands over his face, and his eyes flutter but don't open. She does it more forcefully, a gentle smack, and then his lips come together, and his eyes slowly peel open. Now that he's waking, her other senses start kicking in and she can smell him. Days away from a shower. And she wonders if he's been here since she left a week ago.

"Come on," she says, yanking on him. He tries to sit, but his torso gives out and he tips toward her. She cradles him.

"He's fine," Myles says again, and Quinn holds back from shouting at him because that won't help the situation, despite how good it might make her feel. She rocks Billy.

"You need to wake up," she says. "We need to go home." He comes around a bit more, and he pushes his arms around her, and she can't tell if it's a hug or a gesture for help. The grip of someone losing something. "Come on, Billy." Quinn crouches and uses the strength of her legs to push them both up, and he comes along with her, though she struggles to keep him steady. They stand that way for a bit until he comes around a little more and then he sees her, really sees her, and his head sinks not from the drugs but from the shame.

She pulls him to the elevator and holds him as it opens back up, props him in the corner and ignores the way Myles is eyeing her as she yanks the gate closed and pushes G for the ground floor. The taxis slow then pass, and Quinn knows they'll need to walk the several blocks home. Every step is an effort. The flights upstairs are injurious. Quinn trips twice trying to keep him from rocking down the steps. Billy pulls himself with all his effort and finally they are in the apartment, and she gets him into the shower, and she washes off all the mess. And she shushes him when he promises he'll never do it again. She shushes him when he starts to cry and when he begs and when he says, *I need you, Q. I need you so much.*

Lulu balloons in a way she never could have imagined. So big that she asks the doctor if anyone ever exploded from this, and even though he laughs, she isn't making a joke. The purple lines are like a kid's crayon drawing across the expanse of her skin. Her belly button pops out like a doorbell. There are constant swirly nods under her skin, the edge of a foot, the curve of a fist. It's both amazing and terrifying. And then the day comes and even though she has thought a few times already that it's happening, when it happens there is no mistaking the difference in the level of pain, the level of pressure. The way it seems like the baby wants to drag her inside out. Lulu rubs the aching swell of her belly as Patrick maneuvers between cars and trucks, rushing to the hospital. She screams out over and over as lightning bolts ripple across her belly and down her legs, inside her. Patrick looks nervously at her when she tells him to "hurry the fuck up." She grabs on to the edge of the seat and breathes through the pain, but it comes faster and faster until there is little break in the waves for her to catch her breath. She gasps for air.

When they finally turn into the emergency room drive, Patrick puts the car into park so fast that it jolts the entire carriage, and Lulu curses. He flings open the car door, hoists Lulu up from under her arms, and shouts out for help. An EMT throws down a cigarette and hurries over. Together, they move Lulu into a wheelchair that has been brought outside. She pushes back against the pain as someone asks her name, tells her to try to relax. And she wants to shout back that she can't relax, that the baby is coming. The *baby*, that imagined thing that's been inside her for so long is coming out now. She hears Patrick give her name, and the scene around her swirls as the wheelchair is spun around and she's hurried inside.

Later, as she's holding the tiny bundle of baby in her arms, she tells Patrick it wasn't really that bad, and he laughs, kisses her head, and shows her the bruises she left on his arm. They stare at the pink-faced baby, and Lulu says, "I want to name him Patrick." Still later, when they take the baby home, to the trailer Patrick rented a month before, Maureen and Hank come by to see the baby and Lulu tenses up when a drunken Maureen starts to dance around with little Patrick in her arms. BB quickly takes him away, already deeply possessive of his minuscule legs and flailing arms.

And just like that, life starts up again. A new version with a tiny crying baby.

Patrick helps change diapers and clean spit up and warm bottles and fish pacifiers out from under the couch. They're back and forth to the laundromat so much that Lulu dreams about the flipping clothes folding over themselves in the front loader. The constant feedings leave her raw and aching. Milk spots grow unexpectedly on her shirts, and she curses because she can never tell when it's going to happen until it happens. The blooms are almost as embarrassing as a wet bed. Something she also does now.

When Patrick tells her that he needs to get back to work, she doesn't protest. She knows now how much diapers cost. But she worries all the same as she watches him load up his bag.

"Be careful," she tells him as she bounces the baby in her arms.

Alone, Lulu lays Patrick next to her on the mattress and kisses each of his fingers and toes, and her eyes start to slip even though she wills them awake. She has never felt so tired in her life.

Lulu's not sure how much time has passed when she wakes to the baby's urgent cries, which sound like the birthday noise-makers kids used to blow into, an unwinding long wail. "Hush, hush," she says, sitting and bringing him up with her. His yeasty smell is something she both likes and dislikes, a fine line between earthy and rancid. She pulls out her breast, and he latches on with a tickling pinch, and Lulu has to shake her head a bit to not fall back asleep as he feeds. She leans against the headboard and straightens her back but her head tips down as she nods off and the baby unlatches as she yanks awake again. "Shit," she says and tries to get him to eat again, but the moment has passed. His pink gums quiver as he wails and wails. She checks his diaper for wetness, but it's dry, and she tries to remember what the nurse told her about how much he should eat and sleep and what to expect in his diapers and who she should call if she needs help. She stands up and jiggles him along with her as she goes to the kitchen, fishes a beer from the fridge and cracks it open. The cold fizz instantly soothes her, and she rocks Patrick back and forth in her arms until he too is soothed.

"That's not so bad then," she says, tucking her chin to him. She opens her shirt and gets him to latch on to the other breast, and he feeds. Afterward, they both nap again. Lulu's breast hangs out because she's too tired to tuck it back in, thinks, *Why bother now?*

She wakes first this time, and it feels like a small triumph. She carefully shifts baby Patrick into the crib Hank gave them and he squirms, lips suckling nothing, but he stays asleep. Lulu's back aches as it has since her third trimester. She rummages through the bathroom cabinet for the painkillers and fishes one out of the pill bottle. She drinks it down with another beer and sinks into the couch, welcoming the lightness that spreads across her belly and back and trickles like water down her legs and arms. She worries only momentarily that she may have peed herself, but when she checks, she's dry as can be. She leans her head back and smiles.

Lulu dreams about the laundry again. The clothes folding over themselves like a beautiful dance. But the tumbling rumbles into her arms, and she opens her eyes to Patrick standing over her. He's yanking her shoulder, and she pushes him off, but then sees he's holding the baby. She smiles at them both because she hasn't realized yet that he's angry.

"What the hell, Lulu?"

"What?" she asks, sitting up, alert now, realizing the seriousness in his tone.

"You're passed out on the couch, and he's crying his head off in the crib. When's the last time he ate? His diaper was a mess."

"Shit." Lulu's breasts ache, and there are those blooms. She crosses her arm over them because she doesn't like how Patrick stares. She motions for him to hand her the baby, pulls out her breast and feeds him.

Patrick watches her, and she turns her face away from him. He won't understand if she tries to explain herself, the electric shocks of pain in her back, the exhaustion. Instead, she nestles her head against the baby's and breathes into the fuzzy crown, murmurs, "It's okay, sweet thing. It's okay."

"I was thinking, maybe we can ask BB to help during the day? I mean, we can't pay her, but on the days she's off work, maybe she'll want to just hang out anyway? She loves him so much."

"Yeah, sure," Lulu says, and now she does look at him and she sees sadness in his eyes and wonders if she's made that happen. "I'm sorry about today. I'm flat worn out."

Patrick comes to sit next to her and puts his arm around her shoulder. He kisses her forehead. "It's going to be okay. We'll get used to this." And she wonders if it's as simple as getting used to the baby. She thinks it's more complicated. Even as he grew inside her, it didn't feel real, but now it's real. Now baby Patrick is here, and she's a mom and Patrick is a dad, and they have to do this right, they have to take good care of him and make sure his life goes well.

BB comes over as suggested, and when Lulu hands her the baby, it's as if a huge weight has been taken from her arms. BB coos to baby Patrick and kisses his fingers, and Lulu can't help but think that BB would make for a much better ma than her. It's been one month now, and they should have had some kind of celebration since it feels like a lot longer than that, a year at least. The first three weeks of utter exhaustion, back pain, and broken emotions. But then the baby, little Patrick in her arms, is a small rescue on the days when Lulu thinks she might not make it. His cries are slowly calming as he gets used to being a breathing being in the world. His arms flail with less frequency, his kicks more certain, less experimental. He knows when he wants to eat and sleep, and Lulu has learned the difference between hunger cries, dirty diaper cries, and an arm trapped in a funny position cries. Her ears tune to a new communication, and she thinks they might just make this work out.

"Patrick's gone to get some burgers," she says. "You want to stay for dinner?" BB nods, holds the baby close to her chest while she rocks back and forth on her feet. Patrick coos for her and toots loudly in her arms. Lulu lights a cigarette and flops down on the couch. She stretches her back, but the zigzag of pain that runs down her hip and into her leg no matter how she adjusts is still there. She sighs out a long stream of smoke and closes her eyes. She promised Patrick she wouldn't take any more of the painkillers, but that leaves her with little choice other than to bear through it. She takes a long drink of beer, wishing it was something stronger.

It's a while later that she begins to wonder where Patrick is. He's been gone for over an hour, she realizes, as she checks the clock on the stove. BB is still rocking the baby who has fallen asleep and is making snuffling sounds in her cradled arms.

"You can put him in his crib," she tells her, but BB shakes

her head and holds him closer. "Where the fuck is Patrick?" Lulu says to no one.

Lulu steps outside as if she might be able to spot him coming, but it's quiet in the trailer park. She swears as she comes back in, picks up the phone, and pages him. She goes to the kitchen to see what they might have to eat. She finds two TV dinners in the freezer and throws them into the microwave. She lights another cigarette and wanders around the small space, BB watching her. The ding of the microwave makes her jump, and Lulu thinks for a just a second that it's the phone, but her mind registers the difference and the small part of her that felt relief is flushed again with worry. She takes out the dinners, burning her fingertips on the edge that's not supposed to get hot. She peels back the wrapping on the cardboard trays, sets them on the table. She motions to take Patrick from BB and lays him down on the couch, where, now awake, his arms reach out into the space above him.

Lulu keeps an eye on the clock as they eat and when they've finished and Patrick still isn't home, still hasn't called, she dials Joey's number and asks if he's seen him. He hasn't but offers to check around for her. Lulu can feel it then, can feel that something has gone terribly wrong. "I need to get some air," she says, and BB nods as she sits by the baby.

Outside, Lulu fishes a joint out of her cigarette pack. She lights it up and walks circles outside the trailer. She pushes ideas out of her mind—that he's left, that he's been in an accident. Her stomach knots up against the food, and she takes another hit from the joint to soothe her nerves. The phone's ringing draws her back inside, rushing because she's so relieved that he's finally responded to the page. And BB hands it to her and it's an automated voice asking if she'll accept a collect call. And she knows this automated voice well, from all the times Maureen has called from jail.

"Lulu, they're only giving me a minute here. I got pulled over and they checked the trunk. I had shit in there still from working today."

"Fuck, why would you do that? Never mind, it doesn't matter. What's happening?" She touches her chest where the wet spots have darkened her shirt, but she's too frantic to care.

"They arrested me. I get arraigned tomorrow."

Lulu grabs the top of her head, pulls at her hair. "How much did you have?"

"Enough to be a real big fucking problem."

"Patrick." His name comes out of her mouth in breath.

"Lulu, I got to go. They're making me hang up, but come to court tomorrow morning, okay?"

The phone cuts off, and Lulu sinks to the floor. BB sits next to her. "He's going to prison again, BB. No way around it." And her cousin's arm is around her. Lulu falls into her hold.

BB stays the night on the couch. Lulu appreciates not being alone. She lays on her side with her breast in Patrick's mouth during his nighttime feeding and runs her fingers over the soft skin of his forehead, gently touching his tiny eyelashes which makes him open his eyes. He watches her back.

"It's going to be all right, sweet thing," she tells him. "I'm going to make sure it's all right, you hear?" His suckling becomes more insistent. Lulu thinks he can feel her desperation despite her calming words. She hums a little though it breaks up in the sadness that clenches her throat.

At the courthouse, Lulu tries to touch Patrick's arm as he passes by, but she can't quite make the connection. His head hangs low when they read the charges. A trial date is set for three weeks from now, and a bail there's no way they can make is listed out by the judge who takes a moment to recount Patrick's record, the juvie, a breaking and entering charge, the recent stint for possession of marijuana.

She's allowed to see him once he's processed back at the jail. They sit across from each other in orange plastic chairs in the visitor's room where guards watch over them and tell them to disengage when Lulu grabs for his hand.

"I'm sorry," Patrick says. "I fucked up."

Lulu hushes him. "Listen, no sense in beating yourself

up about it. Joey's going to try to get an attorney, no court-appointed shit for this. I can't get ahold of Digger, no surprise there."

"Lulu, I'm going to jail for some time. They impounded the car. With my record." He shakes his head, and she wants so much to reach out and touch his face. "We got some money in the account. It'll get you through a few months. But you promise me you won't do anything stupid, right? Ask JP for money when you need it." Lulu looks away, nods.

The trial never happens. A plea bargain is accepted for seven years, because they're told it could be twenty. There's evidence that's impossible to refute, no matter the quality of attorney. A duffel bag full of class A drugs. Too much for personal use, no reasonable doubts about that. Lulu cries quietly in the court-room as the plea is entered, while baby Patrick suckles a bottle, unaware in BB's arms. Patrick's head hangs low as he's led past them and out of the courtroom.

At the trailer, Lulu takes out a piece of paper and does some easy math. She looks at the number, calculates how long their meager savings will last them, and presses her hand to her chin. BB looks away. Lulu knows her cousin doesn't approve of what's about to come.

Billy leans against the sink, dragging a razor over the edge of his chin, and Quinn snaps a shot, capturing his concentration, the naked torso, and the dragon tattoo dipping into his low-hung jeans at his hip bone. Her heart aches in a new way she can't un-derstand, and it feels like each time she has this sensation there's another level of excavation and she wonders when it'll hit a core, a pit, somewhere inside so that it stops. For weeks now she's had dreams that she can't find him, that she's all over town looking for him, but he's nowhere. In these dreams, she can't be sure if he's missing or avoiding her and the pain of both wakes her from her sleep with wet eyes and a racing heart. She snaps a few more photos, then sets the camera down and joins him in the small wedge of bathroom space, slips her hands around his waist from behind him and presses her cheek to the hollow between his shoulder blades. She can hear his heart like this, the bass drum and tinkling cymbals of reverberation. *If I can keep him like this*, she thinks, *he'll never slip away.*

He shakes the razor off under a stream of water and sets it on the side of the sink, turns to hold her close against him, and wipes a small cloud of shaving cream that clings to her forehead, transferred to her from his chin. His kiss to the top of her head makes her knees weak, and she holds tighter, presses into him until their bones are digging into each other and their chests rise and fall with the same tempos of inhales and exhales.

Quinn looks out into the apartment where their things mingle in piles that no longer feel like hers or his. She loosens her hold on him and leans back to make space. She studies the small lines that have formed around his eyes and mouth from years of that smile that has always been infectious. She runs her hands down his bare arms and stops at the small marks near the crook of his elbow. Her thumb runs around one in a tiny orbit with the cratered bloom of bruise there.

"Again?" she asks, and she says it quietly so as not to ignite the fight that is a constant undercurrent in their relationship.

But he sighs and his muscles tense up around his jaw and she knows there's no gentle way to have this discussion. "Once or twice," he says.

She holds his arm and turns it out. "That's more than once or twice." The marks always tell the truth. "There's a rehab place that Eric told me about."

"Why are you talking to Eric about me?" Billy pulls his arm away, and Quinn rubs at her eyes. He pushes past her out of the bathroom, and she wants to follow him, to trail his movements, but she stops because she also doesn't want to be that kind of woman.

And then she thinks, *But I am that kind of woman*, and she finds him in the bedroom, on the bed, his arm over his eyes. "Will you lay down with me?" he asks. She moves to do so because she's never been able not to. She pushes a notebook off the bed and shifts one of her cameras from the pillow and then she's next to him and they lay side by side. "I haven't felt connected to you," he says, and Quinn leans up to study his face. He reaches to touch her chin, and she wonders how they can be feeling the same way and then she has to push down a response that sits somewhere near the tip of her tongue because she hears his words as if they're blaming her for what's come between them.

"Listen," Quinn says. "This is getting out of hand."

He rolls onto his back, runs his fingers through his hair. "Quinn, it's nothing."

"This is not nothing." She fights the quiver in her voice, the tears that hover at the edge of her eyes. The bloom of blue bruises and circular sores on his arm yawn in the space between them.

"Okay, it's been a little out of control. We've been working a lot. There's a lot of pressure over this next show. I'll get it together." He can't meet her eyes.

She tries to put out of her mind the way she feels time slipping from her, the ways she worries that if she steps away, if she moves to the side, Billy will disappear from her life entirely. Already, he feels like a ghost most days, like something spectral and conceptual, and she aches for the days when he was solidly there. She grabs the Polaroid from the floor near the bed and shoots two photos of him. He groans in protest.

"I want you to see how you look to me," she says. The images slip one after another from the front of the camera. She sets them on the bed next to him.

"Q, just lay with me," he begs, and she moves the photos to the floor, lays again next to him. She touches his stomach lightly, tries to connect to the part of her that once wanted him so badly, but it feels lost to the drugs, to Myles, to everything else in his life. She curls into his chest, rests her hand on his heart, and he wraps his arm around her, pulls her closer. If she tries, she can find in her mind a younger version of him, but she feels like she's constantly reaching for it. They are memories that refuse to cooperate, refuse to enable her. And so, they stay vague and translucent, no matter how much she tries to color them in.

But then his touch, the right pressure, the places he knows well. And even though it's been some time, they fall easily back into it, the sudden push and pull, a tugging wrestle, and Quinn thinks how much sex can seem like struggling. When she comes, years flash before her eyes, a flickering film that ends with a dark explosion that sucks all the light of the moment. She gasps as she pushes off him, rolls onto her back and stares at the ceiling.

Billy drifts asleep with his arm bent around her, while Quinn stays awake at his side. She has sunken parts of her, submerged them where they're hard to find now. She tries to fish them out, to lure them back, but they remain weighed down. And it's then that she realizes how lonely she's been, in this empty space, waiting for things to be how they had been, waiting for them to be recognizable again, or waiting for them to move on and let her be free. So, she lets the tears come, lets them drip down her cheeks and pool around her neck and soak into Billy's chest. She slips out from his slumbering grip, dresses, and quietly closes the door behind her.

Eric is on the phone when she arrives at the gallery, and he waves her to sit. She listens as he negotiates an art shipment. She flips through an *Artforum*, trying to find some actual art among the plethora of ads. The phone call takes some time, and she mouths to him, *I'm hungry.* He smiles and nods, holds up a finger and finally ends the call a few minutes later.

"Museums," he says. "They're such a hassle. What are you hungry for? Did you eat breakfast? I skipped it and now I'm starving."

Quinn watches him rush around his office with his usual wiry energy. "You're exhausting me. How about a proper hello?"

He stops, sets down a folder he's holding and comes to where she's sitting. Quinn stands, and Eric plants a kiss on both of her cheeks, pulls her into a hug and holds her tight. She's needed this hug so badly, more badly than she realized.

"We have a lot to go over today," he says. "But food, come on." He grabs her hand, and she lets herself be led.

The early fall air makes it too chilly to sit outside but warm enough for a window seat. Quinn slips into the side that lets her look out onto Canal Street. They order dumplings and tea, and Eric starts in immediately on pricing for her upcoming show.

"Rizzoli wants to do a catalog on The Bowery Boards as well. I thought we could pitch a launch of that alongside a smaller show either at my gallery or somewhere else. And San Francisco and Chicago are interested in the Lost Boys Series since it did so well in LA and Philly. We should take advantage of that to get more attention around this new work you're doing."

Quinn nods her head, but she's finding it hard to focus. A part of her has remained with Billy, twisted in the bedsheets and stuck in the tucked corners of the pillows. "Honestly, whatever you think is best."

"It'll mean a lot of work in addition to your practice over the coming months. You're okay with that? What's your semester load?"

"Just two classes. It all sounds fine to me." She sips green tea and looks out past him, watches a cabbie and a pedestrian exchange words with pointed fingers chopping the air between them. Next to Eric's seat is a small shelf built into the brick wall. It holds a waving kitty sculpture, a book on the I Ching, and an empty incense holder. These little things distract her.

Their dumplings arrive, and Eric settles onto the loose cushions that make up the back of his seat. He rubs his hands together as he studies the food, then breaks his chopsticks. Quinn's eyes run over the etch in his cheeks, the slight shadow of hair coming through his skin that now carries small flecks of gray, and the way his blush-colored lips seem painted onto his pale skin. She likes to study him anew each time they meet. She is always finding something interesting. Today, it's a freckle near his lip that she somehow never noticed before. She touches the softness of his black cashmere sweater at his forearm. He looks up at her and smiles.

"Hey," she says. "Thanks, you know, for everything you do for me." She leans back and breaks her own chopsticks, picks up a dumpling. Eric watches her. She knows he holds back on asking if she's okay.

"You know, I was thinking recently," he says, "this is my longest relationship with a woman." He waves his chopsticks between them, and she finally smiles.

"I'm honored, I think."

"Something is up with you, though. You want to talk about it?"

Quinn squints at him and swallows a mouthful of food. "Actually, I lied." She takes a deep breath. "I think we should pause this."

She can feel his immediate alarm. "Which part of this?"

"All of it," she says, and she hates the words even as they're coming out of her mouth. "Billy is using again, and I feel like it happens every time I'm away for a show. I just…I need to pause and help him."

Eric sits back and sets his chopsticks down, puts a hand on hers where it rests on the table. "Quinn," he says, but then stops. She can tell he's holding in his words to be sure they come out right.

"I know," she says. "I know. But I'm watching him kill himself, Eric." She looks away, and her foot flexes hard in her shoe. "And Myles is just making it easier and easier. I'm fighting. I'm like in a war, it feels like."

Eric nods his head. "Okay," he says. "I understand. What can I do to help?"

Quinn shakes her head. "I don't know. I don't know at all."

"Do you trust me to handle your work? To do these upcoming things for you? I know you need to pause, Quinn, but I could keep working on it for you. We'll put your current project on hold, but I can keep things moving forward with the work that's already done. I can approve the galleys. I can do the installs, and we can have you just come for the openings. In and out."

Quinn exhales and nods. "Yeah, that would be helpful." She closes her eyes to keep the tears back behind the lids. Eric gives her the time she needs to regain her composure. When she opens them, he's watching her.

"You're not alone," he says. "Okay? I'm right here. I'm always right here."

TIME TRAVELING

VARIOUS

Eric moves a strand of Quinn's hair away from her mouth and tucks it behind her ear. They're sitting on the couch in his office where they've sat so many times over the years. It's the same couch he's always had, and she can feel the slight groove that she's sure she's worn into the cushions herself. She can't imagine anyone else sitting here like this with him, though she knows she's not the only one. She leans against him so she can feel his heartbeat on the edge of her cheekbone. He holds her head close to him, and his palm feels solid, reliable, loving even.

"What do you need?" he asks.

"I don't know," she whispers.

He rests his chin on her head and she waits for him to say something, but he stays quiet instead. And she thinks about his question, but she doesn't know how to help herself, let alone ask anyone else for it. She feels like she's standing, stuck in one place, unable to move, unable to find a way forward. She turns her head, and they stare at one another for a moment, then Quinn touches his cheek, pulls his face toward hers, and their lips connect. They shift and she grabs the back of his neck, softly but forcefully. His kiss is deep, and it lingers in a way that reminds her that he's not hers and she is not his. He stops and clears his throat and tilts his head away, but Quinn pulls him close again because she's desperate for this, for a feeling that will jolt her out of the place she's in. This time, the kiss is more urgent, less tender, and she pushes into it because she realizes how long she's wanted to do this, how many times in their simple goodbye kisses she's wanted something much more. She can hear his breath catching, can't find her own, but doesn't care. She won't let him move away, holds him there, and then when they finally do separate, they're both desperate for air. And she wonders if this is what she's been after, this feeling. The sensation of being alive again.

Eric pulls her close to his chest and she relaxes into his hold, realizes how much tension she's been holding in her entire body and lets herself relax. It's as if he collects her pooling, the way he adjusts to hold her even closer. And she wonders how bones and muscles and skin can collapse like this. She's never considered that her fire could melt her very self.

"You know, you were never a stranger to me," Quinn says, and she can feel Eric's mouth on the top of her head, the warmth of his breath. His sigh on her skin sends shivers down her spine. She wants to kiss him again, but she thinks that moment has passed, that they may never have that moment again, no matter how much she may want it. His shirt is soft, and she nuzzles into it for a moment, welcomes the way his strong body underneath feels solid and safe. She squeezes him and then slowly slips from his hold. Her bones and muscles and skin come together again, lifting her up and away. Standing, she adjusts her shirt and smooths her pants, runs a hand through her hair. Eric sits with his arms propped on the back of the couch, watching her. His look is something between bewildered and concerned. And she thinks he may collapse if he moves his arms, because she knows exactly how that feels too.

"Where're you going?" he asks.

"I don't know."

They stare at one another for a long moment, until Quinn looks away, and Eric stands to follow her as she's moving toward the door. "Hey," he says, gently catching her arm. "Stay." But she leaves.

Outside, Quinn slips to the sunny side of the street, puts on her dark sunglasses, and walks several steps, as she sometimes will, with her eyes closed, trusting the sidewalk and her instincts, and feeling only the air on her face, all else muted. When she opens her eyes again, she's at the corner, and she thinks how easy it is to make life invisible like that, to shut off all you see if even for a moment. She stops there, watches the cars pass and the people pass, and she feels the rush of the images, the immediacy of color, of light. She sees it in frames, like photographs, like things that are being captured over and over again.

At the apartment, she stands in the center of the room, looks around at the mishmash of her and Billy's things. And she thinks how easily they have fallen into this, how she used to think that at some point in her life there would be a demarcation. Alone, together. But that's not at all how it happens. Untangling this now will be a challenge, but she knows it's going to be necessary. She thinks she'll talk to him about it when he gets home, but she waits up, eating Indian delivery and studying contact sheets, flipping through a camera catalog far into the night, and when it's three in the morning and he's still not back, she goes to bed. Alone in the dark bedroom, she stares at the ceiling and thinks about earlier in Eric's office, and she whispers, "Fuck" into the space above her.

In her dreams, she has lost her sight and she scrambles to touch things, desperate to find the edges of the world around her. It troubles her night, wakes her early, and leaves her exhausted and cranky. She makes coffee and wonders where Billy is, and there's the ripple of worry. It's a constant thing now, something that she feels like a jolt in her spine. She pushes images out of her mind, of him hurt, of him high somewhere. She showers, but the warm water does little to soothe, and in her occupied mind, the razor slips and cuts a sliver into her ankle. She curses as blood drips onto the bathroom tiles. She clings toilet paper into the wound to stop the bleeding. Twice she thinks she hears the door, but when she rushes out of the bathroom, there is no one there.

Quinn finally heads to her studio, buying a bagel and cream cheese from a cart on the corner of Avenue A and Sixth Street. There she runs into Myles as she's wiping cream cheese from the corner of her lip. She's so used to seeing him with Billy that for a moment she conflates the view of him with relief that Billy must also be there. But he's not. Myles kisses her cheek, and she asks if he's seen Billy, though she hates the way it sounds coming from her mouth.

"Saw him at Tiny's last night, and then he left with some other people." Myles's eyes are framed in dark circles. He avoids her gaze and wipes at his nose. She knows he's been out all night as well. "Well, hey, my bed is calling," he says, and she can feel his eagerness to get away from her. He looks over his shoulder as he walks away.

In the darkroom, Quinn has a hard time concentrating. She gets the first mix wrong and ruins two prints before realizing her error. She washes out the bath and starts again. The chemicals sting today. They find their way into the recesses of her sinuses and eyes. She swipes the back of her arm over her face. She processes a small print of Billy working in his studio because she needs to see him now, wants to see him after a night and morning of waiting to see him. The rack is full, so she clips this one on the line to dry and she sits for a bit while the others are in the bath. In the dark redness of the room, she stares at the photo of him, her eyes tracing his jawline and the muscles in his back as he leans toward a canvas. But there is none of the rush there used to be, none of the twitter of excitement inside her. There's only worry. A constant, nagging worry that trips her up, tightens gravity, and makes her feel like the earth is spinning off-kilter. She knows this is what it feels like when something is ending.

All morning Quinn hopes he'll come, waits for the knock on the door. But nothing. She finishes processing in the early afternoon and digs change out of her pocket. When she steps outside, it takes her eyes a moment to adjust to the brightness of the sunshine. Somehow in the darkroom she has forgotten that it's a beautiful day. And somehow this beautiful day seems wrong to her. She wishes for clouds to cover up the light. She drops the coins into a pay phone and dials the apartment number, the 2 sticking so that she has to hang up and try again twice until it works.

Billy answers several rings in. He sounds strained, tired. "Hey," he says, and she tries to find the way she loves the gravely tone of his voice, but she only feels relief to hear him at all.

"Hey. I just wanted to see how you are." *I will not ask him where he was,* she thinks.

"I'm fucking fried. Stayed up all night working at the studio."

The lie stings. "Sorry that I woke you."

"Nah, it's all right. How are you?" His voice softens, and Quinn leans against the payphone stand because it softens something in her too. She touches the peeling edge of a band sticker, presses it back against the metal wall.

"Working," she says.

"When you coming back?"

Quinn tallies in her head what she has left to do, though she thinks she could leave now, she could just walk straight home to see him. Leave the baths and the racks and the rolls. "Like two hours, maybe a bit more."

"Okay, Q. I'll be here."

They hang up. Quinn taps the phone against her forehead because the conversation was so incomplete that she can't bring herself to hang up despite the insisting dial tone.

An elderly man scolds her for holding up the phone, and she quickly puts it on the receiver, moves away. He mutters *bitch* under his breath. She wants to shout at him, wants to kick at him and curse at him and tell him he has no right to call her a bitch, but he is old, with old clothes, old shoes, old teeth. Instead, she imagines that he's had enough of all this and she also kind of knows how that feels too.

When Quinn arrives home later, Billy is asleep. She takes a photo of him and watches the crest of his chest move up and down in deep breath. His hair is a tangle around his head and neck, pasted to parts of his brow in sweaty patches. He snores. And the rumble is reassuring, something she can hear from all places in the apartment, tracking him to where he is. She clears an overflowing ashtray near the bed and picks up two coke baggies and some ripped rolling papers from next to it. She thinks, *He's not even trying to hide it.* In the living room, she taps a cigarette out and twists it in her fingers, tries not to smoke it since she's trying not to smoke anymore, which suddenly seems very hard to do. She opens a beer and sits on the floor with her back against the couch and her feet propped up on a chair and she flips through an exhibition pamphlet for a recent show featuring several of their friends. The risograph ink leaves marks on her fingertips. She wipes them on her black jeans. She goes into the bedroom again. Billy's eyes open in slits and he reaches out his arms for her, beckons her. Quinn sinks into the bed next to him. He tucks his hot forehead into her breasts.

Days pass, Roxy Music is on the record player. Billy sings softly along to "More Than This," rocks Quinn a bit in his arms. It's the lyrics she's always loved.

"Billy," she says, but he presses his lips to hers, and they're soft and gentle, and they listen to the song until it ends and the needle scratches against the inner label. And his lips are still touching hers, not kissing but breathing together, passing back and forth a whispery warm breeze. She thinks how he has always been like air for her. But maybe Alex was wrong all along. Maybe she was really water. Something that washed, flooded, extinguished. And like any other swelling body, she's leaving behind the imprint of her currents. Sinking some things and floating others. She sees it in the glossy edges of his eyes, feels it in her own heavy heart.

"I love you," he says, and it's so quiet it passes with that breath through her own and the words dissolve somewhere around her center.

She lets his hands trail down her sides to her hips, to the front of her jeans where he unbuttons, unzips, and carefully, slowly, pushes them down. And though they've done this hundreds, maybe even thousands of times in their lives, this time feels different from the rest. There's a sadness to it that she knows means it's the last time, the final time. She memorizes each pressure point, every cling and thrown back motion and arched movement. Afterward, they lay together, Billy behind her, their limbs curved like a seashell. She trails her fingers down his arm, past the marks that raise and flatten like any uneven surface. And she feels the separation slowly, like a peeling off of one thing from another. A gasp in her breath as her lungs breathe without his, a surge in her pulse as his blood flows away from her heart, a shiver as his skin becomes his own and she's left again as one thing. She won't know yet, can't know yet, about the small piece of him she takes with her, that little souvenir, an insistence that he'll always be remembered by. Soon, it'll rap and wriggle and pulse, but for now it merely lingers long enough to give itself a chance in the tumbling darkness inside of her.

Quinn stares out the bedroom door at the boxes of things that she's collected, her photos and camera parts, clothes, art works, some books. There's no need for the other things—furnishings and whatnot. Alex has all of that already.

"I'll see you soon," she says at the door when Liv and Alex arrive to help her load her things into a taxi. Billy nods and there's a war in his features, and she knows this is his war, not hers. She closes the space between them one more time and kisses him gently goodbye.

The ride across town is quiet. Quinn sits in the middle, her knees resting against theirs, a box on each of their laps, a full trunk. That her life can fit in this car, like this, is both reassuring and terrifying. At Alex's apartment, they unload the boxes into the spare room that was first Gene's meditation room then Alex's writing studio and is now Quinn's bedroom. They return to the living room.

"Is this a tequila shot situation or a champagne occasion?" Alex asks as he heads toward the kitchen.

"Champagne," Liv answers. "I mean, it's actually a tequila shot situation, but since it's only noon, I think we should go with the champagne."

Quinn sighs and sits on the couch. She taps a cigarette from a pack on the coffee table and rolls it around in her fingers since this is what she does now that she's quit smoking. "I hope I did the right thing." The finality of her decision weighs on her, in the same way it had before, the times when she'd rush back to him because leaving him felt like breaking off a part of her soul and handing it to a stranger. She's not sure what life without him looks like; what she is without him. And she worries, as she always does, that her floating will sink him.

"It was the absolute right thing," Liv says, coming to sit next to her. She takes the cigarette from Quinn and puts it back in the pack, holds Quinn's hand instead. "It's easier to see from out here, you were so in it. But for sure, without a doubt, right decision."

Alex returns with a bottle of champagne and three glasses with the stems hooked in his fingers. The cork hits the ceiling fan when it pops and sends a sprinkle of dust down on them from its wobbly blades. Quinn catches it like snowflakes and laughs and it's the first time she's laughed in a while and even though this isn't even that funny, she can't stop laughing. It pulls muscles that have laxed in their disuse and she touches the corners of her mouth and says, *Ow.*

Liv raises her eyebrows, and Alex says, "Don't be judgy. Do you know how hard it is to have high ceilings? And who has a ladder in New York City? Impossible."

The math never adds up. Just when she thinks she has it right, there's always something that comes along and sweeps her clean again. Just when she thinks maybe, *maybe* there's something else she can do, another job, any other job than this, there's a doctor's bill or a broken appliance, or Patrick outgrows his clothes, or *something* eats up the tiny heap of cash again.

Lulu hands over the stack of bills to Digger, who touches his fingers to his tongue then flips through them. "It's short," he says.

"It's not short," Lulu says. It's never been short, not once.

But he counts it again in front of her, pronouncing each increasing amount like she's an idiot who might not understand, and at the end, he says, "Short."

"Let me see that." She takes the money back from him, counts it herself, twice, and he's right, it's short. "Fuck," she says. "How the fuck did that happen?"

"I told you a million times, you can't trust no pill head."

Lulu sighs. "Yeah, I know. I didn't." But she did. She did not count the last deal; she shoved it in her pocket and assumed it was fine since it has always been fine. "Oh, fuck," she says.

He nods toward the door. "Go back."

"And do what?" Lulu asks.

"Get the rest of it." He pockets what she's given him, no cut yet for her until she makes it whole.

Lulu curses again, a stream of obscenities that seems to amuse Digger. She doesn't want to go back. She never wants to go there. Their desperation has a smell—acidic, metallic. The addiction milks their skin and leaves them shaking, begging. She hates it. She hates all of it. But she's short, and she'd rather go back there than owe Digger anything. Plus, she needs her cut.

She drives Patrick's old car, out of impound a long time now, but still with the broken steering that causes her to grip fiercely to the wheel so it doesn't go off the road. It wants to pull over, to give up, but she won't let it. She needs it too much. The old factory is in the neighborhood of her former foster care, and as Lulu drives by, she cranes her neck, as she always does, to see if she can spot the new house owners. Doug and Kathy were run out of town years ago. Who would live where a known child molester once did? She's curious to know, but she's never seen anyone around, just some cars and an occasional bike in the driveway.

Lulu pulls in behind the building and because she's only just been there, there isn't the usual rush around her car. No zombie-like hands gripping for her when she gets out. She's grateful for that. But still, she should have unloaded the rest of her stash at

Digger's since it's not unlike these people to pry open the trunk, rip through the seats. It's too late for that now. She locks her doors and hopes for the best. She steps around broken bottles and spent needles, and pushes open the graffitied metal door. It wheezes on rusty hinges.

"Hey," she yells out into the darkness. "It's Lulu." By now they have no doubt found their places in the rooms on the second floor. They're surely deep in the haze of the OCs she just sold them. She hates being the purveyor of this evilness. She takes a few steps inside, lets her eyes adjust to the murkiness. This used to be a pencil factory and the smell of graphite is still strong, though not strong enough to overpower the other scents.

"Rosie?" she tries again, louder. Her voice echoes back at her. It's unusually quiet, too quiet. She walks carefully up the metal stairs to the second floor where old mattresses have been pulled into corners of what used to be offices. But they're empty. The place must have been swept. No one is here. Lulu swears again, and the little heap of cash that had been forming in her underwear drawer loses yet again. She'll have to pay Digger from her own pocket.

Lulu gets back in the car and sits for a second, closes her eyes. She's tired, exhausted really. She could sleep right here, sitting straight up. She almost feels the nod of it, the impulse, so she snaps her eyes open, turns on the radio, and tunes it to classic rock, a Fleetwood Mac song. "Rhiannon."

Lulu pulls back onto the road, speeds past the old house, still no one there. She's dying for a cigarette now, and at a stop light, she gets one out, puffs it alive. The light turns. Patrick's car groans with the effort of acceleration up a small hill. She nearly drops the cigarette as the car swerves toward its favored side, and she's forced to correct the wheel. And then it's almost immediate, the way the lights flash behind her, the reds swirling in the rearview mirror, which she's never adjusted for her own height. They circle her forehead in the reflection.

Lulu twists against the cuffs, trying to wiggle them into a

spot that doesn't cut into her skin. They've secured them too tightly. The officer pushes her head low to get into the car, but she catches the edge of her forehead all the same and it sends a shock down the side of her neck. She would rub it if her hands weren't bound, and she thinks how ridiculous handcuffs are when there's two cops with guns lording over her. Where's she going to go?

"You can't do this," she shouts because now she's angry. "I have a kid." She kicks at the back of the divider, leaving a scuffed shoe mark. The passenger cop turns around, tells her to knock it off. The cop car smells like rank cologne and she wonders, only briefly, who was in here before her.

"God dammit!" she screams again because she should not be here, because she can't be here, not with little Patrick waiting at the trailer in BB's arms. And she doesn't scream *fuck*, but it's the only word that comes over and over again to mind. She pounds her feet on the floorboard where they make a satisfying rumble like thunder, and she thinks she could kick her way straight out to the street below if she tries hard enough.

"I swear to Christ if you don't knock it off, I'm going to shut you up myself." The cop smacks the Plexiglas between them. She hopes it hurts his hand.

The backseat narrows her view, tightens up her lungs, and takes the breath from her. Lulu gasps, trying to stop herself from hyperventilating. Her face is flushed red. She can feel the heat coming from her cheeks. She thinks there's something wrong back here, that they somehow have cut off the air supply because as hard as she tries, she cannot catch a breath, and she tries to tell them that they're suffocating her as she leans hard against the door, pushes her torso with all her strength to try to force it open, pushes so hard that her head feels like it could explode with pressure. Her shoulder aches from the contact it makes with the door. And then all goes dark.

She wakes to a slap on her cheek, and for a moment she forgets where she is, but as soon as it registers, the rush inside her rears and she starts to panic again. The cop is hovering over her in the backseat. He pulls her up to sitting, holds a plastic cup of water near her lips, tells her to drink. It rushes the back of her throat. She coughs.

"Worked yourself into a tantrum," he says, and his thumb trails the bottom edge of her lip. She whips her head away. She wants to say it's their fault for shutting off her air, for binding her arms and treating her like an animal. "Come on." He pulls her out of the back of the car by her upper arm. She can already feel the bruises and scraped skin from the cuffs that have now dug deeply into her wrists. Her shoulder tugs and gives. A yanking pain courses down her back, links up with the ever-present sting in her lower back, and she stumbles trying to walk through both.

She's left on a hard chair inside the precinct, while the cops talk, joke, and she wonders how they can banter when her son is at home, and she is here. But she knows they don't care, no one cares. Lulu's head slumps to the front and she closes her eyes, tries to imagine she's home with little Patrick, tucked in the bed, him lying at her side. And if she concentrates enough, she can feel his slight weight, the still chunky arms that cling around her neck, his whispery milk breath saying, *Mama*.

Lulu lifts her head, but it takes great effort. "Can I make a call?" she asks, but no one pays her any attention, and so she says it again, louder. One of the cops who brought her in leaves the group and comes to her.

"After we process you," he says.

"My son's at home," Lulu says. "I need to call home." The cop looks at her and for a minute she thinks maybe she sees some sympathy, but he shakes his head instead.

"Should have thought about that before doing what you were doing." He walks away.

Lulu's head tilts to the right, and she hopes the tears that she feels welling in the sides of her eyes will just stop, since she can't push them away with her bound hands. She wants to explain to the cop why, *why* she was doing what she was doing, that it's all for little Patrick. That it's only ever all for him. But there is no one willing to hear her pleas.

Lulu tries to stay calm as they take her belongings, make her change clothes, roll her finger in ink, and press it into a register. Free of the handcuffs, she grabs the tops of her arms, squeezes as if she's being hugged. She is dragged to do a photo and then pushed into a room where there's a pay phone for her to use. She has no change, so she calls her trailer number collect, and she's reminded of how many times her own ma has done this and the thought drags her to another level of weary. "Pick up, BB," she whispers. "Please pick up."

BB answers in the usual way, with silence. Lulu rushes to fill the empty space with her words, tells her that she was caught dealing. The words rush out of her so fast that she can't remember what she's already said, thinks she's now repeating herself. And each time she says it, it becomes more and more real.

When she finally stops talking, she has to ask, "You're there, right?" and BB murmurs an affirmation. "You have to ask Joey to come down to the courthouse tomorrow. I need him if they set me a bail. BB, is Patrick okay? You can take care of him? I need you to take care of him for me, okay? There's money in the trailer. It's in my underwear drawer. Just look and you'll see. BB, don't let Maureen take him, don't let her anywhere near him, you understand? She's been on my case about him, like she knows anything about anything. Don't let her get her hands on him, please, *please*. And whatever you do, do not let social services take him. He cannot go to foster. Please, you understand?" Lulu stops to catch her breath because the panic is back and is once again rushing her and she worries the air will leave next and the room will turn her into darkness.

And though she doesn't want to hang up, wants to hold on to the connection to BB forever because it feels like all she has left, she also thinks about the ticking collect call and the always dwindling cash. Regretfully, she hangs up.

Lulu spends the night on a hard bed that's really more of a

bench with a thin bedroll over it. It carries the same scent as the back of the cop car, and again she wonders who was here before her. The cell is all concrete, mean-looking blocks on the walls, rough stained floor, no windows. She's the only person here, and in the dim light, she lets herself go, lets the tears stream down the sides of her face and pool under her neck, tickle the back of her ears, wetting her hair. She is not one to feel sorry for herself, but tonight she's as close as she'll ever get because why, *why* is it always her? She's not the only one doing the things she's doing, so why is she the one here, in the cell, when all she's trying to do is survive? It's not fair, she thinks, but then she wonders what fair means anyway. What a stupid word and an even stupider idea.

"Patrick," she says, quietly even though there is no one with her, no one even nearby in the precinct. "I need you." This brings another stream of tears, and she thinks maybe she can find some piece of him like this. She imagines him lying in his cell too, his head on the hard bedroll, his arm hooked over his stomach like hers. They had finally found a rhythm, visits on Tuesdays and Fridays, touching the tips of their toes together through their shoes since they could do that and not be called out by the guards. It looks accidental enough. And she thinks about the days in juvie, the swinging hands as they walked past one another, the slight touch of their fingers, so subtle so as to not attract any attention. And how those tiny touches felt like explosions. "I need you," she says again, softly, quietly, into the darkness above her.

She knows she's going to jail for some time. The oxy will be a felony possession charge. Lulu tries to calculate how much that haul compares to what Patrick was caught with, but instead her mind sticks on little Patrick, now old enough to know when she's not home, old enough to know how to ask for her. The rushing panic threatens, and she swallows down a few breaths to tame it. She wonders if it's possible to die from this feeling, or if she will die here, lying on this hard bed, alone, because all the air is once again squeezing from her lungs. But then it eases and something automatic takes over. The breath comes. She tries to give it more space, lure it deeper into the darkest recesses of her body, into the areas that hold against her and ache when she forces it further.

She thinks there is no way that she can sleep here. Not like this. But sometime later she feels a pulling up sensation, a dip from just under the edge of sleep to awake, and realizes she has in fact slept, some. She keeps her eyes closed, wonders what time it is, and then there's another dip back to sleep, and this is how her night goes by, nodding in and out until someone flips on the overhead lights and the cell washes in ugly yellow-white light that forces her eyes open.

"Rise and shine," a new cop says, unlocking the cell. Lulu hurries to straighten her jumpsuit and run her fingers through her hair before she's once again cuffed and led out.

BB is in the courthouse in the third row with Patrick on her lap, along with Joey, Maureen, and Hank, who sit close but not too close. They, too, hear the charges and the tone of the judge as he recounts her juvie record, her poor choice of employment, as he sets a bail too high for any of them to manage. And it's like déjà vu except it's her in the jumpsuit, and it's little Patrick's hand she misses when he reaches out for her as she's walked by in cuffs. And now her head hangs low because she can't bear to look at him. She can't bear the fact she's let him down and he doesn't even know it yet.

Quinn looks at the crudely printed directions sitting on the passenger seat. They're bent and bent again and the creases obscure some of the inky print. A birthmark-like shape of dried coffee takes out the final words, but she knows that part. She takes her eyes off the highway for a moment to pick them up and double-check the exit number, bringing the paper close to her face before dropping it back down again. She's done this several times already, though she can't commit the number to memory, keeps second-guessing herself. She printed the directions over a month ago, and she's read them, folded them, stowed them, re-read them, re-folded them, re-stowed them several times since. But now she's at the exit, and she swerves the rental car off the highway and up the steeply inclined off-ramp, stops at the intersection. She takes a deep breath. In the years between then and now, little has changed, though she can see the crest of a Walmart farther down the road that was not here before, and the church has been entirely demolished. A Burger King sits in its place. The gas station has grown a Taco Bell appendage.

Quinn pulls into the diner parking lot and takes another deep breath, hopes it will steady her shakiness. She leaves her camera in the car as she makes her way inside and takes a seat at the counter, maybe the same seat she had taken years ago. She can't be sure now. She adjusts herself, shifting to even out the weight of her pregnant belly. The bulge she somehow manages to forget until it catches on edges and sinks her sideways in seats. The waitress is cleaning up dishes from a trucker who has just left, and she calls over her shoulder, "I'll be right with ya, hon."

"No rush," Quinn replies. She runs a hand over the bulging belly, tempering a kick from the baby.

The woman brings a menu and a glass of water. "Where you coming from?" she asks. "We don't get a lot of tourists around here."

"New York City," Quinn says. "Just passing through."

"Ah, we do get a lot of just passing through. What're you hungry for?"

Quinn glances at the woman's name tag, Barb. "I'll take a chicken sandwich and a ginger ale."

"You got it." Barb writes the order on a pad and rips it off, clips it to the metal edge of an overhang behind her where the kitchen is. She tends to two more truckers who come in, and Quinn takes in the diner. She remembers the yellow Formica countertops and the brown vinyl stool seats.

Barb returns with the ginger ale and silverware wrapped in a thin napkin. Quinn studies her thick, dark hair, the slight creases around her eyes and mouth. Her cheekbones are high, and her skin is warm and tawny.

"You got a name picked out yet," Barb asks, nodding toward Quinn's belly.

Quinn rests her hand there. "William, if it's a boy. Willow, if it's a girl."

Barb tilts her head. "Those are nice names. I got a boy myself, Joey—well, JP he likes people calling him now."

Quinn smiles. "Actually," she says, "I'm not just passing through." Barb's eyebrows raise, and Quinn continues. "I'm looking for someone. I was here about fifteen years ago and met her and wonder if she's still living here. Her name is Lulu."

Barb's eyes squint a bit as Quinn says this. "You have any more than that?"

"Well, her mom worked at the motel, I think. And she lived in that trailer park."

Barb studies her then shakes her head. "I know who you mean. But she's long gone," she says. "Family moved out and no one's heard from them since." With a ding, Barb turns around and grabs Quinn's food, places it in front of her.

Quinn sighs. She picks up her sandwich but then puts it down again. "No one knows where they went?"

Barb's lips purse. "Nope. I mean, it happens around here, you know?"

Quinn taps her fingers on the countertop. "She had a cousin, BB. The girl had these scars." She touches her lip, and Barb nods.

"Also gone."

"Shit."

"Why you looking for her anyway?"

Quinn looks away and says, "Just wanted to see how she's doing." She wonders, as she has many times over the years, if her phone call to the police did anything at all.

"I'm sure she's just fine, but it's sweet of you to come all this way to say hello. You let me know if you need anything else, okay?" Barb seems eager to move on.

Quinn nods and picks up her sandwich again. The truckers steer clear of her when a new group comes in. They take seats at the opposite end of the countertop or in the slight rows of booths. Barb doesn't return, but she's left the check with the food, and Quinn counts out the cash and leaves.

She sits behind the wheel for several minutes trying to decide what to do, and while she's tempted to grab the Canon and go into Riverdale Estates to shoot, it doesn't feel okay to her. Instead, she angles into the gas station, fills up the tank, and then winds back out of the town and onto the highway, heads east. The baby kicks, and she frees a hand to rest on her belly, says, "It's all going to be okay. I promise."

Lulu listens to his breathing, the slight hiss that drags after each inhale from the asthma that's mostly under control but can flare up when he gets too excited. She watches the way the ridge of muscles in his bare back fall with each exhalation. There's a pinkish twist of skin from where he wiped out jumping off the swings and another sickle shaped near his hip, though she's not sure what happened there. There's an oval burn on the back of his calf from a thrown cup of coffee and a train track of healed stitches over his left eyebrow from the only fistfight he ever got in. She knows most of the parts of him, was there as many of these memories were etched into his skin, but some are still a mystery. From time to time, she finds a freckle, or a birthmark and she thinks, *Well, what's this now?* The sun is starting to stream in the window, and he stirs, rolls onto his back. There's some of the boy still there when he's sleeping like this. It softens the lines around his eyes and mouth, smooths out the skin. His lips have always been a rosy pink, and his lashes are dark and long, longer than hers even. He opens his eyes, and he smiles, says quietly, "Hey."

"Hey," she says.

He opens his arms, and she snuggles into them, lays her head on his chest. It fits perfectly in the indentation of his breastbone. He's been wearing a new cologne and it smells musky and unfamiliar. She likes it. "You slept in."

"I did?" he asks, turning his head now, glancing around her bedroom, dislodging her a bit. Suddenly more awake. He takes work seriously, refuses to be so much as a minute late. "What time is it?"

"Eight."

He rests back again, seemingly relieved. "That's not sleeping in, Lulu. That's like the middle of the night."

She laughs. "What time you got work today?"

He whispers, "Ten," and kisses her bare shoulder, her temple, and then the top of her head. She never would have imagined he'd become a used car salesman, but he's done well with it. Was the top seller the month before. Still, it's not enough to get out of the trailer park. Not enough to right years and years of close to nothing, to save. But it's honest work, legit. No one's going to jail over used cars, and for that, Lulu is thankful.

He doesn't like to talk in the morning, even though she does. He's never been a morning person. Even when they were young. She can easily picture him cranky on the school bus with his mess of uncombed hair, swiping the tired out of his eyes, not yet ready to start the day, not yet ready to deal with whatever it had in store.

"JP," she says, tapping his arm with her fingertip. Then "Joey?" because she's always liked that name better.

"Hmm?" His eyes are closed again.

"I love you." She says it so quietly, like she's tiptoeing, because it's an incantation that's unleashed a cosmic backlash on her in the past. She can't lose him too. So, she's careful about letting on, careful about accidentally inviting harm here. She can be with him but only part of the way.

"I love you too, Lulu." His arms tighten around her, draw her closer. He moves her leg over his, shifts her on top of him. And they stay like that, like layers, nearly aligned.

☙

When he's four, Quinn thinks, *This is the age I was when my mom died*, and the whole year feels agonizing, like there is always a lurking shadow.

At five, his chubby cheeks thin out and his face takes the shape of his father's and though he likes to smear paint across the big blank canvases in the studio, she never leaves him alone there.

At six, he's old enough to wonder why his dad doesn't show up, isn't where he said he'll be, disappears for hours, days, months.

At seven, they sit side by side in folding chairs that slightly sink into the mossy spring ground in a community garden that cuts the corner of a Lower East Side lot. Quinn holds her own dad's hand and drapes a protective arm over her son's shoulder. Across the street, there's a respectfully silent game of dominoes outside the Latin Social Club. Liv gives the eulogy that Quinn cannot. Quinn's voice has locked itself up, stuck in the bitter confusion of her mind. She can only stare at the small box of ashes that sits, for this short time at least, in a garden plot, later to be scattered in the East River under the cover of night.

Billy's parents do not attend. They gave up on him after the first hospitalization, years ago, when William was merely the size of a peapod, thrumming behind her belly button. The ease of their back-turning has made Quinn unwilling to open this life to them.

After, they cross the street to a dive bar where stacks of empanadas and tacos await. William falls asleep easily in a cracked booth with Quinn's coat folded under his head. He's never had a problem sleeping, and she thinks that's because she's taken him everywhere with her, crossing the country and the Atlantic for exhibitions and projects. His spritely smile always at her side.

Eric finds Quinn and his arm around her is rescuing. "I've been time traveling," she whispers through her broken voice, and he touches her arm, links his hand in hers where it rests on the bar.

"Where's it taking you?" he asks.

"To better times." She smiles, and the tears slip easily out of her eyes.

Hank's hand is cold, despite the warm room. Lulu touches it each time he groans and wiggles his fingers toward her, because she knows that means he wants to be sure she's still there. He can't speak. He can't see. But she's learned his new language, the tiny movements and shifts of muscles, the grunts and growls. The stroke has left him mostly paralyzed. The cirrhosis has colored his skin a sickly yellow. Maureen's death has taken away his own will to live.

The intubation makes him look like he's yawning around the mouthpiece. It covers his nose like a gas mask. Lulu watches as the machine's accordion bag bunches and releases, as each calculated breath rises and flattens Hank's chest.

"It's all right, Hank, I'm here," she says, grasping his hand. She leans in closer to the hospital bed. "It's okay, Pa," she says, testing out the word she has never used. It forms foreign in her mouth, doesn't sound like a word at all, more like an exasperation or an accidental puff of air. "Dad," she tries instead. And she's sure she feels his fingers tighten, just a little bit.

Hank is connected to various monitors that beep and flash. She's learned their language too. She knows which one tells the nurses his blood pressure, which one measures his oxygen level, which one beats out his heart's rhythm in zigzags across a screen. The others that feed him, hydrate him, and rush a cocktail of pain killers into his veins. Nurses come on the hour to check in. They squeeze the catheter bag, frown at the darkness of the collection there. They don't need to tell her that it'll soon be over. Lulu can tell that herself.

She drags a chair closer to the bed so she can sit. "Thank you, Hank," she says, somewhere near his ear. "You watched out for me." Her elbows rest on the bed. "You're in a pretty bad way. You need to let go now. It's okay. I'll be okay."

Lulu's voice catches on the last words. She squeezes her eyes shut, hard, so hard that she sees dark spots when she opens them again.

There's a rasp, audible around the reliable inhale and exhale of the machine. Another rasp. She grips his hand and runs her thumb over the bony back of it. He squeezes, and she smiles. And she feels the slip like that, like letting something drop off a high ledge. A quick sweeping away. And gone.

QUINN BRADFORD: A RETROSPECTIVE

2019

Lulu is dragging a cart mindlessly down the cereal aisle at Walmart when she sees BB stocking the end cap. Her cousin is shuffling several boxes in her arms and one of them fumbles to the floor. She places the others on the shelves and picks up the stray box, but already BB's boss is there and he's standing over her in a way that Lulu knows is no good.

"Nobody wants no dented cereal box," he says, and BB slowly stands and inspects the box. "You know, we only give you a job because you're a retard and we get extra money from the state for it. But that don't mean we can't fire you. Plenty a retards in this town to take your place."

BB looks at the ground, and Lulu is up on them before she can think to do otherwise. "What in the holy hell did you just say to her?" But it's not really a question, and she ends it with a shove to his chest that sends him backward into a frozen food island behind him. He lands hard against its side and is shouting for someone to call security. BB's holding Lulu's arm, keeping her from further attack and neither realize a large security officer has arrived until he takes Lulu by the shoulder and moves her toward a room at the back of the store. BB tries to follow, but she's shut out.

"Get your hands off me," Lulu shouts. The security officer forces her to sit in a plastic chair while he dials a phone hung on the wall. It doesn't take long for the cop to arrive, and it's one who knows her well when he does.

"Lulu," he says. "Why am I not surprised?"

"She assaulted me," the boss tells him. They recount what

happened from both of their perspectives. But Lulu can't deny his side since he's already forming a bruise where he hit the frozen foods.

"Come with me," Officer Clark says, and she follows. There's no need for cuffs and all that mess. He knows she's not going to run for it.

BB is waiting outside the room and immediately tries to help Lulu, but Lulu shakes her head, says, "It's okay."

On the way to the car, Clark says, "That guy's a piece of shit, but I have to take you away or he's gonna make a fuss." He has her sit up front. Lulu wonders if that means she's off the hook, but she knows it's never that simple. Clark makes small talk as they drive. She's sure they're heading to a nearby strip mall since that's the only thing out this way. He's on and on about the weather and Donald Trump and the illegals at the border, and Lulu struggles to follow since she doesn't really care about any of that stuff. They make the predictable final turn, and Clark pulls behind the abandoned buildings. "You know what I need you to do, right?" he asks.

Lulu sighs, says, "I'm not doing that kind of thing anymore," thinking maybe it'll mean something to him. Her eyes sweep the broken concrete parking lot, its faded lines, the sprigs of leafy green weeds starting to reclaim it. And she thinks this looks how she feels inside, and if she tries hard enough, she swears she can feel the slinky green fingers twisting up her organs, pushing at her belly button, rushing under her skin. She shivers.

Clark is staring at her, and she drops her eyes to the floorboard, to her knees. "You think this is the time to take the moral high ground?" he asks. "I got no problem with taking you in. You want to go to jail? What you did back there was assault." He touches her arm, and she pulls it away. No, she does not want to go to jail.

Lulu looks at his hands, at the wedding band, and she thinks of all the wedding bands she's seen on the men who have had some version of this moment with her. She sucks in her breath and nods. "Okay," she says because this will be easier than any of the rest of it would be.

Clark unzips his fly, and Lulu knows the fastest ways to get men off like this, and she does them all, trying to hurry along the process. Her hand slips over his skin. He lets go a few minutes in. Lulu sits back, looks around for something to wipe her hand on and picks up a McDonald's napkin from the console. She reaches for the door handle, but he stops her, says, "I'll drive you home." He rearranges himself, zips back up.

She doesn't need to give him directions. They all know where she lives. Lulu watches out the window as they drive through the back part of town, past Digger's old house which makes her cringe thinking about how many hours she spent there, over the cratered country road that cracks every few years under the pressure of tons of truck tires and mean winters.

"What're you doing for work these days?" Clark asks as if they're old friends, and maybe in some twisted way they are.

"Well, I was cleaning the motel but just got fired from that," Lulu says. "Pay was shit anyway, but it was something, right? Most places aren't too keen on hiring an ex-felon who never finished high school." Lulu thinks about the motel rooms, their constant state of distress. Lipstick marks on the bedsheets, cigarette butts on the carpet, broken booze bottles in the tubs. The thick rubber gloves always pinched her skin. The cheap powdery insides left red splotches on her hands.

"Why don't you take that paper." He motions to a rolled-up newsprint between them. She picks it up. "Check out the classifieds, who knows. And stop beating on people, okay?" He pulls over just shy of Riverdale Estates, dropping her off outside the motel. Lulu tucks the newspaper under her arm.

She walks past the rooms, knowing all too well what's going on inside them. It has never changed. There's a buzzing in the quiet, and Lulu looks up at the wasp nest that has been built and rebuilt over the years, always clinging in the same corner near room six. It threatens above her head. And there is the queen. She hovers on the edge of the hive, clenching a worker in her pinchers. Identical but for her bulk. Lulu watches her squeeze and squeeze and squeeze. And Lulu can't yet move because moving will make what just happened real. Moving will make her have to think about the small savings she has that won't last her more than a week or two. She'll have to think about the sagging carport and the broken stove and the crumbling steps and the cracked window and all the ways things are falling apart that she's just not able to fix.

Finally, she moves. She twists through the trailer park, keeping her eyes averted from her neighbors, thinking maybe they can tell, somehow, maybe they know what she's just done. And it's a feeling she hasn't had in a long time. The shame of it is almost more than she can take.

Jacko greets her at the trailer, nosing around her legs as she steps inside. Lulu washes her hands, twice, cracks a beer, and sits on the couch. She scratches the dog's rear end, and he shimmies around before coming to rest at her feet. She pinches the beer can between her knees and accidentally opens the paper up to the arts section. She's about to flip to the classifieds when a photo catches her attention. She drops the can but doesn't move to pick it up even as the beer flows onto the floor, even as Jacko starts to lap it up. She stares at the photo, her breath catching in her ribs, her heart pounding. Because it's *her*. It's her as a child on the lap of one of the truckers, and she remembers it suddenly like it was yesterday. She remembers the photographer, remembers the moment the photo was taken and the trail of smoke from her lips and the way she imagined the woman's eyes behind the camera were staring at her. And the longing, the longing that someone would see that photo and come help her. Lulu looks at the caption now, sees her own name there and the four little letters are almost a confusion because her brain takes a minute to remind her that's really *her*, that Lulu in *Lulu and the Trucker* is her.

Lulu knocks on Joey's door, pounding out her anger at the newspaper that's tucked under her arm. She's sweating now. It mixes with the newsprint, and she curses as she sees the inky ghost it leaves on her skin. It takes a moment for him to swing open the trailer door. His hair is a mess. She wonders why he's still asleep in the middle of the afternoon. But then she realizes it's only eleven, and it's the weekend. Her mind is swirling. "Wait until you see this," she says, barging past him and flopping down on the couch.

She lays the paper out flat next to her. Joey pushes at the corners of his eyes and squats in front of her to take a look. A fake gold chain swings against his chest, knocking into *LB* forever etched to the side of his left nipple. She touches the top of her right arm where his initials are too and thinks about the way they giggled all the way up until the tattoo needle hit his skin and he cursed at the pain.

"Wait, what is this? I don't get it."

"Think way back. You remember me telling you about that photographer who came here a long time ago? She took a bunch of photos of me. Well, she caught this one too." Lulu taps the paper with a chipped nail.

Joey picks it up and sits down next to her, squints as he reads the small print. He has needed glasses forever but refuses to get them. "Shit, Lulu. Seems to me she owes you some of that money."

"I'm not sure how that all works, but it says it was sold by the current collector. Sounds like she didn't get none of it either. But it's not even the money, JP. How could people look at that picture and think that was all right? Why didn't they ask about me? Or come to talk to me? And what kind of pervert spends that much money on a photo like that?" Her face is flushed with anger now and embarrassment even though she knows she has nothing to be embarrassed about.

Joey takes two beers out of a small fridge and hands her one, cracking open his own. "Lulu, people don't give a shit. Better for them to make up their own stories in their head about you, about us here. They don't want to know us. No one ever pays us no mind. Why do you think we got the problems we got here? Who's watching out for us?"

Lulu takes a long drink and gestures for Joey to hand over the paper to her. She holds it up close and for the maybe hundredth time since she first saw it, scans over her younger self. She can feel that trucker's hands on her, the calloused palm on her soft tummy, the other hand, unnoticeable in the photo, cupped under her butt. That exhalation of smoke and her heavy-lidded eyes already thick with understanding that this was all there would be for her. And she feels like she's always been that girl, always carried her along with her, somewhere tucked up in her like a separate thing.

"What do you want to do about this?" Joey asks, belching into his fist.

Lulu sighs. "I want to go see her. And not for money, before you get any ideas. I want to ask her why she never did nothing to help me."

"How do you plan on finding her?"

Lulu squeezes the paper in her fingers, pushing out the small print below the article that lists information on the exhibition mentioned. "Says right here she'll be giving a talk at the museum in two weeks. I'm gonna be there."

"I love this photo," Emma, the associate curator, says to Quinn. They've finished doing a final walk-through of the show.

"It was a big moment." Quinn sips a seltzer water, eyeing an image of Billy and Myles in their studio, Myles's arm draped over Billy's shoulder, both with youthful grins.

"I mean, who knew that second that you captured the beginning of such an incredible collaboration between them. And they look so young."

"Well, they were young." Quinn tries to smile. She sees something else in the photo though. Through the optimism, the excitement, the eagerness, she sees the moment she was about to lose Billy. "Sometimes it's painful," Quinn admits to Emma, "being surrounded by all these memories." She looks around the room. "I used to say that I did this work because someday it would feel like time traveling; you know, like I was making images that we'd return to like this. And I guess it worked, except that I didn't understand at the time how much it might hurt to come back."

"Do they all feel that way?" Emma asks.

Quinn considers, then answers honestly. "I don't know. Because also sometimes it doesn't hurt too. I can look at Gene and feel the bliss of his courage and his beauty one day, another I'll picture him in the depths of his illness, dying. Same image, drastically different responses. So, I don't know."

"I wonder for my generation if it'll even be possible. With social media and the way we share images, how like everything is an image now, will we be able to time travel too?"

"I think so, maybe? Though you've time stamped your memories in a way we never did. You know it's interesting because it's not linear. My mind jumps years, hops around untethered. I'm twenty-three or fifty. I can look at this photo and be back in that studio like it just happened. And it doesn't matter when it happened, it just matters that it did."

"But humans want to chronologize. I mean, we literally created calendars and clocks, you know?"

"It's true," Quinn admits. "Which has never made sense since it's not at all how life actually works. I feel the same today as I did when I was thirty and when I was forty. Then I look in the mirror and I'm like, *Wait, what happened?*" She touches her cheek. "You know, we want to create these trajectories but really it's more like we're traveling down a long river that can sometimes drag us under or push us up on a shore." Emma's head tilts. Quinn stops talking since she knows she's confusing, but she's not sure how else to explain the feeling like you're every age, you are your entire life, all at the same time. There's probably some school of philosophy for this meandering, but she doesn't have a name for it.

"Maybe I'll quit Instagram," Emma says and laughs a little.

Quinn chuckles. "I've enjoyed working with you," she says, placing her hand on Emma's shoulder.

Emma smiles. "Same, Quinn. Will Eric be joining us for dinner tonight? George has been asking."

"He says so, but we can never be sure until he walks in the door."

"We'll consider it a yes. Do you mind being back here at five forty-five? We'll allow people in at six."

She nods, and Emma says goodbye. Quinn continues to stare at the photo of Myles and Billy in their studio. Myles's arm angles around Billy's shoulder, their smiles so wide, so bright, so excited, and she whispers his name, *Billy*, and she swipes at the tears that fill in the corners of her eyes. She thinks now that they have miscategorized this section. *The Beginning* should really be called *Everything*. She scans the other images in this section—Liv and Micky on the dance floor at Mudd, Micky crouched on a dusty stage, Liv in her studio with paint on her cheek, Billy smoking a cigarette at Coney Island, Alex lounging in the Greenwich Village gay club, Myles walking away from her. And so many other photos chronicling their early days together, before acclaim, before any kind of real recognition, and the many others who came into and out of their lives as they made their way through a city that no longer exists.

Quinn checks her phone for the time and hurries home to get ready for the evening. She takes a taxi to her apartment in the West Village where William is waiting, scrolling through his phone. She leaves him in the small living room and quickly changes into tight black jeans and a creamy cashmere wrap, while also listening to the messages on her phone on speaker mode. The fourth message is from Myles, and it stops her in her orbit of getting ready.

"Q, good luck tonight. And. We should talk."

She means to hit the option to delete but saves it instead and swears under her breath. She pulls her hair from its knot and shakes it out down her back, inspecting it for any messy spots, then sprays a light mist of perfume on her wrists and neck. The softened muscles from an earlier massage start to wind again, and she rubs at her neck. It's a constant pain, a nudging reminder of how many years she's carted a camera around her neck, over her shoulder. Its slight weight slowly disrupting the circle of muscles around her upper torso, putting her on a first-name basis with a slew of Canal Street masseuses who regularly walk on, pound on, and pummel her aching body in poorly lit back-alley spots.

William is waiting for her in the kitchen when she comes out. He finishes a finger of bourbon. "I called a Lyft, but he's coming around the block, so we have a few minutes." He pours another slosh of bourbon into the glass and hands it to her. She thanks him and sips. The warmth seeps down her throat and immediately calms her nerves.

"This is exactly what I needed," she tells him.

"I can tell you're nervous."

"I just want this to go well, you know?"

"It already is," he says.

She sighs. "I appreciate your help on this show. It would have been too much, I think, without it. It means a lot to me that you're here."

William smiles. "The car's outside. We better go down." He grabs her purse for her while she finishes her drink.

Quinn is surprised to see a line outside of the museum when they arrive. "Lot of high heels and sequins," she says and wonders if her black jeans and cashmere are too casual.

"The donors," William says. "Don't worry, the cool kids will come too."

Quinn chuckles. "This makes me feel old," she admits.

"Mom, you're sixty-two, that's hardly old."

"I didn't say I *am* old, I said I *feel* old."

"Well, this is your night, so we should probably get out of the car now."

He exits first and takes her hand to escort her out. Emma is waiting at the door for them, and she's beaming. Quinn realizes this is a big night for her too, maybe even more so than for Quinn who has already had her fair share of attention over the years.

From there, the night is a rush. It reminds Quinn of her first show at Patty Arnet Gallery, the whirlwind circuiting of the room, shaking of collectors' hands, kisses to cheeks, nods as guests give their own interpretations of her work. She's relieved to see Liv and Micky and other friends she put on the guest list. Someone hands her a glass of champagne, and she's toasted to before the guests slowly begin to disperse. It's only when the room clears some that Quinn sees Eric staring intently at one of the photos in The Bowery Boards series. She approaches and taps his arm. He turns and kisses her on the lips, touches her cheek. His look is tender and content, and she loves this look. She knows this is also a big night for him. She hopes she's made him proud after all he's done for her.

"Congratulations," he says. "You were busy when I got here so I just made my own rounds. How are you feeling about it all?"

"Good, good," Quinn says. "A bit tired from so much interaction, but the night's still young. You're coming to dinner?"

He nods. "Wouldn't miss it."

"We better get going before we give William a nervous breakdown."

Eric takes her arm, and they find William and Emma waiting near the door. It's a short drive to the museum director George's apartment where a dinner is being hosted in Quinn's honor. This is the kind of stuff she dislikes but the art world loves. She thinks back to the days of drug-fueled afterparties and wonders if that still happens in this sanitized version of New York City. She imagines it does not.

They take the elevator up to a lavish Tribeca residence that Quinn has been in before, a guest to other artists' being feted this way, and she is immediately swooped up in conversation with George who wants to introduce her to several museum donors. There is polite conversation, comments about her work, her career, the exhibition as a whole. Someone pushes an iPhone at her with the *Times* review, released after the VIP opening hours, as is tradition. She skims it, acutely aware of the eyes on her and the museum's press person saying loudly, *Such a great review! Congrats, congrats!* She can't concentrate on the small type, so looks to Emma instead who is smiling at her and mouths, *It's really good.* Eric finds her and escorts her away from the group, always her rescuer in these moments. She takes a drink he hands her.

"Thank you," she says and leans on him. He puts his arm around her waist and pulls her close.

"It's a great review," he says. "We can look at it together later. But you can relax now." She nods and takes in a deep breath, lets it out, and sips her drink.

When it's time to sit for dinner, she's annoyed to find that she and Eric have been seated at separate tables. She meets his eye in the adjoining group, and he shrugs, winks at her. Emma is seated at her left and one of the museum donors she met upon arrival to her right. There are courses of food that are designed into bite-sized curiosities, remarks are made, gratitude is given, and then the dinner is over. Quinn finds Eric and William, and they hail a taxi.

"I didn't eat enough. I never do at these things," Quinn says.

"Diner?" Eric suggests, and William groans.

"You guys go," he says. "I'm going to go out for a bit. Congrats again." He kisses Quinn's cheek, waves at them both and walks away from the approaching taxi.

"Diner for sure," Quinn says, getting into the taxi and moving across the seat to make room for Eric, while she directs the driver to Fourteenth Street. He puts his hand on her knee, leans over and kisses her lightly on the lips. It's a kiss he's given her thousands of times in their time working together and yet, as it sometimes will, it sets a small flutter in her belly.

"Big night. Are you pleased?"

"I am," she says, and she puts her hand over his, squeezes. "I know I complained a lot during this whole thing, but I'm really happy with the result."

"It's a beautiful show," he says. "You should be proud. It's kind of incredible to see so much of the work together like that, even for me. It's powerful." Their heads tilt to touching at the temples.

"Thank you," she says and snuggles against him a bit. He cups the other side of her face in his hand, and she loves this tenderness between them, the way it's been there since nearly the beginning.

The drive is short, and Quinn thinks they probably could have walked instead. Eric pays with an app on his phone and nods at her with a smile, showing off his technological advancement. She laughs.

"I'm always astonished that this place is still here," he says when he gets out of the cab. "I'm forever waiting for it to turn into a Kiehl's or something."

"Hipsters love diners, Eric. You know that." Quinn grabs his hand and swings it in the night air. They still come here from time to time after all these years, after the first time Quinn saw him here the night of her exhibition at Patty's. They take a seat at the counter and order beers.

"Beer and pancakes, I still don't know," she says.

"It's a perfect combination. It just costs a lot more than it used to." She chuckles, and he sips from the bottle. "You want to talk about *Lulu and the Trucker*?"

Quinn sighs. "Myles left me a message today. He wants to talk to me about it. But what do I have to say to him? He sold a piece of work that wasn't his to have. I realize he lost all his money on bad investments but fuck him anyway."

Eric puts his hand on the back of her neck, and it helps ground her because Quinn can spin out of control over this very easily if she lets herself. She tries to push it out of her mind, tries not to think about Billy's final betrayal.

"Anything I can do?" Eric asks, and she can see the edge of regret in his eyes for bringing it up. But he couldn't have known how deep her well of anger runs on this. She's hidden it mostly well. She shakes her head. "Not unless you know any hit men?"

He laughs. "I've been out of the mafia game for a while, sorry." He squeezes her shoulder tenderly, the one he knows always hurts her, and it lets up under his grip. And it lets up the tension of the topic too.

"Did you know how much I was crushing on you?" she asks, because she's happy to change the conversation. "That first time I saw you here and you came back to my shitty little apartment to see my work. And I kept thinking, Fuck, here's this amazing gallery guy with me, in my apartment." She laughs. "I thought maybe you'd try to sleep with me if I invited you over." Quinn feels a small surge of heat in her cheeks and is almost surprised that he's still able to make her blush.

"Oh, I know you did," Eric says and presses his shoulder against hers. "And believe me, I wanted to. But I saw your work and I thought, This is about way more than sex." He smiles sideways at her, and she grabs at his chin.

"You never told me that before," she says, twisting his face to hers. She lets go.

Eric shakes his head but continues to look deeply at her. "We were so young."

"I was so young," she says. "You were thirty."

"Careful. I'd kill to be thirty again and so would you."

"Well, you still look good to me." She kisses his cheek, and he now pulls her chin around to kiss her lips and it lingers.

Their food comes and breaks them apart. Eric orders two more beers, despite Quinn's protest that she has a class to teach in the morning. She shakes her head as he pours thick syrup on his stack of pancakes. She spreads a small bit of butter on hers.

"This is so good," she says. "Way better than whatever we just ate."

"Yeah. What's going on with this micro-eating thing lately? I'm not into the food as art bullshit. That salad course was literally a shred of cucumber wrapped around some herbed cream cheese. Give me chicken and waffles instead."

"You're so lowbrow." She swipes a drip of syrup from his lip. "I really wish they would stop with these parties. I get it, they need it for the donors, but I have nothing to say to someone who works in investment banking or whatever these people do. Our worlds couldn't be more different."

"Ah and yet they're the ones who collect the art that allows you to eat at such grand places as Good Stuff Diner." He twirls his fork in the air, and Quinn scoffs. She's about to respond when his phone rings. It's on its second round of tinkling bells by the time he fumbles it from his suit jacket pocket. Quinn catches the name on the screen, *Celia*, when he fishes it out. He silences it but doesn't answer.

"How's she doing?" Quinn asks.

"She's fine." Eric takes a large bite of food, and Quinn has known him long enough to know this is what he does when he doesn't want to be asked questions. And she wonders, like she has many times in her life, what it's like to be married to Eric Hoffman.

Patrick is at the trailer when Lulu gets back from her job interview. Jacko's head is on his lap and they both jump up when she comes in. The dog rushes her, his cropped tail zigzagging in excitement. She nuzzles his thick pit bull snout and scratches him behind the ear on the spot he likes best. She slips out of the Payless pumps that have cut a line into the back of her heel and kicks them to the side of the room. And for a second, she remembers being young and hating how Maureen would do the same since Lulu would always trip on them rushing through the trailer.

"How'd it go?" he asks, handing her a beer.

"It went fine, thanks," she says, "but it's minimum wage."

"Mom, most jobs are."

"What are you doing here?" she asks, coming over to kiss the top of his head while she cracks open her can. His hair smells like shampoo.

"Did you forget what today is?" He cocks his head in her direction, and he looks so much like his pa that her heart nearly bursts.

"Of course not," she says, sitting down on the couch and propping her stockinged feet on the coffee table. Her big toe presses through a hole that's slowly worn into a crater throughout the day. Her toenail polish is chipped red.

"Well, I know it's a hard day for you, so I wanted to come by, make sure you're okay."

"How did you get to be so sweet?" She pats the couch for him to sit by her, and he does, and she leans on him for a moment, puts her head on his shoulder.

"I wish you could remember him," she says. "You look so much like him."

"I know," Patrick says. "You always tell me that."

She smiles. "I can't help it," she says. "How was the drive up?" It still stings that he prefers to live near his adoptive parents in Lancaster, but she understands that. They're the ones who raised him after all.

"It was fine. But tell me about this job." He looks concerned. He knows the trouble she's in since losing the cleaning job. There's no secrets between them. She never saw a reason to pretend to be something else when he had such little expectation of her anyway. He'd found her several years ago, and when he showed up on her doorstep, she thought she was seeing a ghost, the way he looked so much like his pa. But then there was some of her there too, the curved bow of her lips, the large eyes and thick lashes. And she could feel that bulk of baby in her arms again, the way his bottom nestled into the crook of her elbow. It was like he handed her a little bundle of himself as he stood at the door, and only then did she realize how much she had missed him.

Lulu sighs. "It's at a fulfillment center out where the mall used to be. I'd be on a line crew filling up boxes with shit people order on the Internet."

"That doesn't sound horrible."

"Better than Burger King. And they have a GED program, so I figure maybe it's not too late for all that." She waves a hand to distract from a small creep of blush in her cheeks. "They didn't blink at my record," she adds, "so that's something too." She sips the beer, appreciating the coldness in her throat.

"Maybe you could move up, you know?" he says. "Like do that job, but then see if they've got something secretarial in the future once you get the GED. But either way, I'm proud of you for trying."

She thinks what a good kid he is and wishes she could take credit for that, but he was already like this when he came back into her life. And she thinks how lucky she is that he forgave her for giving him up to his foster family. They were nice people who came to see her in jail, to talk to her about what they could offer him that she knew she would never be able to. She had asked JP and Hank to go check on them, make sure they were legit. And they were because her son turned out damn fine, finer than he would have with her looking after him. But those were dark days. Days where she felt like the prison walls were closing in on her, like she had no more reason to live. Days where BB refused to see her, and Maureen was nowhere to be found.

"You stop by Aunt BB's? She'll want to see you."

"Already did." Patrick sips at his beer and shifts it from hand to hand. She hopes he's not bored here, tries to think of what else to say to him. She wants to tell him about his pa, but in the past, that's upset him, so she doesn't. But her mind wanders there anyway, today, on the anniversary of his death. And the phone call that came in the night, telling her he'd hung himself in his jail cell. He was on the sixth year, so close to being done, so close to being out and with her again. She had just gotten out herself. But something had shifted in that time she was also locked up, when she couldn't see him. JP carted letters back and forth for them and she could feel Patrick slipping away in his notes, but she couldn't get to him to do a damn thing about it.

"There's something I've been meaning to give you," Lulu says, standing now and moving to the back of the trailer to fish the photograph out of her drawer where it's resting under layers of underwear and stockings. She studies the Polaroid as she walks back to the living area. It still looks good after all these years. Maybe a little darker around the edges. She hands it to him.

"What's this?" He sets his beer down and wipes the wetness from the can on his jeans before taking it from her.

"A photo of me as a kid—at ten, well, almost ten." He studies the photo. "This photographer from New York City came around one day and she took a bunch of pictures and gave me this one of myself. She's a big deal now, this lady. Quinn Bradford, got a fancy show up at a museum in New York City right now. I thought you might like to have it."

"Thanks, this is really special." She watches him study the photo. He smiles, and it's enough to melt her a bit around the knees. She has so little to give him, and she's happy he likes the Polaroid. She doesn't tell him about the other photo with the trucker. It's a nice moment between them now. She doesn't want to ruin it with that.

"I could eat, how about it?" she asks, and he nods, and they make a plan to go to the diner, and she knows this is all she really needs.

Alex kisses both of Quinn's cheeks and angles into a narrow space across from her. He's grown a mustache that makes him look more serious, and she's about to comment on it when he says, "I'm going to need a can opener to get out of here after the lobster roll I plan on eating." Mary's Fish Camp is packed despite the odd hour of the day, but it's Quinn's local spot and they always make room for her. Today they've squeezed in an extra two spaces at the edge of the seating bank and the couple next to them shoots a dirty look when Quinn sits. She mouths, *Sorry*, even though she's not sorry. She's hungry, and she's excited to have Alex home again.

"How was France?" she asks, and Alex squishes up his nose. She wants to laugh because only Alex could squish his nose at Paris. She has missed him dearly, she realizes, though he's only been gone a month.

"I decided it's no place for a boy from Brooklyn." He inhales deeply and looks around. "Jorge will need to come to me next time."

"That's quite a long-distance relationship." Quinn smiles and raises her eyebrows. She's known him through many men, though none seem to last very long. "Do you think it can hold up?" She poses it as a playful question, though she deeply wants him to find someone to be with.

"Absolutely not, but he's so damn sexy, Q. I'll let it play out." They pause conversation to order food and wine.

"Did you at least get the writing done that you were hoping to?" Quinn asks once they've handed over their menus.

Alex waves his hand, and she knows that means no. "Enough about me," he says. "How was the Whitney opening? The *Times* review was incredible."

Quinn smiles and sips a glass of white wine that's been placed on the table. Things feel restored with Alex in front of her. And for a moment she wants to just bask in the lightness of it, the way her heart feels full again.

"The opening was good," she finally says. "And I'm looking forward to the public programs since there's been some great conversation coming up from this show. But, you know." She wonders how much to share since he has his own heartbreaks in the photos. "Well, it made me miss Billy something awful," she admits. "My heart is really hurting." She touches her chest, as if she can feel the ache that's there. And she does since it's always sort of there, like a little splinter in her that she can't quite fish out.

Alex takes her hand for a moment and his palm is warm, soft. "I understand that. I promise I'll see the show, but there's a part of me that's dreading the Gene photos. Sometimes I can completely forget about him sick, and the memories of healthy Gene are glorious."

"I keep feeling like the show is incomplete in some way. Like there's a vacancy of sorts."

"It's the lost ones," Alex says. "So many of the people in

those photos are gone. Gone too soon, too young. Billy, Gene, Tisha. I think your vacancy is them."

Quinn stares out the window at Charles Street, at the young people passing by in their yoga pants and top buns, the dogs being walked, the strollers bounding effortlessly over sidewalk cracks, and she wonders if the vacancy is New York City itself. She has slowly changed, along with the neighborhood around her, but now she feels foreign to the same streets she walked hundreds of thousands of times over the years.

"Do you want to talk about the auction?" Alex eyes her over the lobster roll that's now been set in front of him. Quinn inhales audibly, shakes her head, but she knows he's not going to let her off the hook that easily because Alex is a person who likes to talk about his emotions even though Quinn is most definitely not. But just the word *auction* is an evocation of Myles.

"I should talk about it, right? But I'm not sure how to control my anger over the chain of bad decisions that led to that sale even being possible. So, for now, I'm just not talking about it." She turns a spoon over in a cup of clam chowder, churning a layer of ground pepper into it.

She watches Alex watching her since she knows if he does this, like this, she'll say more, and so she sighs and says, "It's not even about the money. The money doesn't matter to me. It's about the fact that Billy left that photo to him. *My* photo. Like what in the fuck was he even thinking?" Quinn realizes she has raised her voice and the couple next to them is now openly staring at her. She mouths, *Sorry*, again and this time she means it. She tastes the chowder, but it's too hot, burns the tip of her tongue. She drops her spoon on the napkin. "I know it's not fair to blame Myles for all of the wrongs in my life, but sometimes it's easier to do that."

"Well yeah, it lets you pretend that Billy was flawless, and he most certainly was not." A chunk falls out of the corner of Alex's roll. He pinches it into his mouth.

"You said that sometimes you only remember Gene as young and healthy. Isn't that the same? I mean, shouldn't it be a benefit of the living to be able to make up whatever history serves their hearts? I like to think of the Billy I grew up with, the kid with floppy hair and punk rock T-shirts. I don't want to think about the heroin or the pills or the coke or the way he chose all of that and Myles over me. Over all of us."

Alex sighs. "It's this exhibition. It's like an exhumation."

"It really is," Quinn says. "I feel like I planted a little bomb in each of those early photos. I had no idea they were going to go off like this all these years later. At the time, I thought I was doing something good for us. Making memories." She waves her hand between them. "How naive was that? And you know what? I can't stop wondering if I gave up on him too soon and that's what caused it all to happen." Quinn stops to catch her breath. She hasn't meant to rant like this.

Alex takes her hand. "You are not responsible for what happened. And honestly, neither is Myles. Billy made his own decisions, he always did."

"I just sometimes think if I hadn't walked away, I could have seen it coming and done something, you know?"

"It's not like you didn't try. I was there, I remember."

Quinn watches his jaw move up and down, the bulge of his throat when he swallows, the way his new mustache twitches around his mouth. She looks away, out the window, anywhere else since she's afraid if she keeps looking at Alex, she might cry thinking about that time. Somehow, she erased parts of it from her memory, processed them out. And she knows that Alex is right. Billy made his own decisions, he always did.

"Sometimes I forget," she says, quietly. Alex takes her hand under the table, squeezes.

He shakes his head. "Quinn, nothing is ever as simple as time likes to make us believe. We all made a lot of choices back then based on what we knew, what we had. Billy too. You can't use present tense knowledge and apply it to the past. But you can learn to forgive. Yourself, and Myles and Billy too." Quinn knows he's right, but she also has no idea how to do that.

☙

Lulu checks the museum visiting hours several times on Jo-ey's computer before making a plan. She pays the fee to get in, trying to put out of her mind the fact that the ticket costs double her hourly wages. She tries to blend in with others as she makes her way to a large elevator bank, watches as someone else pushes the button for the sixth floor where the show be-gins. She studies the people in the elevator, a girl with the right side of her hair buzzed off, a guy with eyeliner on, a mother in expensive leather pants and her teen daughter with purple hair and a nose piercing. She wonders if they're looking at her too, if her Walmart jeans and no-brand sneakers give her away, as not one of them. As not one of anything.

The doors open and she's the last one out. She surveys the room before deciding where to begin and then simply does what the others are doing, which is to read the wall that intro-duces the show. She gets part way in before she loses patience with the artsy words she doesn't know and instead makes her way into the exhibition. And it's immediate, how the photos find her before she even finds them. She knows *Lulu and the Trucker* won't be on view since the article said it was sold as the exhibition was being planned, but she's nonetheless startled to see so many pictures of her hometown, the boarded-up church, the diner missing one of its lights, and the strands of trailers where her friends and family still live. And there is another photo of a nine-year-old, almost ten, Lulu standing outside the motel, self-consciously running a hand through her hair. *Lulu at the Motel.* And then another inside her trailer with BB next to her. *Lulu and Her Cousin BB.*

She looks around at the other visitors and wonders if they can tell it's her, but of course they can't. That little girl is foreign even to herself now. And then there's BB, alone in the photo at an angle that highlights the bloom of scar on her lip, that pain-ful mark that has slowly resolved with time and gravity. Lulu reaches out to touch the glass, to touch that twist in her cousin's skin, but a security guard steps up and tells her not to do so.

Lulu wanders away from the Riverdale photos to the other

subjects and studies those just as closely, tries to conjure up the backstories of the people there, wonders who they are, their fears and hopes and dreams. She wants them to feel like real people. Makes them real by giving them lives in her mind. "Alex and Gene in Bed," she whispers, reading the card on the wall. Her eyes stray over the intertwined limbs, the heads bent close and the tangle of blankets like little mountains around them. A cross hangs over the bed next to what looks like the blanched skull of a desert mammal. A loop of silky banner drapes around the four posters of the antique bed frame. She's not sure which is Alex, imagines he's the one with thick black hair and then she sees it, the sadness in his eyes, how subtly it lingers in the lines around them and the way he seems nearly pained as he looks at the other one, the one she thinks is Gene. His hand grasps Gene's arm above the elbow, as if holding him away or about to pull him close. And Gene, his eyes are closed, and his head is tilted back and there's a smile there, a satisfied smile as if he has everything he could ever want. Lulu can't take her eyes off that photo. That one leads her to more, *Gene on His Birthday*. *Alex and Gene Dancing*. She makes her way through the whole group. And then the final one, *Alex at Gene's Funeral*. Lulu presses her eyes to keep the tears from coming out.

She checks her watch. The talk is in an hour. She spends every second of it with the photographs. She makes her way down to the next gallery, where she finds the Times Square series. The range of emotions in the photos is stunning. The girls come to life in the frames, laughing, eating burgers, smoking, hugging, crying. She feels herself in all of them. She sees her own life in each of the instances.

As the time nears for the talk, Lulu starts to feel anxious about what she will say to Quinn Bradford. She rehearsed many times, but she's still unsure. She sits briefly on a bench in the gallery and tries to breathe deeply to calm herself, but her head spins with the anticipation, and she worries she may pass out. In her mind, she practices what she wants to say: *Why didn't you help that little girl? Why didn't you ever come back for her?*

But already a cloud of doubt is forming because it couldn't have been that simple, could it? What would Maureen or Hank have done if the photographer came back? What more could have come about than what happened when someone called the cops?

The gallery is filling now with people she assumes are also going to the talk, milling about before the event begins. She swallows hard against a lump in her throat. She should have agreed to let BB or Joey come with her; both had tried, but she had thought she should do this alone. Now, here, in this place so removed from her own world, she longs for one or both, someone to hold her up for a moment as her knees weaken. She takes a deep breath and shakes her head, shakes out the thoughts that are rushing at her, like watching her whole life pass before her eyes. She closes them when Patrick flashes there, closes her heart against the pain there. She stands like that for a moment, eyes closed, feeling other people around her, the slight motions of bodies and accidental brushes and murmured words, and she worries that if she opens her eyes, her whole life will spill out of them, flood like rivers down her cheeks and onto the ground and drown everyone around her.

A gallery attendant announces the talk will begin shortly and ushers guests out of the gallery. Lulu feels them pass by like fish in a stream, and she tries then, she opens her eyes slowly, carefully, controlled. She joins them in their flow. They wind down concrete stairs to the basement where she finds a seat near the middle of the theater at the aisle and shifts her knees to the side repeatedly for others to squeeze past her. She doesn't want to feel trapped or too close or too far away. The entire space fills, and Lulu tries to count the number of attendees but keeps losing track. There's movement on the stage, and Quinn Bradford takes a seat alongside another woman. Lulu immediately remembers the photographer, and though she's looking at a much older version of the woman, there's still so much of the younger lady there as well. Her swagger, the way she swung the camera up to her face, the thin, shapely legs in very short shorts. And her wrists. Lulu could still recall the twist of the pale skin and the bones that seemed exotic to her as a little girl. How she had longed to be like the photographer, to be beautiful and cool.

Another woman takes the stage at a podium and welcomes everyone. The group settles in, quiets down. She quickly runs through the backgrounds of the speakers and then all attention turns to Quinn, and Lulu holds her breath as she hears that voice again, its soft timbre, the way it's both reassuring and forceful. And it's too much, the rising tide that she feels rushing inside of her. Lulu grabs her purse and hurries out of her seat, letting the auditorium door clang shut behind her.

After her talk, Quinn greets friends who have come and meets new people who hang around afterward to introduce themselves. William taps his watch across the room, and she knows they're due to meet Eric for dinner soon, but she finds it hard to gracefully slip away in these moments. She finally frees herself and tells William she'll meet him in the lobby as she follows Emma to the administrative offices to fetch her things.

She's coming back down the cement stairway when she sees the woman standing in the gallery, alone, in front of the Riverdale photos. She stops and watches her through the glass wall, wonders what she's thinking as she stares so intently at the photographs. She considers going inside and introducing herself, but that seems self-indulgent. But there's something familiar about the woman, the arch in her back, the cock of her hip, the purposeful tilt in her shoulders. Quinn watches only a moment longer, then hurries down the stairs to find William, who has already called for a car and is tapping into his phone, likely to Eric to let him know they're running late.

"Sorry, sorry," she says as her son takes her elbow and leads her out of the museum and into the waiting car. "Where's dinner?"

"Little Park," he says. "Eric should be there already. You're pretty late."

"He knows to expect that." She leans into him in the backseat. "I still don't understand how you became so punctual. You do not get that from me or your dad. Billy was late to everything. Can you imagine before cell phones? We'd just go looking for each other."

William smiles. "I'm also not an artist."

"Oh, so you think artists are always late?"

"Artists live in their own worlds, Mom. The rest of us sort of orbit it, you know?"

"I guess so," she admits, but something about it makes her feel badly. "Have I not given you enough attention?"

William sighs, shakes his head. "That's not what I'm saying."

"It's true I've been selfish, William. I know that. I made a decision at some point that I would live my life for me. And I never quite figured out how other people fit into that, you know? But I love you to fucking bits. You're a piece of me, so you have your own special place and it's not in any orbit, it's the whole solar system."

"I'm not sure that metaphor works."

"Me neither, but you get what I mean?"

"I do."

Quinn kisses his forehead and moves the hair out of his eyes. As always, she finds Billy there in the contours of his face, in the curls of his hair and the angle of his chin.

William leaves her at Little Park and adds another stop to the Lyft, telling her he's meeting up with Emma. Quinn raises her eyebrows but simply says, "Have fun," and wonders why he didn't just leave with Emma from the museum, and then she realizes how much he's been holding her hand through this entire thing and in her mind, she gently lets it go.

Eric is in mid-drink of a glass of whiskey when she arrives at the table. He smiles as he swallows and stands to kiss her. It's a spicy kiss, and she lets her lips linger on his for a moment. They sit.

"How was the talk?"

"Good, I think? A few people stuck around with more questions, so I'm sorry I'm late."

He waves at the air. "I'm sorry I didn't make it. I had to finish up some business." He's about to say more when the server comes and hands them menus, takes an order of wine for Quinn.

"What are you thinking?" she asks. "I'm going to do the risotto."

"Sirloin," he says and closes the menu. He's about to say something again when the server returns with Quinn's wine and takes their order.

"Is there something you'd like to say?" she asks, laughing.

Eric shakes his head. "I should know better than to try to give news before ordering."

She raises her eyebrow. "Oh, what's this news and if it's bad, please just wait until I've had two glasses of wine."

He smiles and touches her hand. "I have something for you."

"That doesn't sound bad."

Quinn watches as he reaches into a leather bag that sits near his feet. He slips something from it, holds it for a moment before saying, "I was going to tell you sooner, but I wanted to wait until this whole thing went through and it was in my hands."

"What are you talking about?" She sets down her wine glass and takes the flat, square package from him. He nods at her, and she opens it up, reaches carefully for the contents and when her fingers feel the edge of the Polaroid, her heart begins to race.

"Is this what I think it is?" she asks. He gestures for her to keep going. She shuffles it out of the package and unwraps the archival tissue from it, and it's there, the image she can never forget, the photo that has haunted her for half of her life, the one that she thought was lost for good into the hands of a stranger. Its edges are darker, as time will do, but otherwise it's been well kept.

"Eric, I don't know what to say. I can't believe you did this for me." But she can believe it, and the tears are already on her cheeks before she can think to wipe them away. He grips her knees under the table. She looks at the photo, and it's been years since she's seen it or held it. And she thinks about that day, as she handed it Billy, said, *Please, keep this safe for me.*

Quinn knows exactly what she's going to do with it.

Lulu stares at the photos until the security guard tells her the museum is closing and it's time to go. She smiles and thanks him, and as he follows her out, she realizes she's the last person in the place. She knows the talk is well over, encountered the small rush of visitors after it finished, overheard conversations about dinner reservations and drinks plans and who was meeting up with who. She knows her chance to speak to Quinn Bradford passed as she stood in front of those photos of her youth, of her home.

She wanders out into the dark night. The air is warm and a breeze flutters around her cheeks and neck. She sits on the steps of a nearby clothing boutique and watches people rushing by, their faces blurred in their urgency, their bodies aching in motion. She lights a cigarette and exhales a cloud into the clear night sky.

It's after nine, and she thinks she should start her drive home, but she can't pry away from where she sits. The energy of the city, the lights and the sounds and the smells pull her, hold her, keep her where she is, and she understands this seduction. She looks around her, really looks around her, at the towering buildings, the shapes of the architecture, the beautiful and the ugly and the clean and dirty and shiny and dull and funny and sad and all the contradictions, all the ways it means to be human, to be a human, constantly moving through these collisions. She tosses the cigarette butt to the ground and heaves up off the steps, walks the few blocks to where she parked the car, relieved to find it still there. She lets a parking ticket flutter to the ground.

On the road, out of the jams and pauses, onto the highway. She watches the city lights exchange for stars, runs her hand through the air that pulses outside the window, and she drives, and she drives, and she drives.

ACKNOWLEDGMENTS

I owe a massive amount of gratitude to Jaynie Royal, Pam Van Dyk, and the team at Regal House Publishing for caring for this book as much as I do and for being incredible collaborators. Thank you especially to Pam for your incredible editorial eye. From day one, I knew I was in good hands with you. Regal House is a very special publisher, and I'm so grateful to be in its community. To my dearest friends Jason Brodak and Nicole Raymond and my loving mom Judi Schlottman, thank you for your unwavering enthusiasm every time I ask if you want to read another version of something I've written. I'm so blessed to have access to your brilliant, well-read minds. Alexandra Franklin, thank you for your insights and excitement for this book. You helped make it so much stronger. Thank you, Laura Marie, for your extraordinary publicity efforts and for doing the things I'm too shy to do. And Paul Morris, thank you for your generosity.

Thank you from the bottom of my heart to Matthew Specktor, Chelsea Bieker, Amy Shearn, Jakob Guanzon, Cinelle Barnes, Rachel Lyon, Wil Medearis, and Stephen Kiernan.

I love you Nathan Bright for taking care of me when I'm in a writing flow and for putting up with the rollercoaster that comes alongside giving birth to a novel. Thank you, truly, for being my person. Paola Zanzo, you have breathed life into me many times and in many ways, and I am so grateful for our friendship. Kambui Olujimi, I deeply appreciate your unwavering encouragement and your help in bringing old New York City back to life.

Priscilla Schlottman, Angel Mthembu, and Rick Schlottman, thank you for your love and support. To all the other Schlottmans, you're a nutty bunch and give me a lot of great content to work with. I love you all.

Alissa Roath and Tina McGuire, thank you for holding my heart. Jewels Dodson, Nathalie Benareau, Christine Stamas, Jennifer Oatess, Michael Gibbons, Alexandra Siclait, Lisa Dent, Eric Micha Holmes, Danniel Swatosh, Sandra Glading, Ed Cibor, Mark Katakowski, and Melissa Rachlcff Burtt, thank you for your friendship and support. It means the world to me. Thank you to my pup Jupiter who cuddled me throughout this process and continues to be my favorite writing buddy.

Thank you to Jets to Brazil whose song "Sweet Avenue" inspired my character Lulu and to Roxy Music whose song "More Than This" inspired the saddest scene I've ever written as well as the book's title. And a very special thank you to Nan Goldin whose photographs encouraged me to move to New York City in 2005 and dedicate my career to working with artists, and to Mary Ellen Mark whose photograph *Amanda and Her Cousin Amy* inspired this novel. In this period when people are increasingly divided, I hope everyone will take time to learn each other's stories.